THE CABIN

ALSO BY NATASHA PRESTON

The Cellar

Awake

THE CABIN

Natasha Preston

sourcebooks
fire

Published by Sourcebooks Fire, an imprint of Sourcebooks, Inc.
P.O. Box 4410, Naperville, Illinois 60567-4410
(630) 961-3900
Fax: (630) 961-2168
www.sourcebooks.com

Library of Congress Cataloging-in-Publication data is on file with the publisher.

Printed and bound in the United States of America.
WOZ 20 19 18 17 16 15 14 13 12 11

For Rachel. I love you, girl!

PROLOGUE

They think they're invincible.

They think they can do and say whatever they want.

They think there are no consequences.

They've left me no choice.

It's time for them to pay for their sins.

CHAPTER ONE

Friday, August 7

"Do you have everything you need, Mackenzie?" Mum asked, watching me stuff clothes in a bag.

"I think so. We're only going for two nights anyway." *Two painful nights of dealing with Josh.*

"Remember to leave the address and phone number on the fridge."

"I don't think the cabin has a landline, but I'll leave the address. I'll get cell reception out there, apparently, and I'll let you know when we arrive."

She nodded nervously and gave me a weak smile.

"Mum, I'll be fine."

"You're spending the weekend with someone you don't like."

"No, I'm spending the weekend with Aaron, Courtney, Megan, and Kyle. It's just unfortunate that Josh will be there too." If I could have uninvited him, I would have.

But the cabin is his parents', so that didn't seem too likely. Or reasonable. He'd invited us all to spend the weekend at his family's cabin since school was out. The UK had finally realized it was summer, and next year, we'd all be going our separate ways for university.

"If you need to be picked up early…?"

I shook my head. "Thanks, but I'll be fine. There's no way I'm letting him ruin a weekend with my friends. Anyway, I need to go."

"I'll drop you off at Joshua's."

"No, it's fine, Mum. I can walk." I grabbed my bag and swung it over my shoulder. "See you Sunday night. Love you," I said, kissing her cheek.

"Love you too, sweetheart. Call if you need anything."

"I will," I replied.

Josh only lived a two-minute walk away, so it wouldn't take me long. I slammed the front door behind me and headed down the path. The weather was superhot, it being the beginning of August, and I was glad I'd opted for shorts and a T-shirt.

When I got to Josh's, everyone was outside his house, cramming bags into cars. Seriously, we were going for two nights, but it looked like Courtney and Megan had packed for a week.

"Kenz!" Courtney shouted, jogging toward me. Her red ponytail swayed and her green eyes danced with excitement. She was the only person genuinely happy about this trip.

Taking a deep breath, I pushed away every ounce of doubt I had about this weekend and smiled. "Hey, Court. Is everyone ready?"

"Almost. Josh will be back soon," she replied with a goofy smile. "Don't look like that," she added when I grimaced at his name.

Whoops, she caught me. "Sorry. I didn't mean that. It's…nice of him to invite us to his folk's cabin."

She took my lame apology with a smile. "He wants things back the way they were."

Did he have a time machine so he could go back and not say those awful things about my friends? Could he take back what he'd done to me? What he still was doing to me?

Josh might be trying to make amends for the past—if we were even to believe it was genuine—but we weren't going to forgive him so easily. Some hurts aren't that easy to get over, and I couldn't forgive someone who wasn't sorry and hadn't changed their behavior. Courtney had forgiven him already, of course, but she never could see what a waster her boyfriend was.

I lifted my eyebrow.

"Mackenzie, please," Courtney said, sighing as she pushed her bangs out of her eyes. "He's trying, and it will mean so much to me if you'll try too. Please?"

I groaned and my shoulders sagged. "Fine. I'll play nice."

Two nights, that's it. You can do that.

"We all will," Megan added, stepping beside us. "Right, guys?" Aaron and Kyle nodded along, agreeing to put their differences to the side—for the weekend at least.

"Where is Josh anyway?" I asked.

"Picking up his brother." Courtney rolled her eyes. "Blake wanted to see him again, so Josh invited him this morning. Technically the cabin belongs to Blake too, so there's not much anyone can do to stop him from coming with."

"Oh," I muttered, not sure how I felt about a stranger joining us. We didn't know Blake, and if he was anything like Josh, the

3

weekend was going to be a nightmare. "So the estranged brother is coming." *Great. This trip keeps getting better and better.*

I had seen Blake before, on about two occasions, when his parents were doing a kid swap, but I'd never spoken to him. Blake had moved away with his dad after their parents divorced. Josh stayed with their mum. The two boys didn't spend much time together while they were growing up, which was probably a good thing for Blake.

Courtney pushed her bangs aside again. They never stayed put, so I didn't know why she didn't just cut them shorter. "They're hardly estranged."

They rarely saw each other; I'd call that estranged. "Why is he crashing his brother's party?" I asked.

"He's lonely?" Kyle offered, making a sad face.

Courtney leaned against Aaron's car. "No, he just wants to spend time with his brother. They both want to."

If Blake was like Josh, I would be coming home early for sure. I didn't even want to breathe the same air as Josh, so I sort of hoped Blake was an idiot too, then I would have an excuse to leave that wouldn't hurt Courtney's feelings.

The warm air blew my long chestnut hair in my face. I brushed the strands from my eyes just in time to see a metallic-black Mitsubishi Warrior—the only car I recognized without reading the logo because it was Kyle's favorite subject—pull up beside me.

Here we go…

Josh was sitting in the passenger seat and his brother was driving. They both had the same dark-brown hair and blue eyes, but apart from that, they looked totally different. Josh definitely didn't inherit the looks. Blake snapped every ounce of drop-dead gorgeous and left nothing for his younger brother. Lucky for Blake.

I looked away and walked around to Aaron's car, wanting to put as much distance between me and Josh as possible. Even just seeing his face made me want to punch him, especially after his demands. Courtney was smart, but when it came to him, she was as thick as a post.

Josh got out of the car. "Hey, guys. You remember my brother, Blake?"

Megan shook her head. "Nope, but hi."

Blake walked to the front of his truck and casually leaned against the hood as if he was bored. "Hey," he said with a nod.

He wore chunky black boots, dark jeans, and a black jacket, making him look mysterious and maybe a little dangerous. His dark hair stuck out in all directions in a messy style that looked like he didn't give a crap—which I assumed he didn't. His bright-blue eyes scanned the group, checking us out one by one.

His gaze was intense and it was like he saw *everything*. I didn't want him to see *anything* about me. "Let's just leave already!" I said, opening the car door and climbing inside. The sooner we got there, the sooner we could get back. Damn, I sounded like my parents on Christmas Eve when they would try to get me to sleep as the clock ticked dangerously close to midnight.

But at least I would get two nights adult free to spend with my friends. That was something to look forward to for sure.

"Err, Mackenzie," Courtney said. "You're in the car with me."

My face fell. I knew what that meant. "What?"

She stepped forward and leaned in the car so we could talk privately. "You're coming in the car with me, Josh, and Blake."

"Yeah, I'm not," I replied.

"Please? Look, I know you're mad at him, and I understand why, but will you try? I really think you two need to spend the car trip together to work through this."

"We really don't, Court."

"This weekend is going to suck if you're pissed at Josh the whole time."

I frowned. I wasn't the only one who didn't like him though, so why was I the only one being forced to make the extra effort? "His brother's weird," I whispered as if that was going to change Courtney's mind.

"Blake is harmless."

I'd run out of excuses. Sighing in defeat, I replied, "All right! But if he pisses me off by making his usual stupid comments, I'm switching cars."

Courtney held up her hands. "OK, OK. Thank you."

"We're taking Blake's car then?"

"Yeah, they must have decided to bring Blake's instead. I can see why." Courtney was a car person; she knew all the different types and models by sight. I couldn't even tell if something was wrong with one—unless the engine actually fell out.

"Blake's driving?"

"His car, so I guess." She shrugged, watching Josh with a loving look that made me want to shake some sense into her.

"I call shotgun," I replied. If I had to be in the same car, at least I wouldn't have to sit next to him. I was aware that I was behaving like a child, but I didn't care. Josh had crossed a line, and I wasn't going to forgive him. Actually, Josh had crossed about a million lines.

I got in the passenger seat before Josh had a chance to say or do anything. He could shove it if he thought I was moving. Blake smiled a little awkwardly and started the car. He didn't ooze confidence, but he looked like he didn't care what anyone thought.

"I'm coming in your car too," Kyle said.

Courtney narrowed her eyes. "You're with Aaron and Megan."

"There's space with you for another, isn't there?"

"Kyle, five in one car and two in another is stupid. No one wants to be cramped in the back."

"Oh, for Christ's sake, Kyle, just get in Aaron's bloody car," Josh snapped, shoving past him. "Pathetic arsehole."

I ground my teeth. Did it really matter which car he rode in? The answer was no.

Blake and I hadn't spent any time together, so we quickly fell into an awkward silence while we waited for Josh and Courtney to get in the car. I bit the inside of my cheek and twiddled my fingers. *Say something to him!* We had never actually spoken to each other before. That was about to change. We had a forty-five-minute car ride to a remote part of the Lake District ahead of us.

"Why do you hate Josh?" he asked.

I was surprised by his bluntness. It was no secret that I didn't like Josh, but I didn't expect his brother to come straight out and ask. "Um, because he's a bloody idiot."

Blake's eyebrow rose, and he pursed his lips. Finally, he nodded once. "Yeah. OK then."

"You don't see him much, do you?"

"Not really. Growing up, my parents couldn't get their shit together long enough to schedule proper visits for us. Most of the time, when they finally got around to it, they swapped us over for a day or two. I think I can count on one hand the number of times I've seen my mum in the last twelve years."

My heart ached for him. I couldn't imagine what he went through as a kid. He must've missed his mum. I would have; my mum was the person I went to with every problem—well, almost every problem. "That's really sad."

He lifted his shoulder and let it drop. "That's how it goes sometimes."

"Yeah, but…" I shook my head. I couldn't imagine not seeing my mum every day, as crazy as she drove me sometimes. Blake must have felt abandoned by his mom if she never made the effort. Maybe that was how Josh felt about his dad? Wow, Josh and deep feelings. That was strange to think about… Everything I'd witnessed of his character had been shallow and selfish.

Josh and Courtney got in the car, and I zipped my mouth. The atmosphere turned tense, like it always was when Josh was around. He knew I wished he wasn't with Courtney after all of the horrible things he'd said about our friends Tilly and Gigi.

He loved that Courtney wouldn't ditch him for treating her friends like rubbish. Bastard.

"Oh, I don't mind you sitting up front with *my* brother, Mackenzie," Josh said sarcastically as he climbed into the backseat.

I clenched my fists. *Don't let him get to you.*

"My car, Bro, and I'd rather sit near a pretty face than your ugly mug," Blake responded.

Smiling to myself, I grabbed my bag of lollipops and offered one to Blake. I should probably have been annoyed at the "pretty face" comment, but that was overshadowed by him calling Josh ugly. Blake took an orange lollipop—my favorite—and gave me a wink.

"Not sharing, Mackenzie?" Josh asked.

I took a deep breath, resisting the urge to jam the plastic stick into his eye. "Sure," I replied, holding out the bag. He took two, probably to annoy me, so I said nothing.

"OK, everyone, please play nice," Courtney whined. "This weekend, parent free, is going to be epic, so will you all make up?"

"You know I don't have a problem with any of them, babe," Josh replied.

"Whatever," I muttered, clenching my jaw.

I watched Blake as he drove. His eyes slid over, occasionally catching me, but he didn't say a word. I found myself wanting to get to know him, but I wasn't sure why. He would go home after the weekend, and I'd probably never see him again.

Still, Blake was gorgeous, and I was drawn to him.

We reached the cabin without bloodshed, so I was pleased

with my self-control—so far. Courtney kept Josh in check by flirting with him and getting him to listen to music. I couldn't wait until she saw through him and his crap. I was going to make sure I had a front-row seat when she dumped his arse.

"This is it?" I asked, looking out the window up at a huge, two-story cabin. It could easily house about ten people.

Blake cut the engine and smirked. "What did you expect? The Ritz?"

"This is amazing. I didn't think it would be this big."

"Three years ago, I would have made some sort of sexual innuendo," Blake replied.

"All grown up now, are we?"

"Nah, that was just when I noticed Josh trying to act the big man and I realized how lame those comments actually sound."

I grinned and got out of the car. I liked Blake and his painfully beautiful face. Maybe this weekend wouldn't be so miserable. Kyle and Aaron bundled bags out of the trunk and chucked them on the ground. Halfway to the cabin I guess. Kyle grabbed his phone and started to film, like he usually did. He wanted to do something in the film industry, and I think he'd be awesome at it.

"Smile, Kenz," he said, pointing it in my direction.

I stuck out my tongue and Aaron made an obscene gesture.

"Nice, Aaron," Kyle said sarcastically.

Megan stared up at the enormous house. You could tell from the overgrown plants and faded window frames that no one had been here in a while. Josh and Courtney had spent all last weekend here getting it ready, but they'd just cleaned the inside.

The cabin was set in a clearing; the woods surrounded it on three sides, and a gorgeous lake ran along the front of the property. The scenery was beautiful. I didn't understand why Josh's family didn't use it more often.

"You happy to be back?" I asked Blake as we walked to the front door at a snail's pace. He dragged his feet like he didn't really want to be here.

Blake shrugged and grunted. "Just here for the booze."

Of course you are.

Josh unlocked the front door and turned to us. Kyle rolled his eyes, guessing what was coming, and I tried not to laugh. We—eighteen and however old Blake was—were about to be given *rules*.

"Courtney and I have worked hard getting the cabin ready for you all, so I would appreciate it if you would respect the place and not leave it looking like a Dumpster."

I bit my tongue. How pompous. None of us were going to trash the cabin and he knew that. Courtney stood beside him like the lady of the manor, eating up the attention. I loved that girl, but she needed a good slap to knock some sense into her.

Josh opened the door and walked in ahead of Courtney. Gentleman my arse! And Court didn't even care; she followed him like a little lapdog.

"I'll grab the rest of the bags," Aaron said, heading back out of the door.

I walked in and my jaw dropped. Wow.

The cabin was beautiful, albeit a little dated. The view of the lake from the family room window was to die for. The sun shone down on the water's surface, making it glisten. There was a large fireplace that I could have stepped into.

Kyle walked behind me, capturing the view with his phone.

"I'm going to explore. Anyone wanna come?" Megan asked, bouncing up and down like a toddler. Her short, overly hair-sprayed bob barely moved an inch. She had already dropped her bag by the bottom of the stairs, which was about as much unpacking as she ever did.

I handed a case of beer to Courtney, who was organizing the food and booze in the kitchen.

"Don't fancy getting lost in the forest, thanks," I replied.

Aaron dropped a load of bags on the floor. "I'll come." He walked out before anyone could stop him and make him help. I watched them walk into the woods. The bright midday sun shone down on Aaron's white-blond hair, making it glow. They both looked happy to be away, and I was going to try and do the same.

"Going for a walk," Kyle said, shaking his head at them as he lowered the phone. He held up a six-pack in his other hand. "Crazy. Hey, Blake, where'd you want the beer, man?"

"In the oven," he replied dryly.

I tried not to smile but failed miserably. I wasn't sure what Blake was doing here. He didn't seem to have a good relationship with Josh, and he didn't seem to be making much effort.

Kyle's mouth thinned in a tight smile, and I could tell he was fighting the urge to say something back. Instead, he narrowed his eyes and spun on his heel. Shaking his head, he walked away. Kyle was a sensitive soul and was never very good with anyone making fun of him.

Then, Blake and I were left in the living room. Alone again. I pursed my lips, not knowing what to say. *Should I even say anything?* The silence was awkward, but it didn't seem to bother him at all. Nothing seemed to affect him. Blake was cool, calm, and almost robotic. But I wasn't naive enough to think that nothing got to him.

"So…did you come here much when you were a kid?" I asked to fill the silence.

He looked over his shoulder, half smiling at me. "You're asking if I come here much?"

"No, I asked if you *came* here much." There was a big difference.

Blake turned his body so he was fully facing me. I don't know if he did it to be intimidating, but it was. He had this cockiness about him, but it wasn't off-putting like Josh's.

"We came here a lot before our parents separated. After the divorce, the place stayed empty, until now."

I didn't know what to say. "I'm sorry."

"Why? People divorce all the time." Before I had the chance to say anything else, he walked outside. There was definitely a lot more to him than he let people see.

"Beer, Kenz?" Kyle asked from behind me.

I turned and smirked. "You know it's eleven in the morning, right?"

"Yeah," he replied, tilting his head, waiting for me to explain.

I smiled and took a beer from his outstretched hand. "Never mind."

Kyle and I sat on the sofa while Josh and Courtney messed around putting things away in the kitchen. "You think we should help?" I asked.

"I offered. You know what Josh is like."

Control freak. We wouldn't do it the way he wanted. How many different ways were there to put food in a cupboard? This was "Josh's" place though, and we were being made very aware that we were just guests. "I'm going to need a lot of alcohol to get through this weekend," I said. I'd promised my parents no drinking, obviously, but we were all parent free and determined to make the most of it. They think we're swimming in the lake, cooking out, and roasting marshmallows around a campfire. We are, so it's not a total lie, but there will be drinking.

Kyle nodded in agreement and raised his bottle. "Let's keep it coming, then."

I clinked the top of my bottle against his and took a swig.

Kyle and I had just finished our thirds when the rest of the group joined us. "Wow, this looks fun," Aaron said, grinning at the bottles of alcohol spread out over the coffee table.

"Yep, Kyle and I thought we should have it all at arm's reach. Cheers," I said, raising my half-full bottle.

"Well, if we're doing this, we're doing it right. I'm well up for getting wasted," Aaron replied, picking the Absolut Vodka. "Everyone's in, no backing out. Josh, shot glasses, my man!" My smile grew. I wasn't a big drinker, especially after last time, with the accident, but I wanted to have stupid, immature fun tonight.

"Err, guys, I don't want anyone throwing up in my house," Josh said in his annoying, stuck-up, I'm-better-than-you way. I had a very sudden, very childish urge to drink until I puked.

Everything he wanted, I wanted to do the opposite. I knew that was dangerous though. I knew I couldn't—and I wasn't stupid enough to do it—but I damn well wanted to.

"Lighten up, mate, come on. We all want this to be a good weekend," Kyle replied.

Josh glared and his jaw tightened. He didn't like to be challenged. "I am relaxed," he growled through his teeth.

Aaron lifted a freshly poured shot glass and raised it to Josh, his own little in-your-face, before knocking it back. I smiled and did the same. And then I regretted it because Josh's eyebrow arched and I knew exactly what he was thinking.

And he wouldn't hesitate to open his big mouth. But before he could say anything, Aaron spoke. "A toast," he said, raising a bottle this time. "To a killer weekend."

We lifted whatever we had in our hands. "To a killer weekend!"

CHAPTER TWO

After about an hour of drinking, I eased off so I wouldn't be flat on my face before it even got dark. Josh and Courtney, the only couple, had gone off to his parents' room, as it was the only double, for a bit of privacy, which meant Josh wanted sex.

Megan and Aaron were in the kitchen. I could hear her laughing at something he'd said. Kyle had gone to the toilet shortly after Josh and Courtney went upstairs, which was ages ago, so I vowed to never use that bathroom.

Blake stretched his legs, kicking his booted feet up on the coffee table. He didn't fit in. He drank with us and joined in with conversation when necessary, but he didn't contribute much. There was tension between him and Josh that went beyond the usual dislike that the rest of us had. They stared each other down if one said something the other didn't like. It was awkward and made me want to leave the room.

They clearly didn't get along, so why on earth would Blake invite himself?

"What do you do back home?" I asked, trying to get to know a little more about him other than his favorite alcoholic drink.

"I work here and there," he grunted.

OK, it was like getting blood out of a stone. "You're not very chatty, are ya?"

He flicked his eyes to me without moving his head. "What's the point?"

"To get to know people, to make friends, to not live like a hermit…" I rewarded him with a charming, toothy smile, which softened his face.

"You think I'm a hermit?"

"Aren't you?"

"No," he replied. "I don't spend much time alone at all."

The spark in his eye told me everything. I turned my nose up in disgust. "Different girl every night?"

"Not *every* night."

Hmm, that didn't make sense—unless his earlier shyness was an act? But why would he pretend to be shy around women? He was obviously proud that he could sleep with practically whomever he wanted.

My stomach knotted at the thought of him hooking up with loads of girls, which was ridiculous. We weren't in a relationship. I hardly knew him. I pursed my lips. "Previously broken heart or just not grown up yet?"

He frowned. "What?"

"I want to know why you use women."

"Can't it just be that I like sex but don't want a relationship?"

"Not usually." A thought popped into my head. "Ah, don't worry. I get it."

Sighing, he asked, "Get what?"

"Get why."

He rubbed his forehead in exasperation and muttered, "Women… What do you think you get, Mackenzie?"

"You don't want a relationship because you lived through your parents' less-than-amicable divorce. You're scared of history repeating itself with you."

He sat frozen for a minute, his face falling, and I knew I'd hit the nail on the head. Mackenzie, one. Blake, zero.

A moment of silence stretched on, and I fiddled with my fingers. Blake narrowed his eyes. "You don't know what you're talking about. I haven't met anyone I wanted to see exclusively, that's all."

"Whatever you say."

His glare turned colder.

Damn it. My stomach turned with guilt. "I'm sorry, Blake. I didn't mean to offend you."

"I'm not offended."

His rough, gravelly voice said otherwise.

His eyes pierced holes into mine, making my heart race. The atmosphere solidified until I could barely stand it. One minute, Blake looked like he wouldn't have been bothered if I'd left immediately, and the next, he looked like he wanted to know my entire life story.

He was beyond confusing. He was also very sexy, so much so that he made every other boy I'd ever fancied look like a gargoyle. But I couldn't figure him out and I didn't like that. There were people in my life I loved and some I didn't much care for, but at least I knew where I stood with them.

"Wanna get out of here for a bit?" I asked.

"Really? You don't seem like the type to offer that," he replied. The spark in his eyes crystal clear, blue eyes was back.

"Get your mind out of the gutter, buddy. You know that's not what I mean."

I thought he'd say no, but he dug his hands into the sofa and pushed himself up. When I didn't move, he smirked. "Don't you want to go…somewhere? Was that a trick question, Mackenzie?" he asked, wiggling his eyebrows suggestively.

"No, it wasn't!" I replied, standing. My heart raced in annoyance and anticipation. "I didn't expect you to take that the wrong way."

His eyes turned darker as his mind wandered. "There's a lot about me you probably wouldn't expect."

I shuddered in delightful anticipation at his tone. Yeah, I didn't doubt that for a second. That was part of his allure.

Blake turned without a word and headed for the door. I followed him out of the cabin and along the path even though I wasn't sure how smart that was. My mum had drilled it into me from a young age to never trust a person I don't know. The forest was vast, we were miles from town, the closest cabin to us was a good twenty minutes' walk, and there I was going off into the woods with a stranger.

He headed into the woods by the river. If he went deep enough, no one would be able to hear me scream. A body could easily be lost here.

I swallowed my nerves.

You're being ridiculous. No more horror films.

"So, what's your damage? Or are you as perfect as you look?" he asked, glancing at me out of the corner of his eye.

"I'm not sure how to take that," I said, and he shrugged. I was sure "perfect" was meant sarcastically. I'm so far from perfect. I've made mistakes and done something I would give the world to change. "No damage. I'm boringly normal."

"No dark secrets you're hiding?"

I tripped, losing my footing. My throat closed to the point it almost choked me. Had Josh told him? No, he couldn't have. There was no reason to. Telling Blake wouldn't fit his agenda. "No, no secrets."

"Liar," he muttered.

I planted my feet. He'd taken about ten more steps before he realized I was no longer beside him. He twisted his head around to find me and smirked.

Rolling his eyes, he said, "Oh, come on, Mackenzie, everyone has secrets."

"Not dark ones."

Except, you do, I thought to myself. *What does he know?*

He stepped closer, his eyes pinning me to the spot. I stood tall as he approached. Twigs snapped underneath his boots until he stopped almost toe-to-toe with me. I tried to ignore the thudding of my heart at being so close to him. His muscular frame and bedroom eyes really did make me want to go to bed.

I bit the inside of my cheek. He was entirely too close and too far away at the same time.

Bloody hormones.

"The secrets you hide from yourself are always the most danger-ous," he murmured in a low voice, almost as if he were speaking to himself.

"I'm not hiding anything from anyone."

"You're too straight."

I let that sink in for a minute. Or I tried to anyway. When it still made no sense, I said, "What?"

"You're pretty open, Mackenzie. You put up with Courtney siding with Josh over you, right?"

I nodded.

"Why? Why not give up on her? Stop trying to fix your friend-ship and make every situation perfect. People will let you down and they'll take advantage. Know when to let go. I can see it all in your eyes. You struggle to keep yourself and everyone around you together. It must be exhausting. When do you let off steam? You're going to go crazy before you're thirty."

My spine straightened. How could he be so right after knowing me for a couple of hours? Either I was super-transparent, or he was really good at reading people. Still, I couldn't let the guy know he was right. I stood my ground and folded my arms. "You know *nothing* about me."

He'd hit too close to home and I didn't like it. There were things about my past I didn't like—a massive mistake that I would take back in a heartbeat if I could. I tried to compensate for that horrendous decision by being everything that was expected of me—everything I now expected of myself.

21

It was exhausting.

The most annoying part was Blake, a guy I'd known for two sodding seconds, recognized that more than my friends and family. OK, so he didn't know *what* had happened, but he knew there was something I was hiding. If I could help it, he would never learn what that was.

"I don't know specifics, but you've got frustrated-teen tattooed all over yourself."

"And what have you got tattooed over yourself?" *Arrogant arse* was my guess.

"The Japanese rising sun."

"Huh?"

He pulled up his T-shirt sleeve, revealing a black tattoo of half a sun.

Oh, he was talking literally. "What does it stand for?"

"No idea. Just liked it."

OK…

"Well, I think it's cool," I said.

Chuckling to himself, he walked deeper into the forest. The trees were a bright, crisp green and leaves blew softly in the light wind as we walked. It was cooler under the trees, and since England was going strong with the heat wave, it was welcome.

"You've known the others for years?" he asked as I jogged to catch up with him again.

"Yeah."

"Kyle and Aaron didn't seem that happy about me crashing your weekend. Megan either, actually."

I shrugged. "They're cool. They just liked the dynamic we had pre-Josh-and-Courtney best. They can be kind of protective, Aaron especially. That guy would literally do anything for his friends. He'd take a bullet for us. Not that I wouldn't. Once a guy grabbed my arse after I refused a dance and Aaron knocked him out cold."

"He sounds more psychotic than protective, but put whatever label you want on it."

"I will," I replied, narrowing my eyes. I could handle Blake's theories about me. What I didn't like was his speaking badly of my friends.

"So, tell me. A group as close as you lot…"

I knew where that was going. "Not me. Josh and Courtney, as you know. Aaron and Tilly had an on/off relationship."

"You never? Not even once?"

"Nope. Girls and guys can be just friends, you know."

"Sure, just seems odd. I've been around groups of friends, and there's always a few who have had drunken sex. Or at least gotten their hands busy."

Oh, that's lovely. "Sorry. No dirt here." Not that kind anyway.

"Wow, Kenzie, you lot really are as straight as they come. You plan some board games for this evening?"

"No, of course not! Sorry, we're so boring, Mr. Excitement. What do you do for fun anyway?"

He whipped around. His eyes were wide and hungry as he grabbed my wrists and pushed me against a tree, trapping me with his entire body. I was stunned. My body wanted to arch into him. I wanted to feel his skin against mine, his tongue in my mouth, his breath on my neck.

Get. A. Grip. Mackenzie.

What was going on with me? I'd never had this kind of chemistry so quickly with someone. Actually, I'd never had this much chemistry with someone else at all. It was his fault. Blake's outrageously good looks and air of mystery short-circuited my brain, and I had to force myself to stay focused. My legs turned to jelly, and if it wasn't for him holding me up, I'd be on the floor.

Forcing myself to get it together, I swallowed, my throat like the Sahara, and whispered, "Sex is the only fun you have?" His body pressed against mine a little bit harder, and I stifled a moan. I could feel the hard muscles of his chest. *Stop. It.*

"No. Sex is the *most* fun I have." His eyes, now on fire, looked right through me, to the secrets I hid away. Still, he stayed pressed against me, his jaw tight, as if he was finding it hard to hold back.

I can't be doing this right now. Or at all. I wasn't the person that instantly wanted someone. I had to build up to that, get to know them first, but Blake made me want to throw all my rules out of the window. Rules I had worked very hard to keep.

He suddenly pulled away from me. My knees felt weak. Gripping the tree, I barely managed to keep myself upright. "What?" I asked, shaking my head to clear the fog of confusion and lust that had swept over me.

"What're the odds of you freaking afterward?"

"High," I replied. Having sex in the middle of the forest with Josh's brother, who I'd only met today, was a terrible idea.

I couldn't quite get that through to my racing pulse and over-heated body though. "Thought so. Come on. I'll show you where I shoved Josh in the river and broke his arm."

What? One minute the guy was all over me, and the next, he was playing tour guide?

I took a deep breath to get my thoughts together and stop being an idiot around him. "You broke his arm?" I asked, running again to catch up with him.

"Accidentally." He smirked. "I'm not a sociopath."

CHAPTER THREE

Two hours later, Blake and I were back at the cabin and indulging in drinking games with my friends. It didn't take long for me to get tipsy again…and then go straight to being drunk. I still knew my name and the prime minister's, but I'd definitely had one too many.

Tipping my head back, I laughed hysterically until my stomach muscles screamed in protest. Everything that was only remotely amusing when you were sober was heightened when you were drunk—so Kyle falling over was hilarious. He didn't even go all the way down—it was more like a stumble—but I was drunk, so it didn't matter. He stood up and looked around as if hoping no one had seen.

I giggled uncontrollably.

"Piss off," he snapped, narrowing his eyes at Courtney as she laughed too.

"Touchy," she muttered, leaning into Josh's chest as he put his arm around her.

Kyle folded his arms. "*Touchy?* Really, Court?"

If Courtney had tripped, she wouldn't have found it funny.

"Back off," Josh barked.

Could we not go an hour without someone arguing anymore?

Pre-Josh we rarely bickered. I groaned and held my full stomach. It was full from stuffing my face with enchiladas, and it was probably the only reason I could hold all of the alcohol I'd drunk.

Blake kicked his feet up on the coffee table and threw his arm over the back of the sofa behind me. Aaron's baby blues turned suspicious as he watched us. I refused to meet his eye and wrapped my arms around myself, not liking being the center of anyone's attention.

My walk with Blake had caused a few raised eyebrows. My friends—minus Court and definitely excluding Josh—seemed to think he was bad news, but that was probably because he was related to Josh and they hadn't really spoken to him yet. If they were giving Josh a second—or tenth—chance, they could certainly well give Blake a first one. Aaron was stubborn and protective though, so I knew he'd be the hardest to convince.

"Oh my God, we're gonna be so hungover tomorrow," Megan whined. She wasn't as drunk as she acted, but she had always been like that. She'd perfected her look-at-me wobble, blatantly tripping over her own feet. She didn't like being drunk and losing control, but she didn't like to be the odd one out, so she pretended. Everyone knew she pretended. I think she knew we knew, but we all went along with it and laughed at silly, drunk Megan wobbling. It was kind of ridiculous.

"More shots!" Aaron announced, pointing to the empty shot glasses on the table. I had lost count of how many we had done so far. But as much as we had already drunk, we were going pretty slow compared to *that* night.

Blake was surprisingly sober for the amount he'd put away. I suspected he drank quite a bit at home to have that kind of tolerance. He walked in a straight line when he got up for more beer.

As the shots kept coming, I started to feel sick. My stomach turned, and every time I swallowed, I felt like my throat was pinching shut. Megan had brought some Italian liquor with her and made us finish the bottle because, as she put it, "If I take that crap back with me, my mother will disown me." I could see why. It tasted of lemon and burned on the way down. It was probably what toilet cleaner tasted like. We also polished off Aaron's bottle of spiced rum.

I groaned and craned my neck. My body felt heavy and weak. I was getting to the sleepy part of being drunk. Everything was swimming and spinning.

"Does anyone else feel weird?" I asked.

God, I'll be lucky if I'm not sick tonight.

Megan giggled. "What, drunk?"

"Sort of. I guess," I replied, pressing my hands to my face. I was too hot. *Please don't throw up.* The taste and feel of it rushing up my throat made me panic.

"Mackenzie, you look green," Blake said, brushing my long hair over my shoulder. If I hadn't been too ill, I would've swooned at the feel of his hand grazing my neck.

My head spun.

"Oh crap!" I leaped up, slapping my hand to my mouth as I hightailed it to the bathroom. Thankfully, I made it to the toilet before bringing up half the booze I'd consumed. I braced my palms against the wall beside the toilet as I finished puking.

Groaning, I slowly pushed myself to my feet, flushed the toilet, and brushed my teeth. I stumbled back into the living room feeling no more sober but way better now that my stomach wasn't so queasy.

"Are you OK?" Courtney asked when I returned.

Josh snorted. "Does she look it?"

I didn't have the energy for a sarcastic comeback, so I flashed him the middle finger and sat back down.

Blake gave me a small, genuine smile that melted me. "You good?"

"Mmm. I'm just gonna rest my eyes for a minute." *Keep still and don't move a muscle.* If I could be a statue, the waves of nausea would go away. Closing my eyes, I felt sleep dragging me under.

"I'm going up to bed," Megan announced. "I'm tired and probably going to have a hangover from hell tomorrow." I nodded against the sofa cushion with my eyes still shut and mentally punched myself. *Do not move, Mackenzie.*

"Err, Megan, down here tonight," Josh reminded. It was Courtney's idea that we should all sleep downstairs like it was a big slumber party. Why it mattered where we were when we were unconscious, I did not know. Of course Josh would back her up. Not because she was his girlfriend, but because it would make him look like a good boyfriend. He wouldn't care if Megan slept outside.

"Shut up, Josh," she said, forcing her words to slur.

"Come on, Megan, you agreed," Courtney whined.

Josh put his arm on Court's thigh and leaned toward Megan. "This isn't your house, in case you forgot."

Aaron scoffed. "How could she forget? You remind us every five minutes!"

"You're a guest, Aaron, so you do what I say, when I say!"

"Bloody hell, Josh, why does it bloody matter where everyone sleeps?" Blake snapped.

Thank you! I thought. At least someone was reasonable.

"Just go upstairs if you want, Megan," Blake said.

I flicked my eyes open in time to see Megan stick out her tongue at Josh and stumble up the stairs. Blake was quiet but smirking at the scene.

You so like Blake. I did—much more than I should.

"What's your problem?" Aaron asked Josh, slumping back against the end of the sofa from his place on the floor. "Ever since Tilly and Gigi died, you've been a complete dick."

Before that too.

I curled up, not wanting to talk about my dead friends with Josh. It made me violently angry when I thought about the things he's said and what he was doing. You can be glad you didn't die, but it's unacceptable to be glad someone else did. I gritted my teeth.

"What's *your* problem?" Josh sneered. "You dumped Tilly just before, remember?"

Aaron's eyes darkened. "You know what, Josh? Drop dead! I swear if you ever say her name again, I'll kill you." I expected Aaron to get up and lunge for Josh. But he just sat there. Was he too drunk to move as well? That didn't usually stop him.

Sighing, I scrubbed my face with my hands. Nights always ended in arguments now and I was tired of it.

"Stop!" Courtney shouted. "End it now."

I clenched my fists. How could she not see who Josh really was? That he was the instigator? Aaron shook his head and took another swig from his bottle of vodka, finishing the last drop. I wanted to get up and leave the room, but I couldn't even raise my arm. My eyes suddenly weighed a ton again. I was so over this. I felt horrible. I probably looked it too. The room spun, and I my limbs got lighter and lighter, like they were going to lift and I'd float off. Snuggling into the sofa with a throw pillow, I drifted.

It only felt like minutes later when I was woken up by the bravest human on earth. I don't come out of sleep gracefully. *This had better be good.* "What?" I growled. Blake's very amused expression was the first thing I saw when I reluctantly opened my eyes.

His eyes lit up and he grinned. "Your shirt."

I propped myself up on one elbow and looked down. My shirt was still on, so I didn't know what he was going on about. "What? My what, Blake?"

"It's…" He traced his finger along my hip bone, where my shirt had ridden up an inch or two, showing a small slice of skin. *Oh.* I tried to breathe normally, but my senses were on overload. His intense gaze was all I could see, and that woody, masculine aftershave was all I could smell. His fingertip trailing over my skin tickled and left me breathless.

I looked around to see if anyone else was awake. Kyle and Aaron were sprawled and snoring on the floor. Courtney and Josh were nowhere to be seen, probably upstairs. Hypocrites. "You woke me up to touch my stomach?" I asked as calmly as I could.

"No, I woke you up to see if you've known me long enough to let me take you to bed yet."

No, he hasn't, but I can feel all logic jumping right out of the window. I've never wanted someone I barely knew before, but Blake is different.

My eyebrows shot up in shock, but my heart raced with excitement. I didn't know Blake, not really, but I couldn't get my brain to function well enough to convince me of that. Before I could reply, Blake's lips touched mine, and that was when logical thought ended. I let him take me upstairs.

Saturday, August 8

I cracked my eyes open and they were immediately stung by the evil morning light. It didn't help that the room was a bright yellow. Groaning, I ran my hands over my face. I felt like I'd been hit by a bus. My head throbbed, and every time I swallowed, I felt as if I were downing sawdust. To make matters worse, this time Blake wasn't waking me up. My hangovers weren't usually this bad. Last night, I had drunk a lot, but nowhere near enough to feel as awful as I did. When had I become such a humongous lightweight? Blake lay on his side, with one arm and one leg thrown over me. He looked peaceful. Whatever weighed on his mind during the day didn't trouble him while he slept.

Biting my lip, I watched him sleep, feeling a bit like a creeper. I had never had a one-night stand, so my experience with the morning after was nonexistent. I knew the general idea was to leave ASAP, but in this situation, that was impossible. We were spending the weekend in the same secluded place, and it's not like I had my own car.

Oh God. *I had a one-night stand!* I tried to calm myself. *It's fine. You're an adult, remember? Adults do this all the time.* But I didn't. Why had I allowed myself to sleep with Blake when I hadn't even known him twenty-four hours?

Shut up, it's fine. You're allowed to be into a guy, to have a good time.

I had to get a grip. There was nothing I could do to change what had happened. But neither of us needed to freak out or make this awkward—and by neither of us, I meant me. We were attracted to each other and acted on it. We were both into it, both consenting adults. It'd be fine. Besides, I felt too ill to worry much anyway.

Pushing myself up, I flopped and fell back against the mattress. My heavy stomach rolled. Oh God. I had no energy. I needed water, aspirin, and to throw up the remaining alcohol that was still sloshing around in my system.

Never again. Never ever, ever, ever again.

My movements woke Blake. He removed his hand from my stomach and rubbed his face. "I feel like death," he groaned.

Blushing because of the situation we were in, I replied, "Join the club."

He smiled at me. "How do you not look like hell in the morning? I mean, you've got that stunning, post-sex glow that's turning me on."

Seriously? "How can you feel like crap and still want sex?"

He replied, "Have you ever seen yourself, Mackenzie?"

His comment made me bite my lip. I didn't think I was that pretty, but I kind of loved how he saw me. Everyone wanted someone to think they were special, and my ex never had. Blake made me feel sexy and appreciated, which was nice, even if I broke my own rules.

"I…" I what? What did I want to say?

Chuckling quietly, he shoved himself up and reached for his jeans. "I need food and strong coffee. Do you know what everyone has planned for today?"

Following his lead, I grabbed my clothes and started to get dressed. I flicked my gaze at him to make sure he wasn't looking at me. He was. "We're going down to the lake to swim. Aaron wants to feed everyone barbecue food all day; then we're making a bonfire in the evening."

Blake stilled. "You're making a fire in the middle of the forest?"

"A small bonfire. We're not setting trees alight."

"At least not purposefully," he muttered. "I'm overseeing that."

"Oversee away. I'm sure Aaron would love the help."

"It's not Aaron I want to hang out with."

Holy…

I bit my lip. "Well, good."

He lifted an eyebrow while staring into my eyes. "Yes, it is."

If he kept looking at me like that, I was going to explode. I already felt too hot.

"So you'll be down at the river all day?" he asked, bending over to pick up his T-shirt and pull it over his head. His muscular back was just as painfully perfect as the front. He must work out because there was no way that body just happened.

"Yeah. You'll come too, right?" I blushed again, hoping I didn't sound desperate, but I wanted to spend the day with him.

He wasn't exactly one of us, but there was an opportunity for us all to be friends if he'd give it a chance. I'd already taken that chance and ran with it. Last night was proof. Blake was confident and caring, a combination I found really attractive. And he wanted to hang out with me as much as I did with him, it seemed.

"I'll come. Though I was thinking we could sneak off for a while."

I buttoned my jeans and folded my arms, but I liked that he wanted me. "You're insatiable," I teased.

Blake slowly stalked toward me. I held my ground, determined not to show him how on fire I was at the longing in his eyes.

His gaze rode over every inch of my body. "Can you blame me?"

I was about to say *forget the food* when a wave of nausea rolled over me. I needed to eat soon to soak up the rest of the alcohol. I also needed to keep a clear head. It would be so easy to get lost in all things Blake, and that was dangerous.

"We can find many opportunities to sneak off, I'm sure, but right now I need to eat some greasy food, or I'm gonna feel horrendous all day." *I can't believe I want to sneak off with him, but after last night I can't help it.*

Straightening his back, Blake walked around the double bed and gripped my arms. "Well, that sounds like a plan. I definitely don't want you feeling *horrendous* all day so…" He slid a hand down the bare skin of my arm until he reached my hand. With a little tug, he towed me out of the room and downstairs.

We stopped at the bottom of the wooden stairs to assess the damage. Bottles, shot glasses, and snack wrappers littered the coffee table and floor around it. There were more empty bottles of alcohol than I remembered. No wonder we felt rough.

Blake stood behind me, his chest pressed right against my back and a hand on my hip. I liked the contact a lot.

"This explains the drilling in my head," he murmured, leaning down to nip my neck. Spinning around, I slapped his arm playfully, laughing. Bad move. My head throbbed with the quick movement, but Blake's boyish grin made my heart swell.

Another bad move. *Don't get too involved with him.* When we went home, Blake would be back off to his dad's, and who knew when I'd see him again. If ever.

A door upstairs opened and closed. I stepped around Blake to watch Megan hobble down. She looked as good as I felt. "Kenzie?" she whispered. "I think I'm *dying*."

Laughing quietly, I replied, "You too, huh?"

"Bloody hell. How much did we drink?" she muttered, leaning heavily against the bannister as she made the final steps downstairs. She hadn't drunk much, but it was still more than she usually did.

"We're getting old," I joked. "We can't handle it anymore."

Kyle was sprawled out on the floor with his mouth wide open, breathing deeply, his jet-black hair stuck out in all directions like a bird's nest. Aaron was curled up beside him, sleeping in the fetal position. They clearly couldn't handle the amount of alcohol either. They were both in the same place Blake and I had left them last night.

Blake watched us with a curiosity I didn't quite understand. I had a feeling he didn't have many close friends, which was a shame, because beyond that I-don't-care attitude, he was a great guy. I thought—from what I'd seen, anyway.

"Where're Josh and Courtney?" Megan asked.

I shrugged. "I don't hear anyone else up, so maybe they're asleep still. God, Megan, I need aspirin."

Kyle's eyes flicked open and widened as he saw how close Aaron was to him. I felt so rough I couldn't even laugh when he shoved him away, making Aaron wake with a gasp.

Aaron looked up, dazed. "What?" He rubbed his eyes and winced. "Christ!"

"I'm making tea. Everyone in?" I asked, receiving grunts in replace of a yes and a look of disgust from Blake. I smiled, remembering what he'd wanted before. "Coffee for you, Blake."

I walked into the kitchen; my head was swimming, and everything looked a little fuzzy. A sea of red flashed in front of my eyes. I blinked hard.

You're losing it.

Opening my eyes again, I stared at the floor. It took me a

few moments to register what I was seeing. Bright, thick blood stretched from the middle of the kitchen to what looked like behind the island.

I gasped. There was so much blood. My heart raced and the ends of my fingertips tingled. The metallic smell filled my lungs and made me gag. My body turned cold and started to shake. *What...?*

"Courtney?" I whispered, not even hearing my own voice over the ringing in my ears.

Oh God, don't pass out, Mackenzie.

Someone came up behind me. "What the..." Kyle whispered, stepping around me. "Shit. Stay back, Kenz."

Blake was right behind Kyle. "What's going on?" he asked.

Against Kyle's orders, I stepped around the kitchen island and my stomach lurched. "No," I cried, pressing my hand over my mouth as bile rose in my throat. Courtney and Josh lay on the floor in a pool of crimson blood.

CHAPTER FOUR

I closed my eyes. *When you open your eyes, you'll see something different.* With my heart in my throat, I cracked one eye open. The image didn't change. There was so much blood. Courtney and Josh were still lying motionless on the floor.

Megan let out a high-pitched scream that didn't sound like it belonged to a human.

This isn't real. I'm dreaming. I have to be dreaming.

"Courtney," I whispered again, my voice drowning in a sea of Megan's sobs and screams. "Josh!"

They didn't answer. My mind reeled. *How? Who? Why?* My body was ice-cold from the shock. My fingers gripped the counter, nails digging into the wooden countertop. I couldn't move. I was frozen in place. I couldn't look away.

Oh God. Oh God. *Do something! Help them!*

Aaron dropped to his knees. His arms hovered over Josh as if he wanted to touch him but was too scared. "Shit," he spat. "Someone do something! Call an ambulance!"

It looked too late for that. Courtney's once-red lips were a pale pink, and her skin was dull and gray. A stream of dried blood stretched from her ear to the floor.

My pulse drilled.

They're dead. They're dead! No, no, no, no!

I dropped to my knees, ignoring the bickering over what to do going on behind me.

This isn't happening.

Courtney's eyes were closed, just like she was sleeping. Maybe she wasn't dead. Maybe my best friend had a chance. If I could get her to open her eyes, she would be OK. *Everything will be OK*, I repeated in my head on a loop.

"Court, wake up." I reached out and brushed her red hair from her face. She hated when her bangs fell in her face like that. *Where was help?* "We need an ambulance right now. Someone call for help. We need help," I rambled. Someone had to wake her up. "She needs help. Someone help her! Please! Oh my God, help her!"

I heard someone drop beside me. "Kenzie?" It was Megan. "She's gone, Kenz. We need to… I don't know." She pulled my arm. I thought my legs would collapse, but somehow I had the strength to stand.

"Who did this?" I sobbed, pressing my hand to my mouth, gagging. *Stop looking!* I didn't want to see this terror, so why couldn't I stop looking?

Kyle spun around. "She's right. Where is he? Or they?"

Dread settled heavy in my stomach. Were their killers still in the house?

Blake gulped, staring at his brother's face. Josh's eyes were still open but had rolled back slightly. He looked how I always imagined a dead body would look. "Where's who?" he whispered.

"The bastard who just murdered our friends!" Aaron spat in reply.

They wouldn't still be here, surely? No one was stupid enough to do something this horrible and hang around. They couldn't be. *But what if they are?*

"We need to go," Megan said, tugging on my arm. Yeah, we do. "Come on. It's not safe. Someone was here. We need go. Now."

"No one is going anywhere!" Aaron shouted. "Kyle, call the police. Megan and Kenz, get the fuck out of this room, and, Blake…don't leave this house."

I watched Blake straighten. His face hardened and his eyes narrowed. "Why did you say that? Why single me out? Why can't *I* leave?"

Aaron arched his eyebrow as if to say, *well, duh.* "Come on, it doesn't take a genius to figure it out."

"To figure out *what*?" Blake spat.

Megan gripped my hand and squeezed until I felt my bones grind against each other. I knew where Aaron was going with this. He thought the killer was Blake.

"The delinquent crashes our trip, and then we wake up with two dead bodies on the bloody floor! What else am I supposed to think?" Aaron snapped.

No. Blake wouldn't.

I wasn't sure why Blake had suddenly become a delinquent in Aaron's eyes. We had no reason to suspect Blake would do something like this. He wasn't Josh's greatest fan, but then neither were we. Loner didn't equal criminal.

Blake strode forward and stopped chest to chest with Aaron. He cocked his head to the side. "That's my *brother* lying down there. Watch your damn mouth."

"Stop it!" I shouted, shoving between them. I'd had enough of them arguing. My best friend was *dead*. How could they even think enough to pick a fight with each other? I swiped my eyes with the back of my hand. "What the hell is wrong with you, Aaron? This isn't helping, so both of you stop." I turned to Kyle and said, "Call an ambulance!"

Kyle nodded and pointed to the phone that was glued to his ear. He was so calm.

I dropped back to my knees. "We should do something! How long do you think it's been? Aaron, you know CPR. Try. Please," I begged. In my gut, I knew it was pointless, but we could at least try.

"I can't. Mackenzie, I can't bring her back."

Try!

Logically. I knew he couldn't. Of course he couldn't. She was stone cold and white as a ghost. It wasn't as if she had just collapsed. Courtney was dead. But what did it say about us if we didn't at least try to help? Courtney's and Josh's blood stained the knees of my jeans, seeping into the denim and turning the blue dark red. Horror movies have always been a favorite of mine and I'd always thought they went over the top with blood, but there seemed to be so much blood here that I felt like I was starring in one.

"There's so, so much blood," I whispered and stroked Courtney's hair as tears blurred my vision. Her face was still perfect, apart from the red trickle by her ear. Most of the blood was below her chest and had spread toward her legs. I could just about make out inch-long wounds over the bottom half of her abdomen. "Do you think they died before? They did, didn't they?" I asked. My voice hitched as I sobbed. Had she been in a lot of pain?

Aaron knelt down and rubbed my back in slow circles. "Before what?" he asked, speaking to me like he would a baby. He was surprisingly comforting. Aaron was usually more protective rather than empathetic.

"Before they…" I took a breath. "B-bled out."

"No more of this," he said gently. "Get up, Mackenzie." He tugged me to my feet and pulled me into a hug that was to console himself as well as me. Whether she died quickly or not didn't change the fact that Courtney had died an awful death. They both had.

They were dead. Gone. My heart shattered that I would never get to talk to my best friend again. I pressed my fist to my mouth and started to heave. Aaron hauled me off to the bathroom.

His fingers dug into my arm as I flopped to the floor. Aaron lifted the toilet seat just in time for me to empty the contents of my stomach into it. Again. Gripping the side of the toilet, I threw up until nothing was left.

When I finished, I sobbed and collapsed against the wall. My lungs burned. It hurt so bad I felt like someone had stabbed me too, right through the center of my heart. My best friend was gone, and I was terrified. This was all so unbelievable and so surreal.

"Do you want to stay in here?" Aaron asked.

Fear gripped me. I grabbed his hand. "I-I don't want to be on my own. Please don't leave me."

"OK, it's OK," he reassured me. "Come on." He helped me to stand up because my legs were made of sponges. I turned the tap on and rinsed my mouth out. The aftertaste of bile and alcohol made me want to be sick again. "Let me help you to the living room," Aaron said.

"No, I want to be with everyone." We had to stick together. We *had* to. I grabbed his hand again and held on to it as if it were my only lifeline. Aaron nodded and we slowly walked back.

Just don't look.

My stomach rolled as we walked into the kitchen. I let go of Aaron and leaned on a counter. From where I was standing, I couldn't see them and I wanted to keep it that way. The image would forever be burned into my memory; I didn't need to see it again.

"The police and ambulance are on their way," Kyle said, still holding the phone to his ear as he relayed information. "I don't know," he growled into the phone "Neither are breathing… They're cold. They're dead. I'm sure of it!" he snapped. His face paled and he closed his eyes.

None of us knew what to do. We were out of our depth. I had never felt so helpless before in my life.

If I could have turned back the clock, I would have gone to that CPR course with Aaron. Hell, if I could have turned back the clock, I wouldn't have drank last night. I would have protected them. How did we all sleep through this? One of us should have stayed sober. We're so stupid.

Aaron stood beside Megan and wrapped his strong arm around her shoulder. Kyle stared at Courtney with wide, shock-filled eyes. I refused to look. I'd already seen enough to haunt me for years.

My body was weak, dizzy, and I felt like I was going to collapse again. I knew I needed to eat, but there was no way I'd be able to keep anything down. I focused on breathing slowly.

"Why would someone do this?" Megan wailed loudly, coughing as she tried to catch her breath. She was hysterical—the way I should have been but wasn't.

I was empty, numb. Was it denial? They were gone. I knew that, but how? Why? This couldn't have happened right under our noses.

"Mackenzie," Aaron whispered, turning from Megan and gesturing with his head for me to follow them.

I shook my head. "I...I..." What was there to say? Nothing could make this better. Nothing.

"Shh, I know." He pulled on my arm, and I let him lead me and Megan to the sofa in the living room.

The door handle rattled just as I sat down, making me jump. It was only then that I saw the flashing blue lights. *Oh, thank God.* Help was here.

Someone pounded on the front door. "Police! Open up!"

Blake dashed to open the door. I couldn't remember anyone locking it last night.

Police officers burst in, and Aaron, Blake, and Kyle wasted no time in explaining what had happened.

They rattled off the story all at once; their voices muddled together, mouths moving at a hundred miles an hour, creating a buzzing sound that couldn't be understood.

One of the officers, a tall man with shaved black stubble for hair and a jet-black suit, held up his hand. "Calm down. Please. Where are they?" he asked, his voice thick with authority, similar to my old high school headmaster.

"Kitchen," Blake replied, taking a breath. "I'll lead the way."

"Stay here, girls," Kyle said, looking between Megan and me before following the guys to Courtney and Josh.

I did what he said because I couldn't face seeing them like that again. Leaning to the side, I huddled into Megan for comfort. Really, I just wanted my mum.

"What do you think they're doing?" I asked.

She shook her head, and her hands trembled in her lap. "I don't know. Where will they take them? To the hospital?"

To the morgue. I squeezed my eyes closed at the thought. "I don't know. Probably," I replied. The protocol for situations like this was not something I was familiar with.

As a distraction, I fixed my eyes on the fireplace and watched the last of the flames struggle to flicker. It'd gotten cooler last night, so the boys had lit the fire. The pale-orange glow was almost out, leaving the room marginally cooler.

A female officer with her hair pulled back tight against her head knelt down in front of us. "I'm Detective Inspector

Julienne Hale, but you can call me Julie. How are you both doing?"

I shook my head. How were we supposed to answer that question? Megan's reply was a strangled sob that sounded like it hurt.

"I need to ask you a few questions." Neither of us replied. I tried to, but when I opened my mouth, nothing came out. She continued. "Can you tell me your names?"

"Mackenzie Keaton," I answered. "That's Megan Haydock." Megan was in no state to talk. She buried her head in her knees and her body shook as she silently cried. "Is there someone else in the house? I didn't hear anyone break in. I would have heard someone, wouldn't I? We didn't look. We were too…" *Preoccupied with our dead friends.* I closed my eyes as a tidal wave of nausea almost took me out.

She smiled, placing her hand over mine. "Mackenzie, slow down."

"Why didn't we hear them? Courtney had a loud voice and her scream—"

"I'm sorry," Julie said, giving my hand a squeeze. "We can do this a little later. You've had a terrible shock. Take some time."

"You will find who did it, won't you?"

She squeezed my hand. "We will do our very best."

That wasn't the answer I was looking for. My friends were lying on the floor with deep gashes all over their bodies and she would do her best?

Blake strolled back into the room and stood beside the fireplace. Leaning his elbows on his knees, he tugged his messy hair with his fingers. From the little I'd seen of him, he didn't show emotion, unless it was a cocky smirk, so I had no idea how deeply Josh's death had affected him. I wanted to get up, go over, and help console him, but I didn't have anything left to give. Every muscle felt like it was made of lead.

"Blake," I murmured softly.

He didn't look up but cocked his head to the side, acknowledging me.

"You OK?"

He didn't move his position or attempt to reply. How was one supposed to answer a question like that anyway?

"We have to wait in here," Kyle said as he and Aaron entered the living room. He shook his head and sat down beside me. Julie walked into the kitchen, leaving us with another uniformed officer who I had a feeling was assigned to watch us.

For the longest time, no one said a word. We were stunned. Paramedics and more police officers—about five or so—streamed past us, but we stayed still. I felt as if I were in a nightmare and needed to wake up. I couldn't think straight. Nothing made sense. Who would want to hurt them? Why attack just them? Why not the rest of us too? And why hadn't we heard anything?

"We slept through the whole thing," I said. Hearing it aloud made it even more unbelievable. "Do you think they...shouted... for us?"

"Don't," Kyle said, wrapping his arm around me. I fell against his side, giving in to my body's need to shut down. He stroked my hair and I was done for. I burst into tears, shamelessly gripping his shirt.

Kyle stroked my hair and sniffled. We held each other tight. "OK. We're OK," he repeated in my ear over and over. But it wasn't OK and neither were we.

I pulled back and offered him the feeblest smile. "I've got you too," I whispered. He was being strong, but he was a sensitive soul and needed support just as much as the rest of us.

We sat in silence while the police did whatever it was they had to do. The door to the kitchen was closed, so we could no longer see down the hall, and we were told not to go back there. The room was a crime scene now. Upstairs was off limits too, so we couldn't get our things. The police didn't want us going anywhere. Were they looking for something in our stuff?

"I want to go home," Megan whispered, clenching her fists over and over and shaking her head. "I want to go home. I *need* to leave this cabin."

So did I, but we weren't allowed to. "Why didn't we hear anything?" I repeated. Drunk or not, surely we would have heard someone break in and stab two of our friends. "Do any of you remember?" No one answered, too caught up in their own thoughts. I racked my brain but I barely remembered anything after Josh and Aaron's argument—the one where Aaron told Josh he would kill him if he mentioned Tilly's name again. I already knew I wasn't going to tell the police that. He didn't mean it, but the police wouldn't take it like that.

Blake stood up and everyone stared at him. The burly police officer, our guard, turned his body to Blake, letting him know he was still watching. "We couldn't have been *that* drunk. None of us drank enough to be that out of it during a bloody murder. It's not possible," he said.

"Well, no one heard anything!" Kyle snapped.

Blake spun around. "I'm aware of that, *Kyle*. What I don't get is why. Or how."

The kitchen door opened and the short-haired detective in the expensive suit raised his eyebrows. He walked into the room, carrying himself as if he owned the place. "We need to have a little chat."

One by one, we all shared a quick glance.

He walked to the fireplace and stood in front of it. He had our attention. Clicking his tongue, he said, "I'll get the pleasantries out of the way first. I'm Detective Inspector Wright. Now, the door. You had to unlock it for us this morning, correct?"

"Yes," Aaron replied, frowning.

Wright clicked his tongue again. "Hmm. The door in the kitchen is locked too. When was it locked?"

"Last night," I said, remembering. "Courtney locked it before we started drinking. Why?"

"Thank you. Mr. Harper," Wright said, turning his attention directly to Blake. "The only doors into the house are that one," he said, nodding to the front door, "and the kitchen, correct?"

"Yeah," Blake replied.

"There is no evidence of forced entry, and since both doors were locked, either the murderer had a key or we're left with another possibility."

I frowned. "What's that?"

"One or more of you stabbed your friends to death." He swung his arms behind his back. "So…who wants to confess?"

My heart stopped, and my mouth fell open.

CHAPTER FIVE

"No," Megan said, shaking her head at the bomb Wright had just dropped.

I couldn't believe it and I *wouldn't*. None of my friends were murderers. We all had our issues with Josh, sure, but none of us wanted him to die. And Courtney—she was sweet, funny, and loyal. She was the best friend anyone could ask for. No one hated her. This was a random attack. It had to be. It had to have been someone else.

"No. You need to keep looking. There must be some way the attacker got in," I said, shaking my head. "Blake, you know this place better than anyone—"

Blake shook his head and took a deep breath. His eyes were wide, scared. "They've checked the doors, Mackenzie. There is no other way in from the outside."

"That can't be true!" I insisted and turned to the hostile-looking officers. "The windows!"

"Are all locked and cannot be accessed from the outside," Wright replied. "No one could get into the property without breaking in, and there are no signs of that being the case."

"*No*," I repeated. "Please keep looking."

"The police don't need to keep looking, Mackenzie. We know who did it," Aaron said and stared at Blake.

"Don't be an arsehole, Aaron," I said. Josh was Blake's brother. He had more to lose than any of us. It couldn't have been him.

Kyle stepped next to Aaron, backing him up. "Who was it then, Kenz? Come on. You know all of us. Was it one of your friends or the creepy stranger?"

Blake folded his arms over his chest, saying nothing. Aaron had thrown a huge accusation at him, and if it were me, I'd be defending myself and setting everyone straight.

"The police come up with one theory, and you start turning on each other?" I threw my hands up in exasperation. I thought I knew my friends better than that. I thought our friendship was stronger than that. "Will you all please stop pointing fingers at each other so we can figure out what happened to Josh and Courtney? The way you're all acting is disgusting. We need to stick together, not rip each other apart."

"She's right," Megan said. "I don't believe any of you could do this."

I felt Blake's eyes burning into the side of my head, but I didn't meet his gaze. I refused to believe I'd slept beside a murderer. I wasn't intimate with a killer. I couldn't have been.

Wright clicked his tongue. "As interesting as all this is, I need you to get into the squad cars now." He looked at each of us when he spoke. I felt naked under his intense glare. It was clear he thought one of us did it. "We're taking a trip to the station, so we can ask you some questions and get a formal statement," he said, pursing his lips, "and then my colleagues are going to search every inch of this house—and your homes." He nodded toward the front door and walked out.

I sat in a small interview room, biting my lip. One of the female police officers had brought me a change of clothes, so I was wearing gray sweats and a plain white T-shirt. My clothes had to be sent off for examination. Even though I'd done nothing wrong and was fully cooperating, I still felt like a criminal.

DI Wright and a pretty female officer he'd introduced as DI Lancer sat opposite me. I refused to have my parents or anyone else with me because it would seem like I had something to hide.

Wright tilted his head. "Tell me again, Mackenzie, what happened last night?"

Leaning forward, I leaned my arms on the cold table. "I don't know. We were all drinking. God, we drank a lot. The last thing I remember is Blake waking me up from the sofa and…" I was going to have to admit that we'd slept together. I wasn't sure why it was embarrassing—it just was. I licked my dry lips. "We went upstairs. In the morning, we woke up and went down to make breakfast. That's when we found…what we found."

"Where was everyone else when you and Blake went upstairs?"

"Megan went up to a bedroom first. Aaron and Kyle crashed on the living room floor. Josh and Courtney must've gone to his room while I was asleep on the couch. They weren't in the living room when Blake and I went upstairs. I assume Aaron and Kyle didn't go find bedrooms because they didn't want to get in an another argument with Josh."

"Argument?"

"Um. Yeah. Megan and Josh had a disagreement about where to sleep and Blake told her to go up. Aaron stood up to Josh too."

"They physically fought?"

"No, of course not. It was just verbal."

"What was the argument about?" he pressed.

"Megan and Josh's?"

The DI blinked as if I had asked a stupid question. There were two arguments. How was I supposed to know which one he was asking about?

"Yes, the argument between Megan and Joshua."

"Well, Courtney wanted everyone to sleep downstairs, but Megan wanted a bed. Josh told Megan that it was his house and she had to sleep where he said. Blake stepped in and told her to go upstairs to bed. It was nothing really."

"What was Joshua's argument with Aaron over?"

I bit my lip and looked at the recorder on the table beside Wright. "At first, Aaron was just sticking up for Megan, but then Josh said something about Aaron dumping Tilly before the accident." I frowned, struggling to remember clearly. Was that it? "I think. He spits that out occasionally. I can't remember exactly what they said, but they shouted, and then Courtney told them to stop."

"And then?"

"And then we went back to drinking."

"Why did Courtney want everyone downstairs?" he asked.

I shrugged. "She said we should all drink until we dropped. I don't think she really cared if anyone wanted to go to bed though."

"But Josh did?"

"Josh is Josh." *Was* Josh.

Wright's bushy eyebrows pulled together. "What does that mean exactly? What was Josh like?"

"He didn't really care about anyone other than himself. He liked to be the big man, and we were all supposed to be in debt to him for organizing get-togethers, like this trip." I dropped my eyes to the table. "And the theme park weekend."

"Is this the trip which resulted in a car accident?" he asked. "Two people died that day, Tilly Moss and Giana Beaucoup, is that correct?"

"Yes," I whispered. "How do you know that?" Tilly and Gigi had been sitting in the back of the minivan when we were hit by a truck.

"It's a small town, Mackenzie." I knew that. No matter what happened and where it happened, everyone in town knew your business. He leaned forward, resting his elbows on the table. "Joshua organized the trip that led to two of your friends' deaths."

"I know where you're going with this. No one blames Josh for what happened. It was an accident." We only blamed him for how he treated us and what he said after.

"How can you be so sure your friends feel the same way?"

I gritted my teeth. "Not forgiving someone is one thing. Murder is another. None of my friends are capable of that."

He sighed. "So that brings us back to you."

Did the detective think I was guilty? My palms began to sweat. "No. I would never hurt anyone. I didn't do it. I swear."

"Let's talk about your relationship with Courtney Young for a minute. You'd been friends for how long?"

I frowned at his use of the past tense. "About eight years. We met when we were eleven." We sat next to each other at school and became insta-friends. We shared a love of the *Twilight* books, trashy teen romance films, and boys. I'd give anything to go back to our preteen years.

"And in that time, have you had any fallings-out?"

"A few, I guess. We never argued for long though. I think the longest we've ever gone without talking was two or three days." It would be longer now. I pressed my fingernails into the palms of my hands trying to offset the pain of losing her, which tore through my chest. I would never hear Court laugh or sing like a cat being strangled again. Bless her, she tried so hard to be the next Britney, but it was never going to happen.

He wrote something down and I thought he was going to ask some follow-up questions, but he changed direction. "How long had Josh and Courtney been together?"

I shrugged. "Around a year and a half, I think."

"You don't seem too thrilled by your friend's relationship with Joshua. Why is that?"

"Like I said before, Josh is—*was*—a selfish person. He brought Court down. She was so much more outgoing and confident before him. After they got together, she didn't have her own voice or opinion. She just backed up whatever he said. She deserved better."

His eyebrows arched.

"That doesn't mean I wanted anything bad to happen to him." Not *that* bad, anyway.

"What happened after Tilly's and Giana's deaths? From what I can gather, that's when the feud began."

"It wasn't a feud. Josh said some things that were insensitive."

"Like what?"

"He said at least it wasn't him and Courtney."

"Who died in the crash?"

I nodded. "Yes. I was glad the rest of us were OK, but I don't know how he could place anyone else's life below his own. Like they were expendable. He said the accident was Gigi's fault anyway, because she got too drunk to drive so Court had to. Apparently, that meant she deserved to die."

"And you hated him for it."

I played with the hem of my T-shirt. I didn't hurt anyone, but Detective Wright was constantly leading me there, wanting me to admit to something I hadn't done. I wanted to tell the truth, but I was scared. "Hate is a very strong word. I didn't ever want anything bad to happen to him, but I wished he would break up with Courtney and get out of our lives."

"How badly did you want him out of your life?" the detective pressed.

"I didn't kill him!" Why wasn't he listening to me? I felt sick.

Wright's mouth twitched. His breath blew across my face. It smelled of stale tobacco mixed with mint. "I'm not saying you killed Josh, but do you know who did?"

"No. I swear I don't. My friends aren't violent though, I know that much."

"Hmm," he murmured. "Did you each have a bedroom to yourself?"

58

"No. Megan and I were sharing; the others had a room each."
But I stayed in Blake's, I left out.

"And you unpacked as soon as you arrived?"

"I did."

"Everyone else?"

I don't know. I'm not their mum! "I'm not sure. Megan didn't.
She never does."

"Hmm." He clicked his tongue. What did that *hmm* mean?
"Who had a key to either or both of the doors?"

"Josh."

"Just him?"

"I don't know. Blake might have one, it being his house too."

I wanted to ask why he was asking, but something stopped me.
Wright was intimidating. He looked like a powerful man. He was tall,
muscular, and had a take-no-shit attitude. He was probably a bit in
love with himself. He squinted at me as if he wanted me to believe he
already knew who the killer was and was just waiting for us to crack.

He tilted his head. "You stayed with Blake all night?"

"Yes."

"He was still there when you woke?"

"Yes. I woke first."

He nodded. "What did you have to eat while you were at the
cabin? Did you cook?"

The sudden change in direction had me concerned. I'd never
been interviewed by the police before. "We all cooked enchiladas."

He stared at me, keeping his eyes focused on pulling truths
from mine. "You all cooked?"

"We all helped, yeah."

Now why was that important?

He gave another short nod. "And the drinks. Let me guess, you all got each other drinks too?"

"Yes," I replied slowly. There was something I was missing, but I had no idea what. I closed my eyes and rubbed my temple. I didn't think like a bloody detective!

"So you all drank, you fell asleep, and when you woke, Joshua and Courtney were—"

"Yes," I replied before he could say *dead on the kitchen floor*. We all knew the outcome by now.

"Not a peep in the night, huh?"

"No."

"Joshua and Courtney were stabbed dozens of times and you didn't hear anything…"

I closed my eyes and took a breath as I was about to throw up. "No, I didn't hear anything," I said, then opened my eyes.

Please believe me.

He arched his bushy caterpillar eyebrow. "I think that's it for now. You're free to go back to the waiting room with the others."

Already? That hadn't seemed to take as long as I thought it would. He looked at me and half smiled. *Oh, he's not done with me at all.* I stood up and walked out of the room, anxious to get back to my friends. As I left, I kept my head held high and walked with confidence, trying to show him I wasn't intimidated. I probably walked guiltily.

Through the glass panel in the door, I could see everyone already out there.

"You OK?" Blake asked, pulling the door open for me from the inside, as I was about to push it.

I shook my head and wrapped my arms around myself. "Not really." Megan sat on the chair, curled up in a ball; Kyle's arm was around her shoulders, rocking her like a child. I smiled at Blake in thanks and knelt down in front of my friend. "Megan?"

Her body trembled.

"She hasn't said anything since she came out of being questioned," Kyle said. "How'd it go?"

"He thinks it was one of us," I replied. Blake had moved to the other side of the room. He stood against the wall, looking out of the window, acting as if he were alone.

Kyle followed my gaze to Blake. "Maybe it was," he whispered.

I narrowed my eyes. We couldn't turn against each other. We had to stick together until the police found out who was *really* responsible. I was about to defend Blake when Wright came back into the room.

"We're going to run a drug test on you too, Mackenzie," he announced as if he'd offered me a cup of tea.

"What? Why do you need to do that?" I asked. He hadn't mentioned that before. They already had the clothes we were wearing and our other belongings from the cabin. I thought they had finished with the tests.

Oh, this is the because.

He rubbed the dark stubble under his chin. "Standard procedure, especially when I have two murdered teens and five more at the crime scene claiming to remember nothing. Take a seat,

Miss Keaton, Mr. Harper. I'll be with you again in a moment."
He stepped out into the hallway.

Blake sat on one of the faux leather chairs, staring into space.
I took a seat between him and Megan. "This is like a dream,"
Megan whispered.

"A nightmare," I countered. "Have you both been tested yet?"
Blake shook his head. "Aaron went first."

Aaron looked up. "Did they tell you what they're testing for?"

"This is the first I've heard of it." I shrugged. "I really don't
know. I've never had to take a drug test before. This is crazy." Did
they test for every drug or just the most common ones? "Have
you seen your mum yet?" I asked Megan.

She shook her head, crying. "I-I think they're all here, or they've
been called, but we can't see them until we've done this." Her
voice wobbled.

Defiantly, Blake stood up and walked to the window again. He
leaned on the windowsill, deep in thought. Soon he would have
to face his parents and they were going to have a lot more to deal
with than just getting him through what'd happened to Josh and
Courtney—they had also lost a son.

"Megan, come with me," Wright said, poking his head into
the room again.

Megan shot me a look as if to say either *wish me luck* or *help*
and scurried after Wright with her shoulders hunched. I ran
through everything that had happened for the millionth time,
but once I'd fallen asleep, I remembered nothing. No noise in
the night that disturbed me. Surely someone would scream

if they were being murdered. If Courtney saw a spider, her scream could wake someone from a coma. I may have been extra tired after drinking and being with Blake, but surely not *that* exhausted.

The door opened and Kyle was summoned. Wright was calling each of us himself. Why wouldn't he send an officer to do that? Did he need that much control that he did the rubbish jobs himself too?

I sat back and closed my eyes. There was nothing new I could remember and it scared me that so much of the evening was either a blur or completely missing. That didn't look good. We couldn't have been drugged. No one else was in the house, unless it had been done before we left for the weekend. Some bottles of spirits had been opened previously.

But who would drug us?

"Blake, are you OK?" I asked once we were alone.

He shook his head. "Me and Josh..." Shaking his head again, he turned to me. My breath caught in my throat. His eyes were dull and he held himself differently. He looked haunted, like he was in physical pain.

You and Josh what?

"What, Blake?" I prompted softly.

"This is going to kill my mum. She'll wish it were me."

I blinked in shock. Sure, Blake had decided to live with his father, but that didn't mean his mum didn't love him as much as Josh. "No, that's not true."

He frowned in despair and bent slightly as he blew out a breath.

In that moment, I knew he believed what he said was true. He really believed his mum loved his brother more and would prefer him to be dead. "She wouldn't want it to be you."

"No, she wouldn't *want* it. But she would want it to be Josh a hell of a lot less."

"Blake, come with me," Wright ordered.

We hadn't had enough time to talk. I wanted to reassure him that his mum wouldn't wish he'd died over Josh. Wright wasn't going to give us another minute though. Blake walked out without another word or even a glance in my direction, and I sat down. My head fell back against the wall. How was I even here? I wanted my parents. Mum could fix anything.

She can't fix this.

When it was my turn, I was led down a short corridor and into a small room with a table like they had in the emergency room. "Sit down, please. This won't take long," a lady told me. She turned before introducing herself, so I guess I wasn't going to get to know her name.

"Thanks," I said, taking a seat and biting my lip.

"Lift up your sleeve."

My eyes widened. "This is a blood test?" I was scared of needles, so avoided blood tests like the plague. Something told me I couldn't opt out of this one though. How would that look?

"Yes. Lift up your sleeve, please."

I shoved the elbow-length sleeve over my elbow and gripped the side of the chair. Why didn't I request my mum or dad come with me? Blood tests were never as bad as I worked myself up to believe, but I still hated having them done. "W-what are you testing for?" I asked.

"Drugs," she replied in very much a "duh" manner.

Weren't they required to tell you what it was exactly if you asked? I didn't push it. I just wanted to go home. I needed to see my parents. What was supposed to be a chilled-out, drunken weekend messing around with my friends had ended with blood, murder, and police. Today had to end.

The needle stabbed my skin. I held my breath and squeezed my eyes closed as I imagined it sinking into my vein. It stung. *This is nothing compared to what Courtney went through.* I swallowed the lump in my throat. Had she been in pain long? Did she pray for death?

"All right," the nurse said, gently pulling out the needle and placing a cotton ball and Band-Aid over the spot. "All done. You can wait with your friends in the front. I believe your parents are here."

"OK, thanks," I replied and hurried out of the room.

I stepped into the holding area. Aaron, Kyle, and Megan sat on chairs by the front door. I sat beside a shaking Megan and rubbed my arms, suddenly feeling cold.

"Where's Blake?" I asked.

Megan nodded to the door to an office. "Speaking to his dad on the phone. He's in Hong Kong, apparently, and trying to get a flight back."

"He doesn't even seem that upset. His brother just died," Aaron said, watching Blake through the glass. "What does that tell you?"

"That he's just seen his brother's lifeless body and he's in shock. Same as us," I replied.

How could Aaron judge Blake like that? There was no set way to behave when you lost someone you loved. Everyone reacted to grief and loss differently. I surprised myself by being so calm. When Tilly and Gigi died, I had been a mess. But I saw them die. We were traveling home, joking around and playing the license plate game that I sucked at. We were hit. I remembered the sound of crushing metal and the screams from my friends. Tiny pieces of glass were everywhere, cutting into my skin. Everything was in slow motion until we came to a stop. I heard Tilly cry until she fell silent and I heard Gigi whisper something unintelligible before her eyes closed forever. But I couldn't move. I was sitting behind them but I couldn't reach. My seat belt had locked and I was dizzy. I *tried* but I couldn't move to help them.

This time was different. This time their deaths didn't appear to be accidents—and my friends and I were also suspects. I couldn't grieve properly while I was being questioned, while their killer was still out there.

We were all in shock. Blake was no exception.

Aaron snorted. "Why do you always try to see the good in everyone?"

Why was that a bad thing? Aaron was too quick to cut someone out of his life. I didn't want to be like that. People deserved a first and second chance.

"It's pathetic, Mackenzie," Aaron huffed.

"That's enough!" Kyle snapped.

Aaron sighed heavily. "Shit. I'm sorry, Kenz. I shouldn't have said that. I guess being trusting is not a bad thing." I could tell by how tight and tense his jaw was that it almost hurt him to apologize. Aaron was stubborn and hated to admit he was wrong.

Wright reappeared and addressed us in the lobby. "You're all free to go," he said, "but don't leave town because I'm going to want to talk to you again very soon." Turning on his heel, he walked out. *That's it?* I would've thought he would keep us for more questioning. His tactics were odd and unnerving.

I stood and took a deep breath. What were my parents going to think? I knew they would believe me when I told them I hadn't hurt Josh or Courtney, but would they believe we were all innocent? They trusted my friends, but that trust was being pushed to the limit. To get through this, I needed them to be on my side and to trust that I knew my friends.

Aaron and Kyle lead us out; Megan trailed behind in a daze. My hands shook as Kyle pushed open the door. All of our parents stood in the reception area talking to two officers. My dad looked like he was about to physically move someone out of his way so he could come and find me. He would hate not being able to do anything. Mum's eyes were red and her pale skin was blotchy from crying. I gulped as her eyes met mine.

"Oh, Mackenzie," Mum said, her voice full of emotion. I stumbled forward; my legs barely carried me to her before I collapsed in her arms. "Shh, it's OK, darling," she whispered softly and stroked my hair.

I gripped her and fell apart.

CHAPTER SIX

Monday, August 17

I could feel all eyes on me and my friends. It'd been that way for the last nine days, since Josh and Court were murdered. My room had been searched and I'd been over my version of events about a thousand times.

People were supposed to be innocent until proven guilty, but whenever I left the house, people watched me, whispering things like, "There she is," "It can't be her," or "It's usually the nice ones, you know." Women who spent their days drinking tea with my mum while they planned yet another village fund-raiser now crossed to the other side of the street when they saw me. It was awful to know so many of my neighbors who'd watched me grow up had written me off as a killer. Written us all off. There were a lot of rumors. The most popular one seemed to be that we all planned it and were now covering our tracks.

Josh's mum, Eloise, welcomed us into her house for the wake. We'd known Eloise for years, so I was confident that she believed we weren't responsible, but Josh's other relatives seemed quick to judge and assume. Megan gripped my arm. Since we'd walked through the door ten minutes ago, she had avoided eye contact with everyone. She was doing nothing to prove our innocence and she didn't even seem to care.

I thought the police would want Courtney's and Josh's bodies longer but apparently not. The healing process could start once you had said good-bye—something my mum swore by. I disagreed. The funeral was the good-bye, but afterward, you had to piece your life back together and find a way of dealing with the absence of that person. After the good-bye was the hardest bit. I had found it so difficult to move on after Tilly and Gigi and felt like I was the only one of my friends still struggling.

"We shouldn't have come here," Kyle whispered, darting his chocolate eyes around the room. He was nervous and on edge.

I straightened my back. "We have as much right to be here as everyone else. We've done nothing wrong. We might not have been Josh's number-one fans, but he was Court's boyfriend. We need to say good-bye too."

"But his goddamn family clearly doesn't want us here," Aaron added, speaking through his teeth.

"We won't stay long. Just long enough to show Eloise and Blake we're here for them."

Aaron scoffed. "We should be looking a little closer at Blake."

Rolling my eyes, I replied, "Why's that?"

"Who is the most likely killer, Mackenzie?"

I shrugged. "I don't know. Some crazy guy out in the woods who got in and—"

Kyle sighed. "No one broke in though, Kenzie. Aaron's right. It has to be Blake."

"It's not him, Kyle."

His eyes homed in on me. "Why not? What's going on with you two?"

I licked my lips, not wanting to tell them about my night with Blake. I'd have to tell them at some point, but now was not the time. They thought he was the killer and it would probably only add to their suspicion if they knew about us. I was sure I'd get comments about how he only did it to give himself an alibi. "What? Nothing's going on. Josh is his brother. I'm sorry if I don't believe the guy is capable of killing his own brother." I shook my head and gritted my teeth. Why would they want to believe that over someone random?

"They're not close and he clearly didn't like Josh," Megan said.

"And we thought he was an amazing guy," I said sarcastically. "Look, let's not do this here. After Courtney's funeral tomorrow, we should do something to honor her. A formal wake isn't what she would want," I said to change the subject.

It was hard enough to be at Josh's wake. I didn't know how I was going to make it through Courtney's funeral. I didn't want to go acknowledge the fact that I wouldn't get to see her again. How was I going to live without my best friend? At Tilly's and Gigi's funerals, me, Megan, and Courtney had clung to each other for support. Now it was just Megan and me, and as hard as Megan tried, she was too selfish to be supportive.

"Can we go soon? Please?" Megan pleaded. Her hair moved today as if she had toned down the hairspray, probably because she couldn't be bothered.

"In a bit," I replied. "We should stay a little while longer, for Josh. Well, unless his mum asks us to leave."

Josh and Blake's dad wasn't there. He hadn't been able to get back from his business trip in time due to issues at border control. I felt so sorry that he was missing his own son's funeral. Eloise should have waited. It was wrong and selfish of her not to. She should have put Josh before her hatred for her ex-husband. I could tell Blake wanted his dad here. He looked around at his family but kept to himself. It seemed as if he barely knew any of them.

Out of the corner of my eye, I saw Blake get up and leave the room. "I'll be back in a minute," I said. He'd barely said a word to me the whole morning, and we needed to have more of a conversation about his mum and how he was dealing with Josh's death than was suited to one-word answers or grunts.

He was in the hallway when I found him, staring up at a large collage of photos in a huge glass frame. Without looking at me, he said, "I'm only in three of these." There had to be more than sixty pictures, and he was right—they were all of Josh.

"I'm sorry."

"Don't be sorry, Mackenzie. He was her favorite, always had been. Even before my parents split, she preferred him. He was her little 'Joshie.' He was the baby, so she put everything into him and I was left with next to sod all."

I was surprised at the tone in his voice. I hadn't realized how deep his bitter resentment ran. He felt like his mum didn't love him.

I looked around, trying to figure out if anyone had heard us, but we were alone. I knew his words would make my friends more suspicious of him. He may have felt a lot of anger toward his mum and brother, but that didn't make him a killer. Getting rid of his brother wouldn't make his mom love Blake more—and it wouldn't explain why Courtney was dead too.

"She loves you, Blake. Josh is gone now. You and your mum have to support each other."

"Why?" My breath caught at the fierceness of his smoldering, deep-blue eyes. "She was never there for me. She was *never* there."

"You've both lost so much. Let this be a chance to bring you both closer together. Don't let Josh's death be for nothing."

"I feel like I'm at a stranger's funeral in a stranger's house." His eyes narrowed. "Josh and I hardly knew each other, and I don't want a relationship with my mother." He turned and walked back into the lounge, leaving me speechless. How could he say that? I didn't believe it for a second. He wouldn't look so beat up if he didn't care.

A hand stroked down my back, and I jumped at the contact.

"Kenz," Aaron said.

I turned to him, though it took me a moment to recover from Blake's words. "Yeah?" I replied.

"I know you're going to blow up over Blake being innocent again, but please hear me out."

I rolled my eyes. "This is getting old, Aaron."

"Please," he repeated.

Sighing, I waved my hand, agreeing to listen.

"OK. Did you know Blake was kicked out of his old high school?"

"So?"

"For fighting."

My eye twitched, and I fisted my hands. "Plenty of people get into fights in high school. I don't think we should condemn him for that."

"Don't you think it's even a little bit strange that Blake, the delinquent son, turns up suddenly and the next morning we wake up to…what we woke up to?"

"No, I think there was someone else, someone with a grudge, who did something to the food and drink so we'd be out of it. Not all of the drinks we took with us were new and food can easily be tampered with."

"I get that you don't want to believe it. I don't either, but what other feasible option is there? We know no one else was in the house. Will you at least consider this theory?"

I shook my head. "No."

Aaron sighed in defeat and said, "Let's go back in." I walked ahead and heard him add, "You'll wake up soon," under his breath.

I ignored him. He could think whatever he wanted; it wouldn't change what I knew, what I felt deep down. Blake was innocent. I did *not* trust a killer enough to be intimate with him.

Aaron and I joined Kyle and Megan in the back corner, out of the way of the receiving line. Dozens of pairs of eyes followed me, but I refused to look at them, knowing I would just see blame and hate behind their gazes. I didn't know everyone here, but those I did acted as if I could give them the plague and avoided me.

"Just a little longer," Kyle whispered, tightening his arms around Megan.

Blake entered the room, holding a glass of something amber. He took a sip and grimaced, then sat between his mum and us. All day, he had barely spoken to anyone and I noticed his family didn't make much of an effort to talk to him, except for his paternal grandparents. No wonder he felt Josh was the favorite.

"Can you *at least* promise us you'll be careful around him?" Aaron said, looking past me to Blake.

My heart gave a little squeeze and some of the annoyance I felt toward him and his "Blake's a bad guy" stance ebbed away. Aaron was worried about me. "I'll be fine," I assured him.

"Promise me, Mackenzie."

"I promise."

"And you'll call me if you ever need me or don't feel safe?"

I frowned. "I will." How on earth was I going to get them on Blake's—our—side? We were all in this together. Aaron nodded once and walked away, toward Josh's cousin, Greg, who was friends with Aaron from the high school football team. I was left speechless for a second time. I felt as if I were being pulled in two directions and had to pick a team. We were all supposed to be on the same team!

I looked over at Eloise and my heart broke for her. She stared at a framed picture of Josh that sat on the small end table beside her. I wanted to go over and comfort her, but what did you say to a woman who had just buried her son? I didn't even know her particularly well.

Blake watched his mum. He looked torn, lost even. *Forget this!* I wasn't going to give up on him that easily. He was hurting, and I wasn't going to let him push me away like everyone else.

I walked across the room and sat beside him. "Hey," I said. Despite what Aaron and Kyle said, I believed he didn't do it. He may have been the odd one out, but that didn't mean Blake was a killer.

"Hi." He leaned his elbows on his knees. "She won't even look at me," he said, paying no attention to our last conversation. I wasn't sure what to say. "Last night when I asked her if she wanted me to do the reading for her, she looked at me like…" He shook his head and sighed. "I don't even know how to explain. I could see in her eyes that she was burying the wrong son."

"Don't say that," I said softly.

"It's true. Hell, I don't blame her. I didn't choose her. I wanted to live with Dad, and Josh wanted to be with her."

"That doesn't mean she loves you any less."

He turned his head to the side and looked up at me. "The glass is always half-full in Mackenzie's world, isn't it?"

Is he serious? "Does it look half-full?" I deadpanned.

"You're trying to be optimistic. That's why you won't accept that one of your friends killed my brother," he said, nodding to the corner where my friends stood huddled together. "Josh and Courtney are dead, but if you can prove your friends are innocent…then the glass is half-full."

"You're way too cynical, even for what's going on here. You have to have people you trust. You have to be positive even when everything feels so negative. Do you trust anyone?"

"Myself."

"That doesn't count."

He sat up straight and shrugged. "Then no."

"That's really sad."

"If you don't trust anyone, then no one can screw you over. You're going to find that out the hard way," he said and excused himself.

Kyle was right. We shouldn't have come. I walked into the kitchen to get my bag so we could leave. It was time to go.

"Which one of you was it?" Josh's uncle, Pete, spat. Pete and my dad were friends, so the way he looked at me with hate made me feel like crap. "Which one of you bastards killed my nephew?"

I shook my head, pressing my back against the marble counter. Was he going to hit me? His face was red with rage and his eyes were wide. Bubbles of saliva gathered in the corners of his mouth.

"None of us, Pete, I swear," I replied. "We wouldn't hurt Josh or Courtney."

"You have the audacity to turn up at his funeral!"

"We haven't done anything wrong."

"Tell the truth," he hissed through his teeth. "Tell the police what you did."

"Pete, please—"

"No," he growled, making me flinch. He looked so furious that I wasn't sure what he would do. "It had to have been one of you. If you had any decency at all, you would own up and put an end to our family's misery. Josh deserves justice."

So does Courtney. "I want that too. You're looking for justice in the wrong place, Pete. I promise you, we didn't do this."

"Your promises mean nothing to me, Mackenzie. My sister might not see what you've done to her son, but I sure can. You will pay—"

"Hey," Kyle snapped. I spun around and saw him at the door to the kitchen. "That's enough." He wrapped his arm around me, pulling me against his side protectively. "I'm sorry you lost your nephew, but we lost two friends. This wasn't our fault."

"You're all liars. You'll rot in hell for this."

"Pete!" I said. It was so unlike him I felt as if he'd thrown a punch. The once joke-a-minute man that had me in stitches when I was younger was cold and hateful. "I understand you want someone to blame. I do too, but we didn't hurt them." I wasn't sure if he would ever believe me. I could tell him a million times that it wasn't us, but he was so wrapped up in what the police said and needing someone to blame that he couldn't see clearly.

"Get. Out," he said very slowly. "Don't ever come back here again."

"Come on," Kyle muttered, guiding me out of the door. Aaron and Megan stood in the hallway with wide eyes. "We're going."

I didn't see Blake before we left, and a quick glance in the living room on my way out told me no one in there had heard Pete's outburst. For that I was grateful.

"What are we going to do?" I asked as I walked to Kyle's car, still holding on to myself.

No one had an answer for me because they all knew that until we found out who had done it, we were all suspects.

CHAPTER SEVEN

Wednesday, August 19

"What's he doing here?" Kyle asked, frowning at someone in the distance behind the leafless trees at the side of the graveyard. The trees had died years ago but had never been removed. I found it morbidly appropriate. Kyle's tearstained face hardened.

I turned to find DI Wright standing just far enough away from the congregation for it to be clear that he wasn't part of the funeral. He wore a black suit and tie, so he looked as if he belonged, but he was focused on us and not the hole in the ground that Courtney was about to be lowered into.

A shudder of disgust ripped through my body. Today of all days, he had to show. How dare he come here and make Courtney's funeral about the investigation and not about saying good-bye to someone we loved?

I just wanted the funeral to run smoothly and to be filled with remarks from people who loved her. Wright hanging around made it all about what had happened. Dealing with everything that had happened was hard enough.

"Can't he give us one day?" Megan asked from behind me. The

detective hadn't turned up at Josh's funeral though, so I didn't know the relevance of him just being at Courtney's.

"He's trying to catch a murderer, Megan." Blake's voice made me jump. He stepped in front of us and looked back at Wright. "Gotta keep an eye on his favorite suspects."

"What're you doing here?" I asked. Courtney wasn't really anyone to him, so I hadn't expected to see him.

"Paying my respects on my brother's behalf," he replied. "I decided to stay with my mum for a while. She's a mess." I blinked in shock. After the things he'd said about his mum at Josh's funeral, I'd figured he'd take off as soon as he could. "I'm trying to help, but I'm not good with emotional women."

"I'm sorry, Blake," I said.

He shrugged. "It's OK."

"Look, after this, we're all going to the basketball court. You want to come?" From the daggers Aaron was shooting at me, he didn't want Blake there, but this wasn't about Aaron.

Blake frowned. "I thought the wake was at the social club?"

I nodded. "It is, but we decided to do something else. We hung out at the court a lot." I raised my eyebrow. "And drank there a lot. It seemed more…fitting."

Blake pulled his lip between his teeth and cocked his head to the side. Finally, he replied, "OK. Thanks."

My heart gave a flutter when he accepted. Liking Blake was dangerous; I liked him already, so he had the power to hurt me. It seemed a lot like chasing heartache but I couldn't help how he made me feel. One smile from him and I was being reeled in.

Blake lived in a different town, so he didn't know anyone around here besides his mum, and she wasn't in any state to support him properly right now. His parents were both grieving. And as much of a mysterious loner as Blake was, he needed someone to be there for him. I had my friends who knew I was innocent, but Blake didn't have that. I couldn't help wanting to be that person—even if I knew better than to jump all in with a stranger I was seriously attracted to.

My attention turned back to Courtney's mum, who was talking about reading Courtney's favorite bedtime story, *Little Red Riding Hood*. Courtney loved it so much that her mum read it to her every night as a child. I blinked hard. Hot tears burned behind my eyes. This was Courtney's final good night.

I took in a deep, shaky breath, and my hands trembled. With every word spoken, I could feel the woman's pain at losing her child, her only child. "This isn't fair," I whispered and started crying. This shouldn't be happening.

I felt weak with grief. Courtney was my best friend, and I would never see her again. My heart shattered as her coffin disappeared into the ground. I sobbed and pressed my hand to my mouth.

Blake's arm curled around my waist.

"We'll be all right," Aaron said, glaring at Blake's hand. "I promise."

I turned my body toward Blake's hard chest, desperate to be consoled. I needed someone to make the ache inside me go away. Blake's body stiffened. Then, after a heartbeat, he held me tight with both arms.

I couldn't bear to watch another person I loved, someone so

young, with so much potential, be placed into the ground. It had been hard enough when we buried Tilly and Gigi. I never imagined I'd lose another friend again so soon. We girls were always together locked in one of our bedrooms, listening to music and rating boys. It was hard going from a party of five to three. It took a long time to get used to not hearing them laugh or join in to tease the latest embarrassing crush. Now I had to get used to it being just me and Megan.

"Can we leave now, please?" I asked as Courtney's family scattered dirt on her coffin. I felt like my heart was being crushed, and I wasn't sure how much longer I could keep it together. "Yeah," Kyle replied. He sniffed as he nodded toward the yellow stone path that led us back to the parking lot. With a deep breath, he added, "Let's go and give Courtney the send-off she would actually want."

"Vodka and beer?" Blake said, raising his eyebrow at our choice of drinks. "Classy."

Megan narrowed her eyes. "Do you want one or not?"

He nodded, and Megan handed him a beer. Blake was right; they were stereotypical choices for underage drinking at the park. But we used to have a laugh messing around and playing silly games here. Everything was easier before we knew loss, when we were still all together. I missed it so much.

We sat in a circle on the grass beside the vacant basketball court, leaving space in our circle for Courtney. I wasn't ready to let her go yet.

"Should we each say something?" I asked. "Isn't that what you're supposed to do?"

Aaron nodded and took a swig of his beer. "Why don't we all say something about them both? I'll start. Courtney was one of the most beautiful girls I've ever known, and she wasn't cocky with it. She was modest and that added to her beauty. Josh…" Aaron said and laughed. "Well, Josh was punching well above his bloody weight, and he knew it."

"I'll go next," Megan said, clearing her throat. She looked like she wanted to be anywhere but here, doing anything but speaking about our dead friends.

She wasn't the only one.

"In the first year of high school, Courtney and I didn't get along. I thought she was trying to drive a wedge between me, Mackenzie, Tilly, and Gigi. It was only when my boyfriend dumped me that I realized I was wrong about her."

Megan licked her lips. "Mackenzie was on holiday and Tilly and Gigi were busy. Courtney had texted to ask if I wanted to hang out, and I told her what'd happened. She turned up twenty minutes later with chocolate and a DVD. She was a good friend, and I'll miss her so much." Megan paused, pursing her lips. "And Josh… Josh said some stupid, terrible things that I'm sure he regretted, but he wasn't an evil person. I wish I had the chance to work through our issues. Maybe we could've all had a better relationship."

Megan wanted to sort things out with Josh? I *never* wanted him to die—to be killed—but the things he'd said, the way he'd treated us, was not OK.

Megan looked to me. My turn.

I put my plastic cup of vodka on the grass in front of me. "I'm not sure where to start. There are so many things I could say, that I want to say. How do you condense years of friendship into a few short words?" Aaron gave my hand a squeeze of encouragement. I sighed. "OK, here goes. Courtney and I were pretty much inseparable all through high school, and I remember how excited we were that we had most of the same classes every year. She was always there for me and never judged me, or anyone for that matter. I couldn't have asked for a better friend, and I can't believe she won't get to grow old with us."

I blinked away hot tears. "We were supposed to rent a flat together. Remember, Megan? We were going to get a posh place in a nice part of the city."

Megan dipped her head and added, "Preferably one that overlooked a football club, so we could watch the guys run around in shorts."

I laughed and wiped a tear from my cheek. That was Courtney's idea. As long as we were near a fun part of town, Megan and I didn't care where we lived. But Court wanted to be a WAG, like Victoria Beckham and all those other footballer wives and girlfriends, if it didn't work with Josh. I was hoping she'd get to fulfil that dream. Court was vibrant, outgoing, and had enough confidence to date anyone…before Josh, that is. "Yeah, I'd almost forgotten about that part."

"What about Josh?" Blake asked sharply. "Aren't you going to say something about him?"

My stomach fell. I didn't like to lie, so I couldn't sit there and say how wonderful he was. But he was gone, and I could bloody well find something nice to add. "Of course I am, Blake. Josh and I had our differences, but I never wanted anything bad to happen to him." I frowned.

Blake opened his mouth to say something when Detective Wright sat down in the empty space beside him. *Where did he come from?*

"Didn't fancy the wake?" he asked us.

"Not really," Kyle replied. "Can we help you with anything?"

"You could tell me which one of you murdered your friends." He looked around, pinning each of us with his stone-hard gaze. "No? Worth a try." He threaded his fingers between each other. "I've just had your drug test results back."

"And?" Aaron asked, glaring at him.

Wright was arrogant. He had something about him, an aura that oozed confidence and made it seem as if he owned everyone. I got the impression that he knew a lot more about the case than he'd told us, and he was waiting until he felt it was the right time to share the information. He'd probably had the test results back days ago.

"You tested positive for Rohypnol."

My jaw dropped. "The date rape drug?"

Wright's thin lips curled to one side. "The very one, Mackenzie. You're familiar with it?"

"Everyone's heard of it," I replied. It was often in the news. It was the reason I got the never-leave-your-drink-unattended lecture from my parents whenever I went out. We were always hearing stories about women who woke up having been drugged and raped with little recollection of how it all happened.

Ice-cold blood pumped through my body. Someone had *drugged* us.

"Someone roofied us," Blake said, his voice loud with anger and disbelief. "Who?"

Wright shrugged. "Again, I was hoping one of you would be able to help me with that, but I won't be holding my breath."

"Wait?" I said. "Did we all test positive?"

"Yes."

"Even Josh and Courtney?" Aaron asked.

"Yes," Wright replied. "Strange, wouldn't you say?"

My heart spiked with the glimmer of hope. "But that proves someone else killed them." We're all in the clear. We were *all* drugged and the murderer used that as his or her chance. None of us could commit murder if we were all out of it. No wonder I'd felt so groggy when I woke up!

"Nothing has changed, Mackenzie," Wright said. "All this proves is that this murder was well planned. *Premeditated.* Whichever one of you has blood on your hands, you have done a very good job of covering your tracks. I'm impressed. Drugging yourself too—after the murders, of course—and hiding among your friends is incredibly clever. I must say this though: as clever as you are, I will find out which one of you is responsible." He pushed himself up. "Be seeing you real soon."

For the longest time after Wright had left, no one said a word. I think we were all too shocked to speak. I just couldn't see one of us as the killer, especially not one so callous.

"Is that man seriously accusing one of us of drugging the rest, killing our Court and Josh, and then covering it up?" Kyle spat.

"He's crazy," Aaron added. "He should be out there looking for the real killer, not making stupid, ridiculous accusations about us!"

So Aaron believed Blake was innocent now?

Megan shook her head and tears filled her eyes. "Someone planned this. How could you hate someone so much? Courtney was… She…" Trailing off, Megan took a deep breath. She wasn't able to finish her sentence, but I knew what she wanted to say.

There was someone out there who wanted Courtney and Josh dead so much they sat down and planned their murders. The killer even went as far as to drug all of us to make it possible. Josh pissed off a lot of people, but Courtney didn't. We had to figure this out and prove our innocence.

I took a deep breath. "OK," I said, trying to wrap my mind around the latest bomb Wright had dropped on us. "Do any of you know someone who Josh and Court had a problem with? Even if it was something stupid, you need to say it now."

I knew Wright would love to pin these deaths on one of us, and his latest theory that we drugged ourselves after murdering our friends would make sense if he could find enough circumstantial evidence or a motive. There was no way I was letting one of my friends go down for something they hadn't done.

No one replied, and I began to grow frustrated with them. Was I the only one desperately trying to figure this out? Did they understand what would happen if we didn't find the real killer? We could face a lifetime of suspicion. I didn't trust Wright to put as much effort into finding the real killer as he was putting into trying to force a confession from one of us. "Come on! I need you all to help me here. We can figure this out. We knew them better than anyone else. You know what's going to happen if we don't, right?" I said, desperately pleading with them to get on board and work with me.

"Yes, Mackenzie, I think we're all aware of Wright's fascination with one of us being the big, bad killer, but what do you really think we can do? None of us have a bloody clue how to catch a murderer," Aaron said.

I clenched my jaw so hard in frustration it hurt. "So we should just give up and accept the situation?"

"No." He sighed and hunched his shoulders. "I just don't know what to do or where to start. This is all pretty new to me."

Maybe we do need lawyers.

"We start by making a list of anyone who hated either of them," I said.

Josh's personality meant his list was going to be long. He'd rubbed hundreds of people the wrong way in the past. Of course, not all of them would kill over it, but Josh's enemies would be the answer here. I was sure of it.

I rubbed the ache between my eyes. "I can't think of anyone who hated Courtney. Can any of you?"

"Are we starting with Courtney so we can focus on who hates my brother?" Blake asked, reading me like a book.

"No offense, but—"

He held up his hand, and I stopped talking. "I get it, Mackenzie. I would have done the same. So…anyone hate Courtney? I didn't. Barely knew the girl."

I shook my head. Kyle, Megan, and Aaron replied with shrugs. No one knew of anyone who didn't like her.

"I feel like we should get a large notepad to list suspects for Josh's killer," Blake said, snorting in a humorless laugh.

"I'll start," Kyle said. "We all know the four of us had a problem with him after Tills and Gigi died because of the things he'd said about them, but we also know it wasn't one of us four who did it. Blake had issues with his little brother too, right, Blake?"

"Right," he replied. "But I didn't kill him either." He looked beside Kyle to Aaron. "Contrary to popular belief."

"Tilly's dad," Aaron suggested, ignoring Blake completely.

"No, he was angry but not at anyone in particular," Megan replied.

After Tilly's and Gigi's deaths, their parents dealt with it in very different ways. Gigi's were devastated but determined to make something positive by starting a charity to support families going through the loss of a child. Tilly's dad was devastated and furious.

Aaron glared at her. "He said he wanted to kill whoever was responsible for the car accident. Come on, we should at least consider it."

Yes, Tilly's dad had said—in the heat of the moment and out of pure anger and grief—that he would kill the person responsible for his daughter's death, but I didn't think he would have followed through with his threat. But we weren't in the position to overlook anyone simply because we didn't want it to be true, so I ran with it.

"Aaron's right," I said, arching my spine and sitting up. "Think about it. We were all in the minivan. We survived the crash and Tilly and Gigi didn't. The truck driver died too, so he couldn't pay. Courtney was the one driving, and Josh was the one who planned the trip and acted like an arsehole after. Maybe Tilly's dad held them responsible."

Kyle scratched at his jaw roughly. "I get that. He lost his daughter, and there's no greater motivation to kill than revenge for your child."

My stomach rolled over. That did make sense.

CHAPTER EIGHT

Thursday, August 20

"So why are you redecorating?" I asked Kyle as I stood in his bedroom. His furniture had been moved into the center and draped with sheets, exposing the dark, midnight-blue walls. Until ten minutes ago, I'd had no idea he was even thinking about redecorating. He had called a little while ago mumbling about needing to make changes and raging about how his room was too dark and depressing.

He'd been pacing since I arrived. I watched him walk from one side of his room to the other, staring at the blank walls. Kyle was very levelheaded, so this stressed side of him made me feel uncomfortable. He was passionate about the things that mattered to him, but we're talking about wall colors here.

His anxiety had me on edge. I tapped the outside of my thighs nervously.

"Just can't stand this shitty blue anymore." He held up a large can of light but *bright* green paint. His demeanor made my pulse skitter nervously.

I smiled through my concern. *Something is really not OK with him.* "Err…Kyle?" He was trading one extreme color for another.

The almost-black blue was dark and moody, and lime green was bright and over-the-top cheerful. It was like he was desperate to force a happy facade.

"You hate it?" he asked.

"I don't hate the color, not at all, but there's no way I'd want it on *every* wall. You'll get a headache after ten minutes."

"I don't care. I need something vibrant. A complete change."

I picked up one of the many brushes he had lined along his chest of drawers. "Yes, it's certainly a change. Let's get started then, I guess."

He grinned. "What would I do without you?"

"Paint it yourself," I replied with a smile and dipped the brush in the can of white.

"You holding up OK? Yesterday was…difficult," he said, smearing paint on the wall haphazardly. Even though this was only a primer coat before things got very green, I still stroked my brush up and down carefully, making sure the paint went on evenly.

Yesterday was one of the hardest days I had ever lived through. Not only was it a good-bye to Courtney, but it had also brought back memories of Tilly's and Gigi's funerals, when I'd felt so lost and empty. And to top it off, my friends and I had learned that we were drugged and framed for murder. Yeah, "difficult" didn't quite cut it.

"It was awful, but I'm all right."

"Hmm, lie."

I stopped and turned to him. "It's not a complete lie, Kyle. Right now I'm doing OK."

"You're focused on the manhunt. When the killer's found, you'll fall apart."

I kept quiet. Kyle knew me so well and had since we were kids. He was always the friend who'd given me the emotional support I needed.

"You know, I'm worried about that, Kenzie. I couldn't stand seeing you the way you were after Tilly and Gigi ever again."

Chewing my bottom lip, I considered what he'd said. I had been a mess when they'd died—a big one. I didn't eat for almost a week and barely got out of bed. It was so hard to accept that I would never see them again or receive a text gushing about the latest episode of *The Vampire Diaries*, yelling about a favorite character being killed off in *The Walking Dead*, or demanding we go to Nando's for dinner. It still was. Sometimes I'll watch something, and my first thought is to text all four of the girls. The truth was, I worried about it too. Even after all this time, I still felt raw over the feeling of complete helplessness. Maybe if I could have moved, I could have done something to help. I'd not felt so useless again until we'd found Courtney and Josh.

"I'll be OK. I have you, Megan, and Aaron." And Blake. Sort of. I think. The list of people I could count on was getting smaller and smaller.

"You'll always have us." He held his arms out, and I practically collapsed into them. Gripping hold of his waist, I held on for dear life. It was just us four now, and we had to stick together. "I'm so sorry, Mackenzie." His body shook as if he was crying, but he made no sound. Kyle was always so strong for me, lying with me until I fell asleep when Tilly and Gigi died, researching the best grief counselors in our area when I couldn't cope, and staying up all night to help me study for an exam. He needed to be able to let it out sometimes too.

"Shh, it's not your fault. We're gonna be OK," I murmured into his shoulder, praying that I was right.

"We're going to be OK" was one of the most overused phrases, but also one of the truest. No matter what had happened, how deeply something hurt you, the world continued to spin, and you would continue to breathe. Things might be awful for a while—sometimes a long while—but eventually, you would be able to function again. I just wasn't sure if I had the patience or energy to wait for that time.

Kyle pulled away and took a deep breath. "We should get back to painting. I think it'll take two coats."

I nodded with a small smile and picked up the brush again. "Kyle, do you honestly believe Blake killed them?"

His arm moved up and down as he stroked the paint onto his wall. It took him a long time to reply. "Look, Kenz, I know you want to believe someone broke in, and I do too, but that didn't happen. We know that for a fact, so yes, I believe it was Blake. We don't know him, and I'd much rather believe it was a stranger than someone I've known over half my life. I get that you want it to be someone else, but I don't think it can be."

It had to be someone else. I didn't sleep with a murderer. But how could I deny the facts? No, I could deny Blake's involvement in their deaths because he was innocent. I had to believe that. I *had* to.

"Did it ever cross your mind that it could be me?" I asked, holding my breath. If he said yes, it'd crush me.

Kyle laughed. "You're kidding, right? Mackenzie, you make me take spiders outside because you won't have them killed. No, I never thought it's you."

I exhaled a huge sigh of relief.

His eyebrows arched. "You think it could be me?"

"No," I replied. "I don't think it's any of you."

"You have a thing for Blake," he said. It was a statement and not a question.

A thing. Sure, I cared about him as a human being. I refused to believe he could kill his brother, so suddenly that meant I had a thing for him? None of the others knew that Blake and I had slept together, and I hadn't realized our feelings were obvious. We'd had sex, and Blake had made me feel things that were new and frightening. I didn't sleep around. Being intimate with someone was special, and I'd let Blake in *way* too soon...though it didn't feel too soon at all. That scared me. The way my body reacted when he was around scared me. But I couldn't tell Kyle any of that. Not one of my friends would ever believe the killer was one of us over Blake. And there was no way I was telling my friends that I slept with a guy the same day I'd met him, because that would surely get back to my parents. My town was tiny, and there wasn't a lot you could get away with.

Realizing I'd been quiet for some time, I sputtered, "I-I don't. Kyle, I barely know the guy."

"You defend him blindly."

"It's not blindly."

"Yes, it is. You said yourself you don't know him well. You're defending a guy that, for all you know, could be a killer. I'd call that blind."

"He couldn't have done it," I snapped.

"Why not?"

Closing my eyes, I let the words spill out. "Because he was with me all night."

Kyle stilled. "What?"

"Don't judge. He woke me up in the middle of the night and one thing led to another. We went upstairs. Josh and Courtney were nowhere to be seen, so they must've been upstairs too."

"Upstairs? Mackenzie, they never made it upstairs!"

I shook my head. "No, I would've known if they were already dead."

"How? You couldn't see through to the kitchen from the sofa. Oh my God." He ran his hand over his face. "Surely you can see what happened? Blake killed them and then woke you so you could be his alibi."

"No…Kyle, no, that's not what happened." I stumbled back a step and pressed my lips together. That wasn't true. Blake wouldn't take advantage of me like that… Would he? "You can't honestly believe that."

"What other explanation do you have?"

"Anyone could've woken up at any point and killed them."

"That's true, but none of us would have done it."

I sighed with frustration. "Can we not talk about this, please? Let's just get your room done."

Kyle pursed his lips, considering my request. He looked to the floor and then back at me. "Sure." Knowing Kyle, he probably wanted to lecture me until I came around to his way of thinking—or have Aaron guard me and keep me away from Blake.

"Thanks." I didn't want to argue with him, not my sweet Kyle. Not the guy who bought me my favorite junk food when I was feeling down and watched chick flicks without complaint—well, much complaint—just because I wanted to. "Have you spoken to Aaron or Megan today? I tried Megan earlier, but it went straight through to voice mail."

"Aaron's at her place. Her grandparents came home from Italy to make sure she was OK, probably why she didn't answer."

I nodded and made a mental note to go and see her in the morning. If Aaron was already with her, she wouldn't need me too, and I didn't want to intrude if her extended family was over.

"So do you really think the killer could be Tilly's dad?" I asked as we worked side by side. Lawrence had said some threatening things. But then, so had Aaron. He'd threatened to kill Josh. It was all talk in the heat of the moment, but if we took Lawrence's threat seriously, then shouldn't we treat Aaron's with the same seriousness?

Kyle lifted his shoulder and let it drop. "Maybe. If he had the opportunity to kill us without repercussion, I think he would have. He desperately wants someone to blame for Tilly's death, and you can't blame the poor bastard for that."

"I know, but to kill someone over an accident? I can't get my head around it," I replied.

"People justify their actions to themselves all the time. I can buy a shirt because it's thirty percent off or just one more drink will be OK because I've eaten a big dinner."

"I'll kill this person because they deserve it?"

He shrugged with the same shoulder again. "I guess."

"That's stupid!"

"Kenz, I'm not saying it's right or the sane thing to do, but people use their own logic to justify all kinds of decisions. Our other option is Blake, but I know how you feel, so let's not argue over him."

It took us four and a half hours to paint Kyle's room twice. My arm ached—*everything* ached—and I felt like collapsing. "Shit. It's *really* green," Kyle said, looking at the bright walls with wide eyes.

"Yep," I replied. "I'm not painting it again for at least three months, so you'll have to live with it or repaint it yourself."

He grinned. "Deal. Hopefully it won't look like I'm living in some animated, Disney forest when the furniture is back."

"Doubt it, but let's see," I teased him. It felt so good to joke around after all of the crying for Courtney and Josh.

We uncovered his furniture and pushed it all back into place once the walls were dry enough. Thankfully, with the furniture, his room didn't look quite so bright, but I still wouldn't have slept there.

"I hate to say I told you so…" I said.

He smirked and nudged my shoulder with his own. "No, you don't. I wanted a change, and I got one. I can deal for a while."

"Maybe we can paint three of the walls white or something? That'll tone it down."

"Yeah, maybe."

"OK, let's get the rest of your stuff put away, and then you're making me some food." Kyle still had football trophies, posters, and a few shoe boxes of stuff left in the middle of the room.

I bent down to pick up one of the shoe boxes, and the side fell open, spilling the contents onto the floor. "Damn it," I muttered and knelt on the carpet to pick up the photographs that had scattered.

"Smooth," Kyle said, dropping down to help.

One photograph caught my eye, and my heart fell into my stomach. "Kyle, what's this?" I whispered in shock, holding up that photograph.

His mouth popped open to form a perfect *O*. Panic surged through his eyes, but he quickly recovered. "Just a picture from years ago."

I looked back at the selfie of Kyle kissing Courtney and frowned. Court's hair was a fierce red, brighter than the hair dye she usually used, because the store hadn't had her usual. I remembered it clearly, because I was the one who had dyed it for her—for the last time, it seemed—just before Easter, three months ago. This photo was recent. "Kyle, this must have been taken in April. Courtney's hair," I said, explaining that I knew he was lying. "What the hell was going on between you two?"

Kyle and I stared at each other, both silently challenging the other. Kyle sighed and closed his eyes. He kept his eyes shut as he very quietly confessed, "We were together."

"Together? You two were together? When? How? I don't get it…"

He cleared his throat and his forehead creased. "Behind Josh's back. In secret. Having an affair. Get it now?"

My shoulders slumped. All the air left my lungs in one big rush. How much did I not know about my best friends? "Shit, what the bloody hell were you thinking? Why didn't Court tell me? Why didn't *you* tell me?"

"Really, Mackenzie?" he muttered dryly.

"Look, Kyle. Court and I have known each other since we were seven, and I would have preferred to see her with you than with Josh."

"Yeah, well, so would I. She wouldn't leave him. She kept saying she would break it off with Josh, but she kept postponing for one reason and then another. Finally, eight months later, she cut me off and chose him."

My eyes bulged. "*Eight months?*" Kyle and Courtney hadn't had just a brief fling; it had been a full-on affair! She was seeing him through most of her relationship with Josh. "I don't even know what to think…"

He snatched the photo back. "Don't think anything. Courtney led me on and screwed me over. I would have done anything for her. I loved her so much, but she chose him. I hate her for what she did to me," he spat. He'd turned cold and withdrawn.

I blinked in shock. The hostility coming from Kyle made me

want to leave. He didn't sound like himself, and I hated that. "Don't say you hate her," I whispered. Courtney was wrong for leading him on, and I was angry with her for hurting him, but she was our friend. And she was dead. It didn't help to be mad at her now.

He stood up and gestured to the mess on his floor. "I've got things to do."

"What? You want me to leave *now*? Kyle, I can't…" Explanations. I needed them. He couldn't just make me leave without talking about this.

"I'm tired, Mackenzie, and frankly, I don't feel like talking about me and Courtney."

Sighing, I got up too. Fine. I wasn't going to get anything out of him, and staying was pointless if he wasn't going to talk. Right now I needed some space too. "I'm sorry you got hurt."

Kyle stared at me, his eyes dark and empty. Finally, he replied, "Doesn't matter now, does it?"

I turned and left his room, eager to be as far away from him as I could. He was clearly torn up over Courtney's death, but I couldn't help but feel betrayed by their secret relationship. And now, my happy, mischievous, caring friend had been replaced by a bitter, spiteful stranger.

I walked to my car in a daze. Just how much did Kyle hate Courtney for not choosing him? How much did he hate Courtney *and* Josh? Yesterday, I would have never thought he could have been capable of murder, but the Kyle in his room just now had been completely different. Was the furious person that I had just met—Kyle's darker side—capable of stabbing two people who were once his friends? An affair. Kyle didn't do that. He was loyal and had morals. Or so I had thought.

CHAPTER NINE

Friday, August 21

I pulled up outside the cabin, and my hands started to shake. I'd not been here since the police carted us off, and I didn't want to ever go back inside. I had to though. There *had* to be something the police missed because I was going crazy. Thinking the people I trusted most in the world were capable of something so heinous was not OK with me. There had to be clues in that cabin. You couldn't murder two people in such a violent and bloody way and not leave some sort of evidence behind.

My phone buzzed in my pocket, and I stilled. I slid the phone from my jeans, and my finger hovered over the screen. Kyle had already called me eight times today and I'd ignored them all. He'd never been so insistent before. On a heavy sigh, I clicked my phone to silent.

Blake's Warrior sat in the driveway, but that wasn't surprising. He didn't really have anywhere else to go to get away from his family, and I thought being at his mum's must have been awkward as hell. He couldn't go back home to his dad's because we all had to stay in town.

Police tape cordoned off the cabin, but the front door was

open, so I guess Blake didn't care that it was a closed crime scene. Neither did I. Usually I was a rule follower, but there was no time for that now. Someone needed to figure out what had happened—and fast. What if the murderer started coming after the rest of us?

I walked into the cabin, ignoring the thudding of my heart, and looked around for Blake. The place was a mess. Everything had been turned upside down. Sofa cushions were on the floor. Furniture had been moved. Photographs had been taken down from the walls and spread out on the side table.

Blake was by the window, staring out in a daze. I cleared my throat. His head snapped around in my direction, and he arched his eyebrow. "What're you doing here?" he demanded.

Not letting him intimidate me, I stood up straight. *Trying to prove to myself that Kyle isn't the killer and find out who is.* "What are *you* doing here?"

"This is *my* cabin. Your turn."

"Looking for…" I trailed off, frowning. I slouched in defeat. Who was I kidding? I had less than no clue how to catch a killer. "I don't know. Anything I can, I guess."

Blake cocked his head to the side. "You're looking for a murderer. What makes you think you'll find any clues that dozens of police officers and detectives couldn't? They've gone through this cabin with a fine-tooth comb, Mackenzie. There's nothing to see here."

"Well, they don't have as much to lose as I do, and we don't know they haven't found anything."

He sighed. "So dramatic."

"What happened here?" I asked, ignoring his comment.

"Police would've been searching for the murderer's clothes. They have the knife. It was one of ours."

"They do?" *The knife! There must be fingerprints on the knife.* "And?"

"And they have the knife," he deadpanned. "We all used them when we were cooking dinner together…and most of the other utensils, actually. Doubt they'll find much there."

"The point is that the killer's prints might be on it too!"

My heart spiked with hope. *Please let them find someone else's prints.*

Blake smirked, lighting up his striking blue eyes. "So what have you got planned, then? Sniffer dogs?"

"Are you going to help me or what?"

"Did I offer?" he replied, frowning.

"Fine, Blake, just stand there and look out of that window. Pretend I'm not here."

"That's hard to do when you're talking to me."

"What's your problem?" He was being a total bastard. "What's happened?"

"Nothing," he grunted. "Just tired of all this shit. I want to know who killed my little brother, and I want all your friends to stop looking at me as if I did it."

"And I want to know who killed my friends."

"Friend," he corrected. "You hated Josh, remember?"

I gritted my teeth. Somehow Blake had shifted the blame onto me when I was the one—the only one—who had his back.

"Fine. I want to find out what happened to my friend and her boyfriend. Better?"

Ignoring that particular response, he asked, "Where do you want to look first?"

My head spun. Being around him was like being a human yo-yo; he'd reel me in and then shove me away. "You're helping now?"

"Don't make me change my mind, Mackenzie."

"Right. Sorry. Well, I've no idea where to start. You know this place better than me. If he or she didn't use the doors, then what about the windows?"

He folded his arms. "They were all closed—*properly* closed—from the inside."

"Yes, I know that, Blake."

"Then why are you looking there?"

I glared. He made me want to kiss him and punch him all at the same time. He was pushing my buttons, and I was seconds from snapping. Why was no one taking this as seriously as I was? I needed to check, just in case. "Just do your own bloody thing!"

Blake's eyebrows shot up in shock. Before he could reply, I left the living room and walked into the kitchen. The kitchen was the most logical place for someone to enter or, at least, exit. The murders happened in the kitchen, and whoever did it would have needed a quick escape.

The sight of the floor that I'd seen covered in blood made me want to run back to my car, drive home as fast as I could, and hide in bed—but I couldn't allow myself that weakness. I didn't want to stop and think. I didn't want to face the reality of what happened.

"Mackenzie?" Blake called. I ignored him and shoved at the little window over the sink. The handle was down, and the window didn't budge. I was hoping the latch was broken and it would open with a little force. The police would have tried that already, of course.

"What?" I replied, shoving the wooden frame with as much force as I could muster. "Damn it!" I slammed my palm against the glass in frustration. "Why won't it just open?" I shouted, my frustration fizzing over.

"Stop." His strong hand gripped the top of my arm and pulled me back. "This is ridiculous. It's not going to magically open, Mackenzie, and you're just going to end up hurting yourself."

I held my finger up as another thought sprung to my mind. "Maybe I'm starting in the wrong place. I should find the murderer before I find out how they did it."

"OK, Sherlock, where are we starting?" If I were Sherlock Holmes, I would have figured it out by now. I had no absolutely no clue, not even a hint.

"A hideout." I turned on my heel and walked out of the cabin, rubbing the ache in my chest. The killer would need somewhere to hide, to wait for the perfect moment. I was sure of it. Sort of.

Blake's footsteps thudded behind me, crunching dried leaves on the ground. "You don't even know where you're going," he said.

"No one knows where they're going before they actually go," I replied, power walking ahead. "If you're just here to annoy me, then please turn around now."

"You can't just go wandering off into the woods by yourself."

I stopped, turned around, and glared. "Why do you care?" Blake blew hot and cold all the time. I had no idea where I stood with him.

He was right behind me, his gaze burning into mine.

I couldn't figure him out. Blake was a mystery and a pretty annoying one.

"Got nothing else to do," he whispered, giving me goose bumps. His proximity made my earlier anger toward him fizzle out completely—almost completely.

"Liar." There were probably hundreds of other things he'd rather be doing, including nothing at all.

His eyes narrowed, clearly disliking how I challenged him. "I want to find the killer too. No one else can give me answers, so why not tag along with Detective Mackenzie and see where it leads me? Besides, I can't stand being at home." His voice lowered at his confession. I could only imagine what it was like for both him and his mom.

"I'm sorry."

He smiled halfheartedly and shrugged one shoulder. "What are you looking for?"

"A shed or cabin," I replied. "Anything the killer could have been hiding in."

"Are you expecting to find bloody clothes and the murderer's ID too?"

"Hoping, not expecting. There any places you can show me?"

"A couple." He walked past me, headed in a different direction. "Do you still know the way to them?"

"Please," he said, turning his head to smirk at me. "I'm a man."

I followed closely behind him, weaving around the trees. The deeper we walked into the woods, the darker it became and the more I wanted to head back. "Are you sure this is the way?" I asked, wrapping my arms around myself.

"What do you think, I'm leading you into the middle of nowhere to slit your throat?"

"That's so not funny, and I don't think that's what you're doing. I think you've gotten us lost. No man would ever admit to that, so I think you're taking us around in circles, hoping we'll eventually come across the cabin again."

He sighed. "Just ahead you'll see a crappy, old shack. Josh and I found it years ago when we were looking for somewhere to play with our water pistols."

"You needed shelter for that?"

"We needed a base. Every good military operation has a base."

I grinned, imagining Blake as a child, running around and playing fantasy games. We started walking again, slower this time. "Quite the imagination you have."

"Had," he corrected. "Life screws you over eventually."

"Pessimist."

"Hopeless optimist."

"How far does the river go?" I asked.

He shrugged. "How should I know? Far, I assume."

"That's a lot of opportunity for someone to dump the evidence in the water. And a lot of forest too. Do you think they've hidden it all somewhere? The clothes, I mean."

"No, they're probably doing their weekly shopping in them," he replied dryly.

I narrowed my eyes. "Bastard."

"The forest is huge. You could lose anything in there. The ground is covered in leaves and crap, so you could probably bury a lot in there too."

"Great. We have no hope." Finding clues seemed impossible. If Blake was right, and he knew this area better than me, the murderer could have already hidden the evidence anywhere in the miles of woodland. The police would need the murderer's clothes to match fibers to.

"Want to explain why we're doing this?" he asked, lifting his dark eyebrow at me. I knew what he was thinking and I couldn't disagree. This was stupid, beyond stupid, and a huge waste of my time.

"Because I have to do something, Blake!"

What else could I do? I'd never been the type of person to sit back and do nothing when people I cared about were in trouble.

He pointed ahead. "There you go."

I frowned, but as I took another step, I could see the side of something wooden. "We're here?"

"No, I took you—"

"All right, thank you!" I rolled my eyes and muttered under my breath, "Sarcastic arse."

Blake grinned wide, flashing his teeth. He was a little too good at shoving his emotions aside. I could do it well enough to function, but Blake could do it well enough to be himself.

We walked closer, and I stopped. *No way am I going in there.* The whole structure looked as if it was about to collapse. It looked like the type of shack you screamed for someone not to go near in a horror film.

"It's creepy," I said as a cold shudder ripped through my body.

"It's an old shed, Mackenzie. What do you think it's gonna do? Bite you?"

I ignored him and nodded toward the door half hanging off the top hinge.

Blake's smile grew. "Ladies first."

"Shut up and go." I didn't understand how he could continuously make jokes when what we were doing was serious. And I hated that I didn't completely hate his humor. "Unless you're scared?"

He rolled his eyes. "Reverse psychology doesn't work on me. This is your crusade. You lead the way, detective."

"Fine." I stood taller, trying to fool myself into believing that I was braver than I felt. "But for the record, you have no balls at all, *princess*." I wasn't sure what his reaction would be, whether he would continue the cocky attitude or bite back, but I didn't wait around to find out. I swallowed my dread and stepped into the run-down shed. Cobwebs plagued the top of the doorway, but the bottom half was clear, maybe from where someone had cleared it recently. I peered inside, but the dust-clad windows prevented much light from coming inside.

I looked over my shoulder and was met by an incredibly smug-looking Blake. "Want me to go first, sweets?" he asked.

"Is that a genuine offer?"

He bit his lip, pretending to think, even though we were both aware that he already knew the answer. He sighed. "Move out of the way." Swiping at the remaining cobwebs with his hand, he stepped inside.

"What's in there?" I whispered.

"No one. No reason for you to whisper."

I took a deep breath, gritting my teeth. "What's in there, Blake?" I hissed.

"Bugger all. Come in."

He could have been lying, and I would walk in to see a skeleton or something, but for some reason, I trusted him. Blake drove me crazy with his attitude, but I knew he wouldn't put me in any danger. Well, not real danger at least. He would probably let me do something like walk into a room with a skeleton to scare the hell out of me.

I took a small step and was halfway through the door when the musty smell made my nose sting. Blake wiped the cracked glass with his hand. A shaft of light poured into the small room, giving enough light so we could see.

The inside of the shed was filled with dust, mud, and more cobwebs. The floor was littered with empty packets of chips and bottles of drink. I frowned. "We're not going to find anything, are we?"

Blake scratched the back of his neck. "If you want to continue looking for someone else, I'm with you."

"But?" I prompted, sensing he had more to say.

"But I think it was one of your friends."

I gulped and shook my head. "No, it couldn't have been. They wouldn't."

"That's what they want you to believe, yes."

"No. I need to keep searching. Check the use-by dates on the litter. Some might be recent."

"And that will prove...?"

I don't know! "Please, Blake," I said. I knew I was looking for a needle in a haystack and searching rubbish was plain ridiculous, but I had to find evidence that pointed to an intruder. I couldn't accept the killer was one of my friends.

He held up his hands. "All right, let's look at rubbish."

I smiled. "Thank you."

This is absolutely absurd. We're checking litter. This investigation is at an all-time low.

Blake knelt down and picked up a faded packet of chips. I wanted to tell him that the bag had clearly been here a long time, but he was doing me a favor. "I hope your friends appreciate you."

"What do you mean by that?"

"You're doing everything you can to prove their innocence— innocence you don't even know is there—including sifting through crap. What're they doing for you?"

"I don't do things to get something in return."

"No, but perhaps you should ask yourself if you're being appreciated a little more often."

I didn't respond, but picked up a crumpled biscuit packet. Gasping, I shoved the packet toward him. "Blake, look!" There was blood on it. Not a lot, but I hoped against all the odds that it was blood to link the real murderer to the crime. A frown slipped onto his forehead as he studied it.

"How long do you think it's been there?" I asked.

"How the hell should I know?"

"Well, does it look like old blood?"

He shrugged. "I dunno."

Outside, I heard a snap and froze. Gripping Blake's arm, I looked at the doorway in horror. "Did you hear that?" I whispered.

"Uh-huh," Blake replied, taking a step forward and tilting his head. I tightened my fingers around his bicep and kept myself rigid, trying to hold him back. He looked over his shoulder. "I need to check it out," he said in a low voice, dropping the bloodstained packet.

Shaking my head, I tugged him closer, but he barely moved. "Don't. It could be them."

"It could be an animal."

"Please, Blake, I'm—" Another snap had me clenching my teeth together and my heart sinking to my toes. "Don't go out there," I discouraged.

Blake reached down and pulled my hand from his arm. "Stay here."

"Are you crazy?"

"Not half as much as I'm starting to think you are." His eyes darkened as he leaned closer. "And don't ever question my mental health again."

I took a step back, away from him.

"Stay here, Mackenzie," he growled.

Holding my breath, I watched him cautiously step out of the shed. I couldn't let him go out alone. What if the killer was out there? It was unlikely, but I hadn't thought something bad could happen at the cabin either.

Gathering as much courage as I could, I stepped into the woods and held my breath. Blake rounded the corner of the shed and almost slammed into me. I jumped backward and scowled as he smirked.

"It was a deer," he said.

"Huh?"

"Deer—four-legged creature that lives in the woods?"

I rolled my eyes. "Yeah, I know what a deer is. Are you sure that's what it was?"

"Well, if not, it was a very ugly person." He reached down and picked up the packet from just inside the doorway. "So you really want to take this?"

"Yes," I replied. *It's just a deer, calm down.* "I think the blood looks new...ish."

Blake laughed and shook his head. He thought I was an idiot, but at least I was being proactive.

"This isn't funny, Blake. Why aren't you taking this seriously?"

"Because you've got us sifting through garbage. I'll humor you and we'll take this to Wright." He stood up. "Now come on, before you find a dead bird and accuse that of—"

"All right, thank you." I turned on my heel and stomped away. Keeping my cool with him was hard, even when he was trying to help.

"Mackenzie?"

"Yeah."

"What will you do if one of them is the killer?"

"I honestly don't know," I said, and tried to shake the thought from my mind. "Will you help me? No one else seems overly enthusiastic about investigating. I need someone," I whispered.

He frowned. "Are you gonna cry? I don't do well with hysterical women, remember?"

"I'm not going to cry. Not yet."

"You've set a timer?" he teased.

I smiled. "When this is all over. Until then, I'm strong Mackenzie."

"Your friends really are lucky."

I shrugged off his compliment. It's what anyone would do for the people they cared about. "So will you help?"

The corner of his mouth pulled up, and he did a little bow. "I'm at your service, Detective Keaton."

I breathed out sharply, relieved that I had someone to go through all this with—even if that person drove me insane most of the time. I knew that, together, we could figure out the truth of what happened.

He reached out and brushed his thumb over my little finger. His touch sent a bolt of electricity through every inch of my body.

"Thank you, Blake," I whispered.

CHAPTER TEN

After leaving the cabin, Blake and I dropped the bloodstained packet off to an amused Wright at the police station and then went back to Blake's house. The second we stepped through the door, I could tell he wanted nothing more than to leave again. He walked slowly into the living room. His mum sat in the same chair where she had spent Josh's entire wake. The TV was on, but she didn't seem to be watching it. She stared into space, not moving at all. I could only tell she was alive by the rise and fall of her chest.

"Hi, Eloise," I said to the statue of his mum. She didn't even blink. I looked to Blake for help.

He shook his head discreetly, his lips thinning. I guessed this empty shell was normal for her now. "Let's go up to my room," he said.

I took a quick glance back at his mom as I followed Blake out of the room. Her eyes were bloodshot and sunken. Her hair was slick with grease and tied into a messy ponytail on top of her head. She looked as if she had checked out days ago and just left her body behind.

"Is she OK?" I asked as we reached the top of the stairs and were out of her way, not that she would have acknowledged she'd heard me if I had asked him right in front of her.

"Not really." He pushed the door open and nodded, gesturing for me to go in first.

Wow, he can be a gentleman.

His room was plain and bare. A dull light blue covered the walls, and there was nothing hanging from them to personalize it. The only furniture was a double bed, bedside table, and wardrobe. A flat-screen TV hung from the wall opposite the bed, but it looked old, probably secondhand from when they'd replaced another one in the house. I imagined Eloise buying a new one for the lounge and saying, *Oh, we can put the old one in Blake's room.* His bedroom reminded me of a cheap hotel room.

"I've never spent much time here," he explained.

"It's fine." I wasn't sure why he felt he had to explain it to me. I didn't care how it looked. "Have you heard from Wright?"

"Nope, but that's hardly surprising since it's been two minutes." I sat down on the bed. "All right, I'm impatient!"

"Please, make yourself at home," he said playfully, teasing me. "He does that on purpose, I think."

"What, not contacting us?"

He plopped down on the bed, making me bounce. "Yeah. You'd think he would be on our case twenty-four seven, so he's not. Whatever we expect, he does the opposite."

"Ah, to mess with us. He doesn't seem like a proper detective."

"I dunno"—he shrugged—"I'd probably be cocky and arrogant if I were a detective."

I snorted, and he rolled his eyes—if he were a detective my arse.

"Moving on," he snapped, amusement clear in his eyes. "What

fun activities do you have for us now? Digging up graves? Sifting through sewers?"

"Why don't you suggest some options if you don't like what I'm doing?" I could've used the help.

"We could talk to Tilly's dad. You know, maybe something he says will tell us more than looking through people's rubbish."

He absentmindedly reached over and stroked the back of my hand with his thumb as he spoke. I wasn't sure if he realized how he was making me feel, but I liked it way too much. Every touch had me feeling like I was falling. I wasn't sure if I was falling *for* him or about to fall *because* of him. At that point, it could have been either.

"I found blood, didn't I?" I replied, my voice wavering while I tried to keep my hormones in check.

"Probably from a half-dead animal, but whatever."

"We'll see. Wright is going to have it tested."

"I thought he would laugh in our faces and tell us to leave."

He didn't laugh, but he was definitely amused by our investigative work. "Um, because he knows I'm right."

"Either that or the blood will be from one of your friends and you dropped them right in it."

My world slammed to an abrupt stop. What if it was? Would that mean they'd done it? No, it couldn't be. "It won't be theirs," I said, my throat closing around the words.

"Whatever you say. My money's on Kyle though."

Did Blake know about Kyle's affair with Courtney? "Why Kyle?"

"He has those dark eyes. They look mysterious slash serial killer."

I laughed. "'Mysterious slash serial killer'? Brown eyes don't make you a murderer."

"It's not the color. Just the way they look."

I shook my head. Blake was no longer making sense.

"So…Lawrence's?" he said. "I'm assuming that's Goldilocks's dad?"

"Yes, and how do you know Tilly was blond?"

"I can sniff blonds out. It's a gift."

"You're a pig!"

He laughed, standing up as I did. "I do know you all, you know. Well, I know of you." Right, he had seen us from the car as his parents had done the child swap. "How far away does Lawrence live?"

"Five minutes. We all live close."

"I hate small villages."

"There's nothing wrong with this village."

"Sure, if you don't mind a bit of murder every now and then," he muttered.

Taking a deep breath, I pushed his words to the back of my mind. I was grateful that he was helping me, but his little jabs weren't helpful. He joked about situations to make people think he didn't care about anything. But that wasn't true. Blake cared, but for some reason, he wouldn't drop the tough-guy act.

"And where you're from is so much better?"

"Towns are better. Fact. Here, everyone knows your business, and they all look at you, wondering what you're up to. In towns, people have lives. In villages, people's lives are other people's lives."

"OK then." We reached the bottom of the stairs, and I frowned in concern. Should we leave his mom alone? "Blake, is she really OK? I feel like we should do something for her."

Eloise sat in the same position, still, motionless. I wished Blake and I had met somewhere else. I understood why he didn't like staying at his mom's anymore. Usually, I was good with grieving people. I could do or say something to try to help, but not with Eloise. She gave me nothing to work with. Crying I could handle. Angry I could handle. An emotionless statue? I drew a blank.

"Has your mum eaten anything? Maybe we should make her a sandwich before we leave," I said as we stopped outside the lounge door.

"She won't eat it even if you make something—never does."

"What about you?"

"I'm a big boy, Mackenzie. I can look after myself." He walked to the front door, and I followed.

"You don't cook," I said. He wasn't that helpful when my friends and I were preparing dinner.

"I can if I want to. I can even use a washing machine."

"Whoa, never knew guys like you existed. My dad still has to ask what setting it goes on if he's forced to do it."

Blake smirked. "He knows. If he pisses you off by asking every time, you won't make him do it. I would have done the same, but it being just me and Dad at home…"

"I've never met your dad."

He unlocked his car and opened the door. "We're not quite there yet."

Rolling my eyes, I got in the passenger side. We weren't together, and right then, that was the last thing on my mind—well, not last, but certainly behind finding my friends' killer. Whatever was happening between us though, it was real and powerful.

"So what's this Lawrence like?" he asked.

"He was really nice until Tilly died."

"Understandable, I guess."

"He doesn't like Josh, so we probably shouldn't mention you're his brother."

He scoffed and pulled out of his driveway. "Is there anyone in this village that actually *did* like Josh?"

"Courtney," I replied. "Look, he wasn't all bad, and no one actually wanted him to die."

Blake's eyebrow arched. "One person did. We're still assuming it was just one person, right?"

I shrugged. "Can't say I've thought too much about that. All I know is that it's not one of my friends."

"Or more than one of your friends."

I narrowed my eyes. "You know, when I first met you, I thought you were all right."

Blake turned his head to me and smirked.

"Watch the road!" I yelped.

"Where does this guy live exactly?"

I gave him the address and sat back, holding on and praying for my life. The accelerator was Blake's best friend. He didn't necessarily drive dangerously; he just liked to put his foot down on the gas and do it frequently.

"What are you gonna say to him? We can't exactly knock on his door and be all, 'Hey, did you murder two teens—'"

"I get it," I said, cutting him off. What *should* we say? After Tilly died, I popped around to see how her parents were and helped them sort out some of her clothes they were donating to charity, but I hadn't been by in months. Perhaps I could use that as an excuse though. "I'll say I'm checking in to make sure they're OK, like I used to. Remember: do not tell them you're related to Josh. I'm serious, Blake."

"Yeah, I got it, but thanks for the reminder."

I didn't talk to Blake for the rest of the short drive; we would have probably ended up bickering, and I needed to stay calm. I was an awful liar and prayed that Lawrence wouldn't see through me straightaway.

As Blake pulled up outside the yellow brick bungalow, my heart started to pound against my chest. I might have been the only one willing to go out there and look for the real killer, but I was definitely the worst person to do it.

"Ready?" Blake asked.

I gulped and nodded. "Let's get this over with." I didn't want to think about Tilly's dad being the killer. I had slept in that bungalow hundreds of times and eaten Lawrence's famous cheese-and-bacon bagels more times than I could count. How could someone I know be a murderer? Murderers were on TV shows. They shouldn't exist in my world. But yet, my best friend was dead.

I walked along the path with Blake trailing behind. He didn't make any stupid comments or try to hurry me. Tapping on the door lightly, I took a deep breath to try and calm my racing heart.

"Mackenzie, what a surprise," Lawrence said as he opened the door. "What brings you here?"

I smiled, going over the reason I'd rehearsed in my head on the way over. "I just wanted to come by and see how you're all doing. It's been a while."

"It has." He nodded and looked at Blake. "And you are?"

Don't say you're Josh's brother. Do not say you're Josh's brother.

I wasn't sure how Lawrence would react if he knew; he hated Josh more than anyone. Blake held his hand out, and Lawrence shook it. "Everyone calls me Spike." He slung his arm over my shoulder. "I'm Mackenzie's boyfriend."

I am going to kill him.

I smiled tightly, gritting my teeth. Spike? Really? He couldn't have come up with a lamer name if he'd tried. We should have discussed who he'd be in the car, but I did not see "Spike" coming.

"Spike," Lawrence said slowly and looked at me as if it to say *what on earth are you doing with this boy?* Believe me, at that moment, I had no idea. "Nice to meet you. Please, come on in."

Lawrence walked ahead, and I took the opportunity to slap Blake's arm while no one was looking. *What the hell?* I mouthed, which only made Blake smile.

"You know your way to the living room. I'll make us some tea," Lawrence said over his shoulder. Blake turned his nose up but didn't ask for coffee instead.

"OK," I replied, turning right into the living room. It was

exactly the same as it had been for all the time I'd known Tilly. Light-caramel walls, a brown sofa, and oak coffee table, but they had replaced the wood-framed clock with a modern one. Tilly had hated that old clock and said it looked like it belonged in a retirement home. She would definitely have approved of the modern change.

Blake and I waited in silence. I played with my fingers, nervously anticipating the conversation we were about to have. We couldn't exactly come right out and ask if he'd committed any murders recently.

Beside me, Blake pressed his leg against mine and then took my hand, silently giving me strength and support. "Calm down," he whispered.

"What if he did it?"

"I don't think he'll admit it, Mackenzie. We'll be all right."

"What if we're not? If he killed them, he's capable of doing the same to us."

Gripping my chin, he tilted my face so my focus was on him. "There is nothing in this world that is going to hurt you while I am here."

"What's happening to you?" I teased, keeping my voice as light as I could. Blake scowled as if he was unsure himself. Lawrence came into the room and set a tray of tea and biscuits down on the coffee table. Blake and I sat up straight. Our moment was over.

"Thank you," I said. "So, how have you been?"

Tilly's dad sat down on the worn leather sofa opposite us. "Not too bad now. Yourself?"

"Not great."

"Right, of course. I'm very sorry to hear about Courtney and Joshua." *Are you?* "You found them, didn't you?"

I gave a small nod.

"I'm very sorry you saw that, Mackenzie. It must be very hard to live with."

Lawrence's voice was cold. His words didn't seem genuine or heartfelt. There was nothing that showed me he meant what he said. I had always got along with Tilly's family, but when she'd died, Lawrence had barely spoken to me—to any of Tilly's friends— for a while. I knew he would have preferred it to have been me, or any of us, who had died that night instead of Tilly—of course he would. I went to see him because it was important to me to be there for Tilly. He was polite and never turned me away, but his demeanor was nothing like it had been before. He'd been polite when we'd arrived, but now that the conversation had shifted, he didn't want me there.

Blake's body tensed beside me. *Not now. Whatever it is, not now!* "I'm very sorry to hear about your daughter, Lawrence. Mackenzie's told me Tilly was a great person."

"Thank you, *Spike*. She was a great person, one of the best. My Tilly was going to be a doctor. All she ever wanted was to help people."

I smiled at the bittersweet memories of Tilly tending to us all whenever something was wrong. She would never get to pursue her dream career, and that was such a shame because she would have been an amazing doctor.

"She would have been great at it," I said. "I lost count of the times she played doctor when someone hurt themselves. You remember when I sprained my wrist a few years ago and she insisted on checking it regularly and changing the bandage?"

Lawrence laughed. "She drove you crazy, if I remember correctly."

"Yeah, I had to keep stopping what I was doing so she could look. There wasn't even anything to really check." I would have understood if it had been a cut she could re-dress, but there was nothing to do. That was Tilly though. Even if there was nothing significant that she could do, she still tried to help.

"Aaron mentioned that too. Do you remember when he had pneumonia at the beginning of last year, and Tilly spent most of the week at his bedside?" Lawrence smiled fondly at the memory. "It was a shame they didn't have the chance to make a go of things. He's a good lad, and it was clear he was in love with her."

Tilly and Aaron's relationship was so on and off, you could barely give it the *relationship* title. Each time they got back together, they were great, but it never lasted very long. They seemed more stuck in a habit than anything else.

"Yeah, they would have been good together," I said. Maybe being older and more mature, they would've stood a better chance, but they'd never get that opportunity. "Aaron misses her a lot too."

"Yes, he's here often to be close to her."

I tried to hide the surprise on my face. *Aaron came here often?* We all visited but not much anymore. He mentioned coming a few times not long after the accident, but then we'd both stopped—I thought. It didn't make sense that he wouldn't tell me he still visited with Tilly's family. We talked to each other a lot about Tilly.

What other secrets did Aaron have?

"He still comes a lot? I didn't know that," I said.

"Almost every week. He sits in her room or sometimes we look through pictures. I was surprised at first. Tilly was always crying over him or ranting at how much of a 'stupid, pissing idiot' he was."

I could hear her words so clearly. She had used that phrase for Aaron so many times.

"It really does mean a lot that he still cares for her so deeply," Lawrence said.

It would appear that Aaron did care about Tills much more than I ever knew, but was that enough to make him hate Courtney for being the unfortunate one behind the wheel the night? And hate Josh for his part in it?

There was something very wrong with thinking Aaron could've been their killer. He may have hated Josh, but he wasn't vengeful. He didn't ever wish harm on anyone. That wasn't his personality. That wasn't me or any of my friends.

"That's nice. I'm glad he comes over. Tills would have been too," I said finally.

Lawrence smiled, but his lips barely curled. "She would be."

"How long ago was the accident?" Blake asked, putting a little too much emphasis on the word *accident*.

"Eight months ago," I replied. I couldn't quite believe months had passed. It still seemed like yesterday. I could still clearly hear the sound of crunching metal, smashing glass, and my friends' screams. The minivan had rolled over before coming to an abrupt stop in a ditch. I had been in the row of seats in front of Tilly and Gigi, and if the truck had hit just a few inches forward, I probably would have died too.

"Eight months and six days," Lawrence corrected. He shook his head. "I will never understand why Giana drank that day."

I bit my lip. She hadn't meant to get drunk. Before losing about fifteen pounds, she could drink about five or six drinks and not feel a thing. She'd only had two beers. And she'd known enough not to drive. That's why Courtney was behind the wheel when it happened.

"She didn't mean to," I whispered. It wasn't Gigi's fault—or Courtney's or Josh's. It was a bloody accident. Why were so many people having a hard time understanding that? We all wished we could rewind time and have a do-over of that day, but we couldn't, and it was just something we'd have to live with.

"I believe that, but the accident happened as a direct result of Giana's drinking. She was a better driver than Courtney." The way he said Gigi's name gave me chills. She was Giana now.

Ice froze my heart. The venom in his tone was the same as Kyle's when he'd told me how much Courtney had hurt him— he seemed so bitter now. I swallowed a massive lump building in my throat.

Tilly's and Gigi's deaths were an accident. We were hit by a truck. The driver was irrelevant when you had a massive truck ramming you up the arse. They never stood a chance, and if Gigi had been driving, it still would have been Tilly that died.

The man sitting in front of me wasn't who he used to be. He was cold and detached. His eyes were empty and had no empathy.

It's him. Lawrence was the killer.

It had to be him. The alternative was unthinkable.

I felt my face burn as blood pumped too hard. Gripping Blake's hand, I shot up to my feet. "We should go. We have to meet Megan soon." Blake frowned, looking at me as if I had lost it. Maybe I had. At this point, going crayon-eating crazy was entirely plausible. "I'll stop by soon, Lawrence."

He shook his head, surprised by our sudden departure. "OK."

I held Blake's hand in a death grip and pulled him through the house and out of the front door. I could barely breathe properly. My lungs felt like they were made of lead.

"Him," I hissed in a whisper. "It was him!"

Blake took charge. With one hand on the small of my back, he pushed me forward, quickly leading me to his truck. "Get in," he said, opening the door for me.

"It's him," I repeated, hands shaking in disbelief.

"You don't know that. He didn't say anything incriminating. The way he spoke about Gigi is the way most people talk about Josh. Hating someone doesn't make you a killer, remember? Don't mess the investigation up by charging into the police station when you're all emotional like this," he said, wiggling his fingers in my direction. "Mackenzie, just sit tight."

"What? We can't just do nothing!" Was Blake insane? Who

knows if the police had even questioned Lawrence on his whereabouts that evening. They may never even consider him a suspect if we didn't speak up.

"We don't have a choice. There's no evidence. If he's pulled in for questioning now, he'll have a chance to make sure his tracks are covered. Please, think about this carefully. Let's at least wait until Wright has the results on that blood back before we go to him with this."

I took a deep breath. He was right of course. Logically, I understood that I could screw everything up if I accused Lawrence without proof, but I was so desperate to clear our names and not have people look at me like I was a monster. I felt like I was crawling out of my skin.

"Fine, you're actually making sense," I replied.

He smiled. "Look, let's go back to my place for an hour before I drop you off at Aaron's, so you can both go to Megan's later. You can't go while you're panicking."

"Yeah, OK. Thanks, Blake."

"Say that again."

I rolled my eyes, looking out the window and smiling to myself. I'd teamed up with a proper idiot.

CHAPTER ELEVEN

I walked up Aaron's driveway and something caught my eye outside his neighbor's house. I stepped back behind the shrubs separating the two houses and peeked through the bushes. My jaw dropped. Aaron was in the back of Wright's car. There was an officer in the passenger's seat too, who was turned around saying something to Aaron.

Rubbing my stomach, which had a knot in it, I stared intently until a second later when Wright pulled onto the road and drove away—with Aaron still in the back of the squad car!

Blake was long gone, or we would have tailed Wright.

Oh God, what's going on? Was Aaron arrested?

I felt like a robot as I planted one foot in front of the other toward Megan's house. My hands shook. I got halfway there when I pulled my phone out of my pocket and dialed. I might trust Aaron, but I still felt sick and uneasy about the whole situation. *Pick up, pick up.* I held my phone so close to my ear that it hurt. "Wright just took Aaron to the station," I said the second Blake answered.

"Oh, I'm fine. Thanks. How're you?"

I sighed sharply and rubbed my forehead. If I could just have one conversation with him that wasn't bloody hard work, that'd be great. "Cut the sarcasm for five seconds. What does he want with him?"

"This probably won't come as a surprise to you, but I'm not psychic."

"Blake," I snapped. "Why don't you take anything seriously?"

"I am. I don't know what Wright wants with him," he replied a little too coolly. Blake had his theories, and for once, I wanted to know one.

"I know you're lying. Why don't you just tell me what you're thinking?"

"Because, Miss Keaton, you take this detective job far too seriously." *And you are too trusting of your friends*, I silently added because I knew that's what he wanted to say to me.

"Just tell me, Blake. Please."

"The blood, Mackenzie. I think they've had the results back and the blood is Aaron's."

I hadn't even thought of that. "No," I snapped. "The blood—it can't be his. Aaron wouldn't hurt anyone."

"Whatever," Blake replied, and I could picture him rolling his eyes. "Just call me when you know more."

I shivered with the cold. The sun had slipped behind a cloud, abandoning me. "Why? What're you doing?"

"Do you really want to know?"

"Good-bye, Blake," I said and hung up the phone, not in the mood for any more of his stupid jokes.

I walked up to Megan's alone and tried to calm myself down. It was probably routine questioning and we would all be called back in too. That was it. I shouldn't let seeing Aaron in the back of a police car get to me.

Before knocking on Megan's door, I sent a quick text to Mum and Dad, letting them know I'd arrived safely at Megan's house, since they needed to know my every movement now.

Taking a deep breath and plastering on a fake smile that I was beginning to hate, I rang the doorbell. I didn't want Megan to know what was going on. It would just upset her, and Blake and I were just sort of keeping what we were doing to ourselves. Besides, he was the only other one that seemed willing to help.

Megan opened the door and visibly relaxed. "Oh, thank God you're here!"

I walked inside, wringing my hands out. Time to act like a normal, sane person. "What's up?"

"My family is driving me crazy!" She slammed the front door behind her and led me into the kitchen. "Where're Aaron and Kyle?"

I licked my lips in preparation for the lie. "Not sure. Did they say they're coming too?"

"They just said maybe."

"Do you mass-produce that stuff?" I asked and pointed to the four new bottles of whatever that Italian alcohol was we'd had the other night. At least it was a safer subject.

She turned and rolled her eyes. "My grandparents keep sending it over. They brought these with them. Mum's pissed because she only just got rid of the last lot."

"Why don't you just tell your nan you don't like it?"

"That's what I said. Come on. Let's go to my room."

Megan's room was small and claustrophobic. There was literally only space for a bed and wardrobe, but she'd tried to create the illusion of space by painting it a light-mint color and hanging large mirrors on the walls.

She sat down on her bed and hugged a pillow to her chest. "Mackenzie," she said slowly.

I sat down and faced her as she nervously fiddled with the ends of her short hair. Something was wrong. I'd seen Megan nervous before, but never around me. She looked like she was ready to bolt for the door.

"What's wrong, Megs?"

"Huh?" she muttered, not even looking up.

"Well, you either have something important on your mind, or you've got worms."

She stopped twiddling hair around her finger. Her chipped purple nail polish poked out brightly between the strands. "My dad's right, isn't he? The truth always comes out eventually."

My heart gave an uneasy thud. "Sure. Usually. Why?"

"I did something, Mackenzie."

"Go on," I whispered, completely unsure if I wanted to know what she had to say or not. If Megan told me she'd killed Josh and Courtney, I had no idea what I would do. But that was just ridiculous—same as the possibility that Aaron had done it.

"Megan, talk to me. What did you do?"

"The night of the crash. I…I spiked Gigi's drink."

I recoiled in shock and tried to make sense of what she'd just said. "You did what?"

Megan sucked in a shaky breath and gulped audibly. "The accident was my fault, Kenz. I *spiked* Gigi's drink."

There was the *spiked* word again.

Shit. Megan *spiked* Gigi's drink. I thought it was strange that she was drunk on so little. It all slotted into place in the worst kind of way. My chest ached. Megan's actions had directly led to the accident. Gigi was the more experienced driver and would've taken the shortcut through the country roads that Courtney was afraid of. I rubbed my forehead.

"You drugged her," I whispered in disbelief.

Megan's eyes widened. "Oh my God, Mackenzie, don't think that. I put vodka in her beer. I have no clue where to get Rohypnol from!"

"Why? I don't understand. What did Gigi do to you?"

She shook her head. "I can't tell you that."

"Are you serious?" I spluttered. "Megan, you can't say something like that and then not explain. Tilly and Gigi *died* in that car accident. This is nonnegotiable. Tell me what happened. Now."

Courtney was the only one not drinking the night of the car accident, because she was on antibiotics. She had just passed her driving test and wasn't confident behind the wheel at all. With little choice and Josh in her ear telling her "a van is no different to a bloody car," she had driven. She'd pulled out at an intersection, and then we had been hit.

"I…I…" She stopped to chew on her lip. "Promise you won't think any differently of me?"

"Just tell me." I couldn't promise her that. She'd spiked Gigi's drink. I couldn't promise anything right now. "Why, Megan?"

"Because whenever we were drunk, we slept together." She said the words in such a rush they blended together. But I still heard her crystal clear.

"What? You and Gigi…you did what?"

She glared. "Don't look like that. You slept with a killer."

Great, Kyle had a big mouth.

I held my hands up. "I'm sorry. I just didn't expect that. I didn't know the two of you were involved."

"We slept together whenever we were drunk." She looked down at the bed, ashamed. I wasn't sure if that was due to sleeping with a woman or what she did to Gigi the day of the accident. It had to be the latter, because she had to know I would be her friend no matter who she wanted to sleep with. "I wanted her that night, Kenz."

"But you're not gay," I blurted out and mentally slapped myself. That wasn't the most important part of what she had just told me, but it *was* true. I had never even heard her mention a celeb girl crush like the one I had on Mila Kunis and Tilly had had on Mischa Barton.

"I know." She shrugged. "But there was something about her. The first time was in the summer, after school was out. I'd just turned fifteen. All of you were on holiday or busy, so me and Gigi were hanging out in her room. We were drinking Malibu, and she just kissed me out of nowhere. At first I was stunned, but then I kissed her back. It was so different than anything I'd ever felt before—softer and more intimate. Anyway, we didn't stop with a kiss, and whenever we were drunk, we'd have sex."

What the hell was going on with everyone? Was I the only one who hadn't slept with someone in our group? First Kyle and Courtney, now Megan and Gigi.

"OK," I said, taking a breath to digest the information. "Why did it only happen when you were drunk?"

"She said I wasn't ready to be out, so nothing could happen, but you know her—she had no self-control when she was drunk. She was half-right; I'm not a lesbian. I still like guys, and I've never felt anything for a girl before or since her, but I just wanted her. It wasn't because she was a girl; it was because she made me feel things that I never knew were possible."

A tear trickled down Megan's face and settled on her jaw. I felt awful for her. The pain in her face and words stole my breath. "It's all my fault. Gigi died because of me. Tilly too. They both died because I was selfish and wanted to get laid!"

I wrapped my arms around her. "Shh, it's OK. You didn't mean for anyone to get hurt."

"B-but it's my fault. I have to tell the police. I-I have to."

I pulled away and gripped her face in both of my hands, forcing her to look at me. Her eyes were wide, scared. "Megan, that will achieve nothing. It was an accident. The collision could have happened if Gigi had been driving. It was getting late, and there wouldn't have been much visibility on the country roads either. It was dark and foggy that night, remember? No one saw the truck."

"But—"

"Think about it. You *spiked* her drink to take advantage of her. Do you have any idea how bad that looks?"

She started sobbing, covering her mouth with her hand. "I know. I get it. I do. I get how it looks, but I swear to you, Mackenzie, I didn't hurt Court and Josh. Please believe me. Please."

I wrapped my arms around her trembling body again. "Shh, it's OK." It so wasn't OK, but I needed her to calm down so we could talk more. "Megan, you can't go to the police. I know you didn't kill anyone. I believe you, but the police might not."

"But I didn't do anything to them," Megan replied.

I pulled back so I could see her and try to make her see sense.

"I should come clean about Gigi. People blame her for the accident, but it was my fault for spiking her drink."

"People blame Josh and Courtney for the accident too." I closed my eyes. God, what was going on? Were Courtney and Josh killed for revenge?

"There are about a million what-ifs, Megan. I could have gone to the toilet before we left, and we would have been a few minutes later and missed the truck. We could have left an hour earlier when Kyle wanted to or pulled over at the burger joint like Aaron wanted. There are so many things we all could have done that would have changed what happened that night, but you can't go back in time. It was an accident."

She nodded, wiping her nose on the back of her sleeve. Her dark eyes were bloodshot. "I feel *so* guilty."

"I think we all do. That's part of being the ones who survived.

Take me through everything that happened that night. I have to know what happened, why you spiked the drink."

Did I really want to hear how much I clearly didn't know Megan and Gigi? We all kept our secrets, but I hadn't thought Courtney or Megan would have kept their relationships with Kyle and Gigi from me. We could talk about things like that—a week ago, I had thought I'd known everything about my friends.

Apparently not.

Megan grabbed her pillow and pressed it into her chest. "It was the last night of the trip, and we hadn't been…together in a few weeks. She kept flirting with me, but when I tried to kiss her, she pushed me away. Do you remember me suggesting someone else should drive back because Gigi drove there?"

Megan had suggested to us during the afternoon before anyone had started drinking. I only had a provisional license at the time or I would've volunteered. Gigi had insisted that she didn't mind and wanted to drive back too. Her stepdad owned the van anyway, so she hadn't wanted anyone else being responsible if anything happened to it.

At the time, I'd just thought Megan was being considerate and wanted Gigi to be able to drink on the last day; I'd had no idea about her ulterior motive to sleep with her again. They'd never acted any differently around each other—not that I'd noticed anyway. But, as I was realizing, there were a lot of things I'd never noticed.

"Yes," I replied.

"When it was decided that Gigi was driving back, I took

matters into my own hands. At the hotel, she said she was just going to have a beer or two, so I put vodka in them," she said, her voice raw with emotion and regret.

"How could she not know?"

Megan smiled. "Probably because you bought the cheap, crap stuff."

I tilted my head to the side and glared. "I'm not forking out for the good stuff when you lot down it in seconds. What happened next?"

"Well, it worked. When you all went out, we went to her room and… Well, you don't want the details. I knew Courtney couldn't drink, so she ended up having to drive, and you know the rest. It was my fault, Mackenzie."

My head spun faster than if I'd been on a carnival ride. "OK." *Think. Take control.* "OK," I repeated. "What you did was wrong. So, *so* wrong, but it doesn't change what happened, and telling people will only make you seem untrustworthy. And if the police find out you spiked Gigi's drink, they're going to think you did that to us too. If you're capable of drugging a friend to have sex with them, what else are you capable of?"

"That's not how it was!"

"I know that. I know you, Megan." *I think.* "But you can't give the police a reason to doubt you."

"What do we do? Kenz, this secret has been killing me. I want it off my chest. It feels good to tell you, but I don't want to go to prison for something I haven't done."

I pressed my lips together as a pang of guilt hit my stomach.

"Talk to me about it whenever you want. Whatever you need to say or vent, just do it to me, OK? We're not going to the police. You made a stupid, stupid mistake, but you didn't mean to hurt anyone."

Her eyes filled with tears and she slowly shook her head. "I don't know what to say."

"Don't say anything. Dry your eyes and plaster on a smile. You need to be normal when you see me out. Your parents can't see you like this."

"You're leaving?" she asked.

I need to leave or my head is going to explode.

"I have to, but don't worry. Everything's going to be fine."

I hope.

CHAPTER TWELVE

I sat cross-legged on my bed in a daze. Two of my friends had hidden big, fat secrets from me. Strike that—technically four had. I knew that if I told anyone else what I knew, I could land Kyle and Megan both in trouble. After all, the secrets they'd kept could be seen as motives.

An awful thought kept popping into my head over and over until I was ready to scream: What if it *was* one of them? Clearly I didn't know my friends as well as I thought, but there was a massive difference between not disclosing every aspect of your life and murder.

This all felt like some horrible roller-coaster ride, and I wanted to get off.

My best friend had been murdered and three other friends could be responsible for it. How could I keep it to myself if I found out one was responsible? And how could I turn one of them in? It was too hard to choose between the people I loved, even if they had committed a heinous crime. I had to choose, and it was so hard because two people had lost their lives, and they deserved justice.

I picked up my phone and called Courtney's cousin, Felicity. We hadn't spoken since a brief encounter at the funeral, and I was hoping she could make things clearer for me. She had grown up with Courtney. Her mum was never around, so she'd practically lived with Court and Courtney's parents until she'd moved away to university.

"Kenz," she said, picking up on the first ring.

"Hey, how are you?" I closed my eyes. *Stupid, stupid question, Mackenzie.*

"I'm doing all right. You?"

"Yeah, OK, I guess. Are you busy tomorrow, Felicity?"

"Not really. I'm packing to go back to uni, but apart from that, sod all."

She was going back so soon? How was everyone starting to move on again so soon?

"You want to meet up for lunch?" she asked.

"That sounds good," I replied.

"Wanna meet at the Lion at eleven thirty?"

"OK. I'll see you then."

"Bye." She hung up but I stayed still, the phone still up to my ear. I hadn't thought she would leave so soon. Courtney had practically been a sister to her. Was the same thing happening to Felicity as was happening to Blake? Was Courtney's mum giving her the cold shoulder, wishing it had been Felicity instead?

My phone buzzed. A number I didn't recognize flashed on the screen with a text message. Keep your friends close and your enemies closer.

"What?" I whispered. Who was that? I held the phone in my trembling hand.

Unsure if I should try to call or reply, I stared at the message, trying to work out what was meant by it—and, more importantly, who could've sent it.

Who is this? I typed my reply and sent it before I could change my mind.

I stared at the screen and waited for the longest time. Seconds turned into minutes, and there was no reply.

What's going on? Is someone trying to mess with me? My mouth fell open, and I dropped the phone. *It's from the killer.* How had they gotten my number? Did I know them?

"Mackenzie?" Mum shouted up the stairs. I jumped at the sound of her voice and grabbed my phone. "Kyle's here. I'm sending him up."

In a panic, I stuffed my phone under my pillow and took a breath. "Thanks," I called.

Kyle had barely left me alone since he'd told me about him and Courtney. I found it unnerving. He knew I wasn't going to tell people, so he shouldn't have been obsessed with seeing me all the time to make sure I wasn't blabbing his secret.

"Hey," he said, closing my bedroom door behind him.

His once-calm and inviting smile now made me feel like I should have something hard and heavy at the ready to defend myself, just in case. "What's up?" I asked and cleared my croaky throat.

Forget about the text message and focus on him. I already knew I wasn't going to tell him about the text. Before I opened up, I wanted someone else to go first. I had no idea if I was the only one who'd received one or if we all had. Kyle was cut up over his relationship—or lack of—with Courtney. That didn't make him a killer, but crimes of passion were common.

Could seeing Courtney and Josh so loved up at the cabin have made him snap?

I wanted to be honest with my friends, but the more I learned, the harder it was to trust them. My heart stuttered with fear and anxiety.

He shrugged and flopped down on my bed, lying on his back with his arms above his head. I smiled a genuine smile—it was so normal of him to slob out all over my room.

"Nothing much. I can't stand being at home."

"Parents driving you insane?" I asked. Mine were doing my head in, but after what'd happened, I was lucky they hadn't locked me in the house or hired a security guard, which Mum had actually suggested.

"Yep. What are you up to?"

Trying to figure out who's sending me creepy texts. Wondering if you're getting them too. "Nothing. You?"

He bared his teeth in a grin. "Just come to see one of my oldest friends."

"I'm not old."

"That's right." His dark eyes lit up. "You're the baby of the group."

I was turning nineteen in five months. Courtney should have turned nineteen two weeks before me, but she would never get to do that. She would be eighteen forever—like Tilly and Gigi.

Kyle and I drifted into an awkward silence. We met when we

were kids, and kids just got on, no matter if they knew a person or not. I wanted to ask him if he really meant the nasty things he'd said about Courtney, and I think he wanted to talk about it too.

I said, "Is everything really OK? I know you're angry at how Courtney treated you. If you want to talk about it, we can."

You want him to slip up.

No. That wasn't it. I believed him. Kyle was sweet. He was my human teddy bear. He wouldn't hurt a fly.

"You'll judge me, Kenzie. You did yesterday and I can't stand it. You don't understand."

"Then make me understand. Come on, Kyle. There's nothing we can't talk about."

Yes, there is. I wouldn't talk about my secret, the blackmail from Josh, or the text.

"Have you ever been in love?" he questioned, knowing the bloody answer.

I'd thought I was in love with my ex, Danny, but he had turned out to be a heartless dick when he'd cheated on me. There hadn't been anyone else since we'd broken up two years ago. Never again would I put myself back in the position I had been in with him.

"No," I replied, feeling a twist in my stomach.

Blake…

No, I absolutely did not have the time or mental capacity to consider my feelings for Blake right then. Besides, I barely knew him. We had incredible chemistry, but you couldn't love someone you didn't know. Insta-love wasn't possible. Right?

"Then I don't know if you *can* understand it yet. Courtney was...everything. She was all I thought about. My whole life had become about making her happy. I thought she felt the same. We were supposed to be together. And then she turned around and kicked me to the curb. You can't imagine how much that hurt. I had all of my happiness ripped away from me, so, yes, I'm pissed at her. I hate her, and I hate that I can't stop loving her. I wish I could flip a switch and not care about her anymore, but I can't, so I'll be angry until I'm over it. I'm more angry at myself that now I'll never be able to set things straight with her."

Maybe I didn't understand how he felt, but I still didn't know if I could hate someone who I loved after they'd died—even if they had hurt me. Did Kyle only want Courtney to be happy if she was with him? If so, that wasn't my definition of love.

"I'm sorry, Kyle," I said, completely out of anything helpful to say. "I'm sorry you're hurt and things didn't work out the way you wanted." Closing my eyes, I felt every ounce of energy being siphoned. I was completely over everything. "God, I'm so tired."

He frowned. "Sorry. I should have called before I came and unloaded that on you. I wanted to make sure we're OK. I don't want what happened with Courtney to mess up our friendship."

"It's OK, and it won't come between us. I should get some sleep now." I hated that he doubted our friendship. Was he worried that I thought he could have done it? I knew he hadn't. But I wasn't so sure about the possible burner phone used to send those weird text messages. Why didn't I feel comfortable enough to ask him?

He kissed my forehead as he stood up. "Bye, Kenzie. Speak to you tomorrow."

I smiled halfheartedly and flopped down on my bed, exhausted. My body felt like it was made of rock. I couldn't have moved even if I'd wanted to. "Bye, Kyle," I replied, yawning.

Once I hung up, I dialed Aaron's number, but it went through to voice mail. *Damn it.* I flicked down my contacts and called the landline at his parents'.

"Hello?" his mum said.

"Hi, it's Mackenzie. Is Aaron in?"

"He's sleeping. I'll ask him to get back to you in the morning."

"OK, thanks."

She hung up first, and I glared at my phone. That sounded a lot more like Aaron was avoiding speaking to me.

There was no way I would get a good night's sleep—not after that text—but at least I would be alone for a while and not have to think.

Saturday, August 22

"What time will you be home?" Mum asked, looking at the clock on the kitchen wall. All morning she'd been my shadow. Time had ticked by so slowly, I'd wanted to pull my hair out, so I was beyond grateful when I had to leave to meet Felicity.

"We're only having lunch. I doubt I'll be longer than a couple hours." I figured that gave me until two before I had to be back or she'd be calling.

"OK," she replied, nodding to herself. Mum found it hard to let me go anywhere, but she recognized that she couldn't keep me locked up, and there was nothing to suggest I was in any danger. She still thought someone had somehow made a copy of the key or picked the lock at the cabin. I prayed she was right.

"You can always call or text, you know," I offered.

"I know, love. I just worry about you. It makes me feel uncomfortable having you out there when the murderer hasn't been caught."

It kind of made me nervous too. Someone was sending me cryptic texts, and I was a person of interest in a double murder investigation. All of that didn't exactly make me feel safe.

Our little village was safe—or it used to be. Everyone knew and looked out for everyone else. I'd gone from having full freedom to having to disclose my every movement. "I'll be fine, Mum, and I promise to let you know where I am." With a bit of luck, I sounded more confident than I felt.

She pushed my hair behind my shoulder and smiled. "You're a good girl, Mackenzie. Say hello to Felicity for me and have a nice time."

"Thanks. See you soon," I said and left before she got tearful and I felt guilty for leaving her sight again. I wish I could've stayed in to stop her worrying, but I had to clear my and my friends' names and figure out who was sending me sinister text messages.

If Megan, Kyle, Aaron, or Blake were responsible, Felicity

could help me go to the police. I'd like to think I was strong enough to do the right thing for Courtney, but turning in someone I loved wouldn't be easy. Felicity could give me the support that I needed.

I saw her as soon as I walked into the restaurant. She sat at the back of the pub, next to a window, wearing a deep-red summer dress and a cropped denim jacket. Her hair fell in tight blond ringlets down to the bottom of her shoulder blades.

Felicity's appearance couldn't have been more different from Courtney's. Court's hair had been stick straight and a fierce red since she was fifteen. She loved the color.

"Hey," I said as I approached the table.

"Hi," Felicity replied, her solemn expression brightening as she stood and held her arms out for a hug. At least she didn't think I killed her cousin.

I hugged her back, and we sat down. "How is everyone?"

"Devastated. I don't want to leave them, but I have so much work to do." She bit her lip and her eyes clouded over. "And truthfully, I can't stand being there. I know that sounds ridiculously selfish, but there's nothing I can do to help. I've never felt so useless before."

"You're not useless. I don't think anyone can do anything right now. They lost their daughter; they need time."

"And what about you? What do you need? Kyle said you're dealing with this well."

My back stiffened. "You've spoken to Kyle?"

She picked up the breakfast menu and scanned the options.

"He's dropped by a few times. The pancakes are a bit hit-and-miss here, aren't they?"

"Sometimes they're amazing and other times they're awful," I agreed. I didn't know Kyle had gone around to see Court's family. He was still angry with Courtney for choosing Josh over him, so why go to see her family? Kyle and Aaron both secretly visited the family of the girl they loved, but it didn't make any sense.

An annoying, nagging voice in the back of my head kept screaming that Kyle was hiding something else.

I'm missing something here.

What if it *was* Kyle? I had known the guy practically my whole life. Surely no one could be *that* blind. But if the last week few weeks had taught me anything, it was that I was so blind it was almost embarrassing.

Could he have sent that text?

"What's going on then, chick? You know it's not healthy to bottle up your emotions."

I laughed and tucked my hair behind me ears. That one I had heard far too often lately. "I'm temporarily bottling. I'll grieve when their killer is found—or at least when we're scrubbed off the suspect list."

She scoffed and flicked her hand. "That's a load of rubbish. I thought it was a joke when I first found out. No one believes it—no one who matters anyway."

Sure the people that really knew us believed we had nothing to do with it, but I still couldn't sleep properly knowing others considered me a killer. "What will you do if they never find him, Flis? I don't know how I can live with knowing they never got justice."

She pressed her lips together and scowled. "I'll hate that, but life does go on, Mackenzie. I know that's harsh and horrible, but it's true. I hope they catch him, but if they don't, it doesn't change anything. Courtney and Josh will still be gone. Nothing will bring them back or make what happened to them OK."

"If they never found out who did it, you'd be OK?" Just the thought made my head spin.

"No, not OK. I want justice, but it won't bring them back. Don't drive yourself crazy with this. You know Courtney would probably say something like, 'Get a grip, Mackenzie. I'm dead, deal with it,' wouldn't she?"

I smiled and shook my head, hearing those words in Court's voice. "Yeah, she would." But that didn't really make it OK to cover up for one of my friends. I changed the conversation. "So how's uni going, anyway? You still loving it up in Liverpool?"

"I do. It's a great place. Not sure I'll stay after I graduate though. I'm thinking of moving back when it's time to find a job."

Felicity wanted to be a nurse and was three years into a four-year degree. It was the same course Tilly would have been starting next year.

"Are there better job opportunities here?" That seemed unlikely. The closest hospital was a forty-minute drive, and there were only three within a comfortable daily driving distance.

"Not really, but I want to be around family. I'm thinking of going into a walk-in clinic or doctor's office."

"Sounds good. Would be nice to have you back this way."

Liverpool was about two hundred miles north and just over three and a half hours away. Felicity didn't get to visit much, so it would be great to see more of her. Courtney's parents would love it too.

"What about you? School going all right?"

I turned my nose up. "It's going. Not looking forward to getting back after summer, especially now. But a friend of the family is a counselor in another uni so I'm hoping to pick up some work experience with her next year while she works in summer school."

"You didn't want to do that this summer?"

"This year was supposed to be our last summer of freedom, so we were all spending it working our way through a before-university bucket list."

She laughed. "Courtney mentioned something about that. How far did you get?"

"We'd done LEGOLAND and camping, which I hated because it rained constantly." Two weeks into summer holidays, and our plans were ripped away. Court and Josh would never get the chance to do all the things we'd planned—or anything else for that matter. Again. I dipped my head and added, "Then the weekend away."

"You don't want to do the rest of the things on the list?"

"One day maybe." For Tilly, Gigi, and Courtney, I would do all of the things we'd planned to, but there were far more important things to deal with before I ticked off any activities from the list.

I also didn't particularly want to do them anymore. It wouldn't be fun. It was just something I felt I had to do now.

"What's this Detective Wright like, then? I've heard interesting things."

"You haven't had to speak to him?"

"I've been interviewed but not by him."

"Oh. Well, where to start," I muttered. "Interesting is one way to describe him. He's like one of those eccentric detectives you see on TV. Not sure if he realizes TV isn't real and that maybe he needs to be grown-up about his career."

"There are no other leads?"

"Apparently not, but he's hardly forthcoming with information. We only know what he wants us to know and when he wants us to know it. I have no clue what he's thinking about the clothes."

She frowned, stirring the mug of tea that everyone received as soon as they arrived whether they wanted it or not. The owners, Mr. and Mrs. Graham, were big on tea, and from the big pot in their hand, it looked like I was getting one soon too. "What clothes?"

"The ones the murderer was wearing. If it was one of us, then they have to be somewhere, right?" She nodded. "They can't find any, of course. But he still won't accept that it means it wasn't us."

"Are you sure? They can't ignore that."

I shrugged one shoulder. "I'm not sure about much anymore. There's been no mention of the clothes though." I scoffed—like he would tell us even if he had found it. "I bet the first we'll hear of any new leads is when someone is arrested. Aaron was called in for more questioning."

"Jesus. This is such a mess," Felicity said, shaking her head.

You have no idea how messy it's gotten. "Yep."

It was a big mess, and I was caught in the middle of it and desperate to get out.

By the time Felicity and I had finished lunch and I'd made my way back home, I was feeling slightly better. Her strength was encouraging, and I knew, without a doubt, that whoever killed Courtney and Josh would pay the price. I would turn whoever it was in if I found out—no matter who it was and how much I loved my friends.

My phone beeped with another text message, and I froze. I'd never been scared of that tone before.

It was Megan, thankfully, asking if I wanted to do something that afternoon. I didn't. So I replied with an excuse and told her I'd see her soon. That would hopefully give me some time to work things out in my head and hopefully figure out what was going on.

As I sent the text, my phone rang. I sighed in relief as Aaron's name flashed on my screen. Did I expect whomever the anonymous person was who'd texted me to start calling now? Honestly, I didn't know what they were capable of.

"Aaron! Are you OK? I tried calling you last night!"

He chuckled. "Mum said you'd called. I'm fine."

"What happened?"

"Apparently, Wright found some of my blood in the woods. It's OK though. I explained what happened."

My heart froze. Oh God. It *was* his blood.

No.

God, Aaron?

No, he wouldn't…

"Start at the beginning," I said, absolutely terrified of his answer. There had to be a reasonable explanation.

"Megan and I went for a walk that afternoon when we were at the cabin. She found what she thought was one of those stupid crystal stone things. I picked it up and it turned out it was an old, very sharp piece of green glass, which I chucked into some shed in the woods."

We hadn't seen the green glass, but it hadn't been particularly light in the shed. The stone must have landed on the wrapper and fallen off when I'd picked it up. "Oh. You never mentioned it when you got back."

There was something about the story that I didn't like, though it was completely plausible and Wright must have accepted it since Aaron was calling me rather than sitting in a prison cell.

"One, I'm a tough man. And two, it bled for a second, hardly bandage material. Wright just wanted me to clear it up. He'll probably want to confirm it with Megan. Can you believe he doesn't trust us?" he joked.

"Crazy, right?" I replied, forcing myself to laugh. "So everything is all right?"

"Yep. I gotta go. My parents and I are off to visit the family soon. I'll be home tomorrow so we'll meet up, yeah?"

"Wait, you're going away?"

"Twenty miles away, Kenz, not to Mexico."

I bit my lip as I walked up my front path. "OK. See you tomorrow."

Aaron hung up, and as I opened the front door, Mum came rushing out of the kitchen. I was home early, but she'd still worried herself sick.

"Hey," I said, grinning like a fool so she would see that everything was fine, even if it wasn't.

"How was lunch?"

"Good. Felicity seems to be doing OK and she's going back to uni for summer classes."

"That's good."

I could tell that Mum wanted to quiz me on every little detail, but she was holding back. She could get a little obsessive.

"I'm gonna go to my room," I said, giving her a quick hug and taking the stairs two at a time.

Dropping down on my bed, I rubbed my aching head. Aaron was visiting family last minute but usually did *everything* he could to get out of family gatherings. Last time, he was ill; the time before that, he'd had a make-believe exam. And I think he'd even used my break up with Danny as an excuse once too.

He hated his extended family because they were judgmental arseholes who constantly put Aaron down for not being a straight-A student. They thought he should be headed to Cambridge to study law, like his cousins were. So him going sounded a lot like he was running, maybe not from Wright and the police, but from his friends. It was like there was something he didn't want us to know.

I dialed Blake's number and laid my phone beside me on speaker.

Hopefully he would make everything clearer—or just turn it into a joke. I'd have taken either one right then. Desperation kinda did that to a girl.

"Do I need to take out a restraining order?" Blake teased instead of a traditional hello.

"It was his blood," I whispered, feeling as sure as I could be that Aaron was the killer. The line went silent. I waited for him to say something. "Blake?"

"I'm here," he said. "Do you want me to come over?"

No annoying "I told you so"?

"I don't know what I want, Blake. How can it be his?" I shook my trembling hands as reality started to set it. "Do you think Aaron killed them?"

"You're asking me?"

"I'm too close, aren't I? I believe them all so much that I can't see clearly. Did Aaron do it, Blake? Please answer me."

"For what it's worth, I don't think so. My money is still on Kyle." I heard Blake rustling around in the background and then the sound of keys jingling. He really was coming over. "Just chill out. We still need to speak to Wright about Lawrence. Aaron's blood in an old shed doesn't prove he's a murderer."

"Why are you doing this? You think it was one of them, so why help me with Lawrence and reassure me?"

"You asked me to, remember?"

"That doesn't answer my question. You could have told me to get lost, and don't tell me you're only helping me because you're bored because I know that's a lie."

He sighed. "Fine. I like that you're so loyal to the people you care about that you believe in them and want to do everything you can to keep them safe. You don't find that much, and it's not a quality I've ever had in a friend. Plus, you're not that bad to look at."

"You had to ruin it," I replied. A small smile pulled at my lips. "Are you coming over?"

"On my way," he said and hung up.

I put the phone down and shook my head. As much as Blake played the I-don't-give-a-damn card, he really did care. My heart soared so high I felt faint. I really did have a thing for him. A big thing.

This will be interesting. The one guy I've felt like I could really fall for and he was brother of a guy I hated—a guy I was suspected of killing. Fabulous.

Blake knocked on my front door in half the time it should have taken to drive to my house. I wanted to yell because he had obviously driven fast, but I was too glad to see him. He led the way up to my room as if he owned the place.

"What did Aaron say?" he asked, sitting down on my bed and lying back against my pillows.

"Please, do make yourself comfortable."

His light eyes darkened in a glare.

I refocused. "He said he was out with Megan and cut his finger on a piece of glass, but he never said anything when he got back."

Blake's chest shook as he laughed. "Guys stop whining—or boasting—about their war wounds when they're about ten, Mackenzie. Do you believe him?"

"Yes," I replied. *I think.*

Rolling his eyes, he pushed himself up so he was properly facing me. All of a sudden, he had his serious face on, and I felt like I was about to get a lesson in who to trust. I didn't like where this was going. "Do you? There's not an ounce of doubt in your mind about Aaron's innocence?"

The way Blake looked at me made it hard to concentrate on breathing, let alone something as serious as murder. I licked my drier-than-the-Gobi-Desert lips and swallowed. "Um…"

"Seriously, Mackenzie, is he innocent?"

"Yes. I believe him. He might be hotheaded, but he's protective of the people he cares about. There is no way he could have ever hurt Courtney or Josh, Court especially. Aaron's uncle used to hit his aunt before she left and Aaron despises violence against women."

He flopped down on his back again. "All right, then. I think you're right too. Aaron didn't do it. It's Kyle. We should delve into Megan a little more as well."

"Megan," I repeated.

"You said 'girl or guy' once. She had the opportunity."

I rolled my eyes. That was one of the stupidest things that'd spewed from his mouth, and that was saying something. "We *all* had the opportunity."

"Shh," he whispered. "I'm going to have a nap. We'll resume this when I wake up."

If I hadn't been sitting down, I would've fallen over. "Excuse me?"

"Mackenzie, I am trying to sleep." He lay back and closed his eyes.

"Why do you want to sleep here?"

"Because I'm scared of the boogeyman."

I sighed. "Fine, Blake. I know it's really because you don't feel comfortable at home."

"Then why did you ask?"

I narrowed my eyes at him even though he couldn't see me. "You're not sleeping here all afternoon."

"Just a couple hours. Wake me when you've cooked dinner."

I gritted my teeth but couldn't help a little smile. *Idiot.*

He fell asleep quickly, and I grabbed a book from my bookshelf and sat beside him. He looked so peaceful. I watched his plain black T-shirt rise and fall on his chest and his closed eyes flutter the deeper he slept. My heart leaped as I watched him, and when he flopped his arm over his pillow and turned his head toward me, it stole my breath.

Not good.

About ten minutes into Blake Watch, he sighed, rolled onto his side, and threw the arm that was over his head over my lap. Desire fired in my belly. We'd been together once, and it had felt like nothing I'd experienced before. It was more than sex, and I wasn't ashamed to admit I wanted to feel that way again.

It was absolutely not the time though. There was so much going on that I couldn't worry about out-of-control hormones, even if they were shouting louder than my desire to catch a killer at that moment.

At eight that evening, after Mum had cooked us homemade pizzas, Blake went home. Thankfully, my parents didn't suspect anything was going on between us because then there would have been more rules when he was over or when I was at his house.

As much as Blake drove me crazy, he also kept me sane. My mum and I watched him drive away from my front door.

"How is he doing?" she asked.

"He's doing all right considering."

"I feel for the whole family, but that boy's been through a lot, especially after his parents' messy breakup and rarely seeing his mum. Must be awful to know your own mother didn't want you back. I don't understand how she could've turned him down."

"Huh?" My scalp felt like it was on fire.

"After the divorce, Eloise said she couldn't deal with Blake's behavior and sent him to live with his dad. If you ask me, Blake's acting out was due to Eloise always favoring Josh. The poor boy had to get her attention somehow and I think he's still trying. He clearly still resents them both."

My pulse thudded in my ears. Blake had never mentioned this, but it sure did explain why he was so angry with his mum and younger brother. That was in the past now though; he wasn't just staying with his mum because he had to stick around. He did still have to stay—we all did—but now he wanted to too.

Shit.

I swallowed what tasted like acid and asked, "How do you know this?"

"Eloise and I aren't close, but we've spoken a few times over the years. I saw how she was with the boys, and Lori from work knows her well."

Oh God. I was hoping she'd tell me it was all just a rumor. My mum wasn't one to gossip, especially not to me. If there was one person in this world I was sure I could trust, it was Mum.

"OK," I whispered. "So she wouldn't let him live with her?"

Mum shook her head. "No, it was more than that. When Josh was about two or three, he and Blake were playing outside in the back garden, and Josh fell in the wading pool. Eloise grabbed him but she blamed Blake. I think Blake wanted to live with Eloise, but she never did trust him around Josh again."

Wow, that must've hurt a lot. Accidents happened, and it wasn't Blake's responsibility to look after his toddler brother! In addition to that, she'd kept him away from his brother too. That wasn't OK. Why hadn't Blake told me any of this?

Rubbing the ache between my eyes, I faked a yawn. "I think I'm going to get an early night. I'm exhausted."

"That sounds like a good plan, darling. Good night."

I let Mum kiss my cheek and then hightailed it upstairs. Closing my door, I started to pace. Blake lied to me about why he didn't live with his mum. Maybe indirectly, but he'd still hid the truth. Eloise was scared for Josh. I hoped it was only because he was scared; otherwise, it didn't look good that his mum thought he could hurt his brother, but if I had to consider Aaron's and Kyle's secrets being motives, then surely I had to do the same with Blake's.

Stripping out of my clothes, I threw on the first pair of pajamas I could find, brushed my teeth, and got into bed. But I couldn't switch my mind off enough to sleep.

My phone rang ten minutes after Blake left. I picked it up with shaky hands, scared of who was contacting me. I was now scared of my bloody phone. Thankfully, I saw Blake's name. Blowing out a deep breath, I answered. "Hi," I said into the phone. "You're home?"

"Uncle Pete's in the hospital," he stuttered and cleared his throat.

"What?"

"He's been… He was attacked."

Attacked? Jumping out of bed, I reached for the jeans I'd thrown over my chair. "I'm on my way. I'll meet you at your house and we'll go together, OK?" I replied and hung up so I could get dressed and get on the road. Blake sounded shaken up, and I didn't want him driving alone. Mum wasn't going to be happy, but I had to get to him.

CHAPTER THIRTEEN

Mum had reluctantly agreed to let me go to Blake's house and to the hospital as long as I was back home by eleven. I gave it an hour before she texted me, needing an update on my whereabouts.

Blake's house was dark when I arrived, but his bedroom light was on and the front door was unlocked. "Blake," I called, making my way upstairs.

He didn't reply, but his door was wide-open. I found him sitting on his bed, staring at the wall. There was no doubt he'd heard me calling him and stomping up the stairs, but he made no attempt to acknowledge my presence. I slowly sat next to him on his bed. I was wary and worried. "I'm so sorry," I said. "What happened to Pete? Should we go to the hospital? I can take you right now if you want."

"My mum found him at his house. He was supposed to come over, but when he didn't show, she went to his. The front door was open, and he was lying on his living room floor. He's been hit over the head with a cricket bat, Mackenzie. His own cricket bat."

"Oh my God." I sat down and covered his clenched fist with my hand. "Do you know what's happening now?"

He shook his head and lifted one shoulder in a halfhearted shrug. "I just found out. My dad offered to come and get me but…"

"But what?"

"I don't think anyone would want me there."

"Of course they'd want you there." It was me who Pete wouldn't want there. "Come on. We need to go."

He looked over, and I saw the raw pain in his eyes. "Why are you here?"

Because you called and because I can't get you off my mind. "Why did you come over when I called you?"

He frowned and looked down at his hands. "Friends now, are we?"

I thought we'd passed that stage when we'd slept together, but I didn't think I needed to bring that up now. "Yes, so get used to it. Put on your shoes," I instructed. "We're going to the hospital."

I could only see the side of his face, but his smirk was crystal clear. "Did you just tell me to put on my shoes like I'm a child?"

"Well, when you decide to act your age…" I rolled my eyes and slapped his forearm. "Come on, Blake. You *have* to go."

"That attack could have killed him. Someone tried to kill my uncle. Do you know where Aaron, Kyle, and Megan are?"

"What?" I replied, laughing in disbelief. "You think it was one of them?"

"How can you not think this is related to Josh's and Courtney's murders?"

I hadn't really thought about it. Court and Josh were stabbed, not hit like Pete. "Let's just concentrate on what's important right now. Get off your arse and get in my car. I'm driving you to the hospital. You need to be with your family."

He arched his eyebrow and muttered, "Family. Right."

"Come on," I said, yanking his arm until he got off the bed.

We arrived at the hospital forty-five minutes later and walked the deserted corridor looking for Ward F, where Pete was according to Eloise's voice mail.

I looked up at Blake. His body was so tense I thought he was going to shatter. "When we get there, I think I should wait outside. You OK with that?" I asked.

He clenched and unclenched his jaw. "I don't need you to hold my hand."

"Of course you don't. You don't need anybody," I replied sarcastically. "Blake, you've been there for me, and I *want* to do the same. There are no ulterior motives here. I'm not doing it to get anything in return. That's just what friends do."

"Again with the friend thing. You really do like me, don't you?" He said it as a joke, but under the teasing I could tell it was a genuine question. There weren't many people in his life that actually knew and cared about him.

"Yes." *I like you way more than I should.* "You're stuck with me."

I rang the intercom outside the locked intensive care ward, and as soon as I mentioned Pete's nephew was here, we were told to come straight in. That didn't seem good to me, like they wanted to get his family in quick to say good-bye before the inevitable.

Blake held the door open as it clicked unlocked. I walked through and turned around. "Ooh, you're turning into a gentleman there."

His blue eyes glared. "Next time, I'm gonna let it hit your arse."

"Sure you will. Go ahead. I'll wait in there," I said, nodding toward the door with a sign that read "Waiting Room."

"You really don't want to come with?"

"Blake, your family will be glad you came. You know how Pete feels about me. He was so angry and hateful; there's no way he would want me there. I'll be right here, and we can leave whenever you want." He opened his mouth, but I reached up and pressed my palm against it, sensing what he was about to say. "*After* you've seen your uncle. You can do this."

He took a step back, and I lowered my hand. With a curt nod, he walked off to be with his family.

I watched the hallway until Blake entered Pete's room, and then I went into the small waiting room. One wall was lined with blue fabric chairs, and the other had a long wooden counter. Exactly what you'd expect at a hospital. There were tea- and coffee-making facilities, but I figured those were for the families of patients to use, so I stuck fifty pence in the vending machine for a crappy plastic cup of coffee.

I sat down and sent a quick text to Mum, letting her know what was happening. She replied immediately and told me to let Blake's family know she was thinking of them. I wouldn't, of course, because I wasn't welcome, but I replied I would tell Blake.

I wasn't sure how long Blake would stay, but I didn't think it would be that long. As much as I was tired and wanted my bed, I wanted Blake to stay more. He needed to connect with the family who were still practically strangers to him. The only family he really had was his dad and paternal grandparents.

Being the only person in the waiting room and with no other distraction, my mind wandered to what Blake had said. Was the person who'd hurt Pete the same person who'd killed Courtney and Josh? Blake thought it was Kyle, but I couldn't see any of them hitting someone over the head with a cricket bat any more than I could see them stabbing two of our friends. Then there was Blake's past with his mum and the fact that he had no fuzzy feelings toward anyone he was related to, besides his dad.

No matter what though, I kept coming back to the same conclusion: it wasn't any of them. I couldn't even force myself to imagine it was. The image of any of them holding a knife in his or her hand, standing over Court's and Josh's bloody bodies, refused to enter my mind.

Blake didn't have the same history or emotional attachments, and he thought it was Kyle.

I had only just finished my pond-water coffee and second round of obsessing when Blake walked into the room. "Let's go," he snapped.

"How is he?" I asked, standing up and throwing my empty cup in the bin.

"Unconscious," he replied and walked toward the door.

I scrambled after him, eager to find out why he was so desperate to leave. What happened in that room?

By the time I got home, it was a little after midnight, and my legs were ready to collapse. I was that exhausted. Blake had barely said a word the whole way home, and I wasn't sure if that was a good thing or not. No matter how many times I asked, he refused to tell me why we'd left in such a rush. Someone had said something to him—that much was clear. But who and what?

I hadn't seen any of Blake's family, but he told me they were in Pete's room. From what I could drag out of him, I knew that Pete was in critical condition. His brain was swollen and he was unresponsive. A machine was literally his lifeline.

The only other thing I had managed to get out of him was that his nan was glad he was there. It looked really, really bad, and I was scared for them all.

Sunday, August 23

The next morning, I woke startled after a vivid dream of Josh and Courtney being stabbed by a faceless killer. I knew they were both stabbed. I'd seen the aftermath and heard the details the police had released, but last night, it was as if I saw it happening. The dream was so vivid I felt sick.

Rolling over, I grabbed my phone to check the time and my face fell when I saw the unknown number again. *Open it, Mackenzie. You can do it.*

Someone had a big mouth.

A big mouth. Pete? Did they mean Pete?

"Oh God, think, Mackenzie," I muttered, rubbing at my thudding forehead. There had to be a connection between Pete and Lawrence, other than a heated exchange after Tilly's funeral. I didn't want one of my friends to be responsible. Josh had been an arsehole about being thankful it was Tilly and Gigi and not him and Courtney who'd died. Pete defended his nephew and Lawrence defended his daughter.

It could be. I wanted to be able to place the blame on Lawrence.

It was time to tell Wright my theory on Lawrence and let him decide what to do with it. We were getting nowhere. I had no idea what I was doing. I'd received a second creepy message, and my head was a total mess. Was I the only one getting these messages? And if not, why had they not said anything? Were they as scared as I was?

We were friends. We shouldn't be protecting ourselves from each other. But that was exactly what I was doing.

Pete had been hurt, and the police needed to start looking at Lawrence, before—in case—something happened to anyone else. Before I dared look even closer at my friends, I would exhaust every other option.

Over breakfast, Mum and Dad required a lot of reassurance that I was OK. It was exhausting. As soon as I finished eating, I grabbed my keys and headed out to my car as my parents headed off to work. I waved to them and anxiously got in my car, eager to get this trip to the station over with.

I gripped the steering wheel tight with both hands as I drove. Nerves rattled around in my stomach and I wanted nothing more than to curl up and pretend it was just a regular summer day. I turned into town and my phone rang. Megan.

Yeah, I was not ready to deal with her, but I couldn't put it off, because she'd only keep on calling. "Hi," I said and put her on hands free, so I could drive at the same time.

"Hey, Kenzie, you OK?"

No, not at all. "Yeah, you?"

"I'm OK. Look, I think we all need to get together. We've not all been together properly, where it was just us, in over a week. Aaron and Kyle are coming to my house at seven tonight for pizza. We need to stick together and not continue to drift apart. You in?"

It all sounded so normal, like any other chill evening. But it felt forced, like we were just papering over the cracks. "Sure, I'm in. I'm driving, so I've gotta go, but I'll see you later."

"All right. Bye."

"Bye." I ended the call and pulled into the parking lot next to the police station. To my right was Aaron's car. *What the hell is going on?* I got out in a daze and saw Aaron and Kyle walking toward me. My heart beat a little too fast.

"Hey," Kyle said, wrapping me in one of his big hugs.

I hugged him back briefly and pulled away. "Hey."

"You've been called in too, huh?" Aaron asked, rolling his eyes.

Called in? He'd been called in again? "Uh, yeah," I replied, not wanting to get into what I was really doing at the police station. If I asked Aaron for details, he might question why I didn't know. It was probably something to do with Pete's attack anyway.

"Will you be at Megan's later?" Aaron asked.

"Yeah, I will. I'll see you guys there."

"Cool," Aaron replied, nodding and opening the car door. Kyle got in the passenger side and started messing around on his phone. Everything they did now made me think there could be a hidden meaning behind it. Knowing Kyle, he was probably just playing on some rubbish app he'd downloaded. You couldn't mask the number you were texting from, could you? No—that didn't make sense. I was just jumpy. They both gave me an effortless wave as Aaron backed out of the space and drove off.

I strode toward the police station, still intent on telling Wright about Lawrence, when Wright and Blake came out of the station's front doors. *Blake is here too. Are Megan and I the only ones who weren't called in?* I took a few steps closer so I could hear what they were saying.

"Yes…very colorful indeed," Wright said, raising one of his dark eyebrows. I couldn't see Blake's face because his back was to me, but I could picture his bored expression.

"Colorful doesn't make you a killer, Mr. Wright. What you're looking for is psychotic."

Wright shrugged. "Perhaps and perhaps you're not the killer. Your past doesn't prove you murdered your brother and his girlfriend. Your police record did, however, make very interesting reading, Blake. I thank you for saving me from a dull evening." He nodded once and went back inside the station.

Blake turned and walked toward the parking lot.

"Hey," I shouted and waved at him.

"What are you doing here, Mackenzie?"

"What did Wright mean about you having a police record?" I asked, jogging to catch up with him. Man, he could walk fast when he wanted to.

Blake's eyebrows pulled together in a deep frown. "Nothing," he muttered.

"Bull!" I grabbed his arm.

He spun around, almost knocking into me. "What do you want? You're all over the place, running around trying to solve a murder. I. Didn't. Kill. Them," he said slowly.

"Blake, I believe you."

He looked into my eyes, trying to figure out if I was telling the truth or not.

"I believe you," I repeated.

"Good. You can drop it then."

Turning around, he walked toward his truck.

Not so fast, buddy! I followed, leaving a small distance between us. Whatever he was hiding in his police record, I wanted to know. Blake unlocked his car, and I tugged opened the passenger door. "What are you doing?" he asked. He sounded bored, and it made me smile. "What?"

"Get in the car, Blake."

He growled and got in, slamming the door.

"Tell me," I pressed.

"I'll tell you what's in my police file if you tell me something that no one knows about you."

"Is that what you always do? Deflect?"

He'd put up his wall. "If I'm going to tell you something only my dad knows, something that I'm not proud of, then I want the same in return," he said. "It's your choice."

"Fine."

"And you have to go first," he added.

I chewed the inside of my cheek and looked out of the side window. I couldn't look at Blake when I told him. It was too personal, too intense. My heart broke as I prepared to talk about it for the first time since I was fifteen. I clasped my hands together as my body froze from the inside out.

I don't want to do this. I don't want to relive this! Can I really trust him with this story? I took a deep breath and swallowed the football-sized lump in my throat. I knew I had to share if I wanted the same honesty from Blake. And I needed that honesty if we were going to figure out what had really happened that night at the cabin.

Opening my mouth, I closed my eyes and waited for the words to form. My heart felt like lead as I whispered, "Three years ago I had...an abortion."

Oh God, I'd said the words aloud. Pain wrapped around my heart and squeezed.

I waited for him to say something, but he was silent.

I went on. "I was fifteen, far too young to be a mom, and *so* scared. My boyfriend at the time had broken up with me a week before I found out and he'd turned...nasty. So I didn't tell him. I couldn't tell my parents because they would have been angry and so disappointed. I didn't want them to hate me. I had no idea who to turn to or where I could go. I was drowning and didn't know what to do. Every night, I cried myself to sleep after praying for help. But no one could help me—or at least, that's how I felt at the time. I'd never been so terrified before and I haven't since, not even finding Courtney and Josh. I was alone and didn't feel like I had any options at all, so I didn't tell anyone."

The fabric of the seat rubbed loudly on Blake's jeans as he turned suddenly in my direction. "Mackenzie, you went through that by yourself?" he asked gently.

I struggled to take a breath and blinked away the sting behind my eyes. *You can do this.* "I-I booked an appointment at the clinic. I didn't allow myself to think about it too much. I pretended I was going for a routine test." My hands shook as I was catapulted back to that day. I could still smell the cleanliness of the clinic and the feel the fear burning in my stomach. "When I took *that* pill, I pretended it was aspirin. When I felt the pains, I pretended they were from my period. The second I did it, I hated myself. I still do. It was the biggest mistake of my life," I whispered. "And Josh was the only other person who knew."

CHAPTER FOURTEEN

Blake reached across the seat, taking my hand in his own. I gulped back a sob at the comfort I felt from his kind gesture.

"Josh knew? How?" he asked.

I bit my lip as a scorching tear burned its way down my cheek. Thinking about it never got easier. "Josh saw me leaving the clinic. He was going to his after-school job at your uncle's office next door. I was a mess. I couldn't believe what I'd just done. It didn't take him long to work out what'd happened." My throat, chest, and heart were on fire.

"What did he do, Kenz?"

I pulled my legs up, wrapping my arms around them in a bid to protect myself from the conversation. "He blackmailed me," I replied. "It was nothing serious, really, mostly things like making me step out of his way when he wanted to get with Courtney, making me pick him up in the middle of the night when he needed a ride, give him money, false references for new after-school jobs he wanted, getting me and my friends to agree to go on trips he knew I wouldn't ever want to go on because we didn't like him."

"Bastard," Blake muttered, clenching his jaw and grinding his teeth.

"Every time I tried to convince Courtney that Josh was an arsehole, I pictured his face—that half smirk and one raised eyebrow, telling me he knew something I didn't want getting out." I took a deep breath. "I wanted Courtney to be free of him, but I couldn't let anyone know what I'd done. I hate myself for what I did, and I hate everything I did to keep it a secret."

"Why have you still not told your parents?"

Blinking rapidly, I looked up to stop fresh tears from falling. "Because I'm ashamed and because it's my biggest regret. I was such a mess inside, Blake. Dating Danny messed me up and just about broke me. I had no self-esteem or self-respect. He cheated constantly, and I never broke it off and never told a soul. My parents would be *so* disappointed in me for having sex so young, for being irresponsible, and for the abortion. I would do *anything* to go back in time and change what happened."

Blake squeezed my hand again. He looked so out of his depth, but the fact that he was trying to comfort and support me meant the world. "Please don't beat yourself up. You were young, Mackenzie."

"So? I was old enough to have sex. I was old enough to deal with the consequences." Well, I wasn't, but I'd made choices, despite knowing deep down I should have been making other decisions. "I just wish I had thought it through before I made a snap decision. Now I have to live with it."

"I'm sorry that you had to go through that alone."

"I make such a big deal out of everyone else not keeping secrets when mine is so…" I shook my head and pressed my forehead to my knees.

"I put a man in the hospital," he said.

I looked up through my eyelashes. "What?"

"When I was sixteen, I was a bit of a fighter. Actually, I lived for it."

"Why?"

"I was angry," Blake said.

"About?"

He smirked. "Man, you're nosy."

I turned my body to face his. "Hey, I told you my biggest, deepest regret that no one else knows. Your turn, remember?" He reached up and wiped a small tear from under my eye, and I stopped breathing for a second. "What happened, Blake?"

"I don't have a good relationship with my mum, which you know already." I nodded. "I was angry with her for not caring enough, and angry at her for loving Josh more. She couldn't handle us both on her own, so she picked the golden boy. My dad worked a lot, so I was alone most of the time. I didn't have many friends—not real friends, anyway. A group of us would hang out on the street, drink, and get into fights."

"Wow, drinking and fighting on the street. And you questioned our class for drinking in a park."

A ghost of a smile pulled at the corners of his lips. "I never said what I did was classy. It was stupid. *I* was stupid. There was this guy mouthing off one night and I lost it. I can't even remember what he said. Anyway, I went too far, and when I was pulled off him, I realized why everyone was shouting so much. He was lying so still. There was a lot of blood." He stopped and frowned, remembering. "That was the last fight I got in."

"Whoa." I blinked, shaking my head to absorb what he'd told me. At least he'd told me the truth, almost, about his Mum not wanting him. "You were an angry kid, but I understand why you were like that."

He took a deep breath and tried to make light of the matter. "All right, no more psychoanalyzing me."

"I imagine Wright was having a field day with that information."

"You could say that. Although fighting and premeditated murder are two completely different things, I think I just got bumped to the top of his suspect list."

"I wouldn't go that far, Mr. Harper." We both jumped at the sound of Wright's voice. My heart skipped a beat and the hairs on my neck prickled. I spun around and saw him leaning against the car beside Blake's. He was standing level with the back windows, just beyond where we could have seen him while talking. Both our windows were open because it was scorching out. He'd heard everything. "But, Mackenzie, I think maybe we should have another little chat."

Wright turned on his heel and walked back toward the station, so confident that we would follow.

My stomach bottomed out. "Oh God, Blake!"

"It's OK. It'll be fine."

"But he's going to think I killed Josh for blackmailing me." *I'm going to be sick.*

"He already thinks that." Blake snorted and then grinned.

"Mackenzie, anyone can see you're not a cold-blooded killer. You're too puny for one. You can barely open my car door."

"Shut up. It's stiff!" I shoved the door open—which was easy from the inside—and got out. Blake followed me, laughing to himself. How could he be calm when I was so sure Wright was going to arrest me the second I walked into the building?

I heard my pulse throbbing in my ears as I stepped into the all-too-familiar police station. Wright smiled and clicked his tongue. "Mackenzie, follow me." Blake's fingers brushed my arm, and he motioned toward the door with his head. Of course, he was going to split. Was it always the way? You always had to do the hard stuff on your own.

"Would you like me to call your parents?" Wright asked.

"No thank you," I replied a little too dryly.

I sat down in the small, boring, magnolia-colored interrogation room. A black desk separated me from Wright. He closed the door and sat down. Leaning on the table he said, "You know the drill," and nodded to the tape recorder, which he flicked on, giving the date and my name. "So tell me about Joshua Harper blackmailing you."

"It wasn't blackmail really. Josh never made me do anything truly terrible. I just wasn't allowed to tell Courtney what he was really like."

The detective's bushy brow arched. "Which was?"

"I've told you this before."

He shrugged. "Humor me."

I sighed. Telling him what I had told Blake in his car seemed like a bad idea, but I had no doubt that I had to repeat it. "Josh was selfish and thought everyone owed him something. I knew he would try to control Courtney. He did control her. She could have done better than him."

"But Josh didn't allow you to voice your true opinion about their relationship?"

"Well…no. He didn't." I bowed my head. "In the end, I told Courtney that if she liked him, he couldn't be that bad. I told her it was her choice if she wanted to date him. I didn't want her to get into a relationship with him, but I didn't want anyone to know that I'd had an…abortion."

"And that's why you killed him?"

I gasped and sat up straight. "No! I swear I didn't do it."

"Josh was the only one who knew. He was the only one who could reveal your secret. With him out of your way, no one would ever know. His death has solved your problem, hasn't it?" Detective Wright pressed.

"I didn't kill him! And if I had, why would I kill Courtney? She was my best friend! I would never kill anyone over a secret. You have to believe me!"

"Here's what I think happened," Wright said and paused for a second to see if I was going to challenge him. There wasn't much point in that. "I think there was an altercation between you and Joshua and you lost control. Courtney witnessed it, and to silence her, you stabbed her too."

"No, that's not what happened! I didn't do it." I knew I should remain calm, but that was practically impossible when someone was accusing you of something you didn't do.

"Where were you yesterday at around eight at night?"

"At home."

"Was anyone else there?"

"Blake was at my house until about half ten, and my parents were in all evening. I didn't hurt Pete."

He held his hands up and smiled. "Just asking." He paused. "So Blake was with you all last evening?"

"Yeah."

"The whole time?"

"Yeah. Well…"

Wright raised his eyebrow and leaned forward. "Well?"

"I mean he was in my house the whole time, but I wasn't with him for all of it." Wright stayed silent, waiting. "I went downstairs to help make dinner with my mum and Blake stayed in my room. But he was asleep and didn't leave the house."

"How can you be sure of that?"

"He would have had to walk past the kitchen to get out the front door, so I would have seen him."

"Back door?"

"The French doors off the living room," I clarified. "My dad was watching black-and-white films all night. He would have seen Blake, and there's no way he would let a boy leave the house without talking to him first."

"So there was no chance he could have snuck out and back in again?"

"No," I replied.

"Did you leave the house?"

"No."

Wright smiled, and I thought he was going dig further, but he didn't. "Let me run through what I think happened at the cabin once more, shall I?" It wasn't a question, and I didn't have any other choice but to listen.

"I think you killed Josh because he was threatening to expose your secret. Courtney witnessed the attack, which meant you had to kill her too. Peter Sheffield somehow—I haven't quite worked that part out yet, but I will—found out what you'd done, so you tried to kill him too."

"No. It's not true. I bet you said the same thing to Blake, but that doesn't mean he did it either."

He smiled tightly, narrowing his eyes. "Sure, but Blake's motive was different."

I blinked, shocked. Was the detective admitting he'd accused Blake in the same way? He made my head spin. I couldn't figure him out. Whatever I thought Wright would do or how he would react, he always did something completely different. It was like it was a game to him.

"You're free to go now, Miss Keaton."

I was free to go. I didn't stay to talk to him about Lawrence—it would look like I was clutching at straws after Wright had revealed his theory, so I had no choice but to keep my suspicions to myself for now. I stood up and left the room, refusing to allow Wright to know he was getting to me.

I walked quickly through the station and out the door. I was in such a bad mood I could have punched something.

"Hey."

My heart soared at the sound of Blake's voice. *He stayed!* He leaned against the brick wall, one leg slung over the other as if he didn't have a care in the world.

"What are you still doing here? Were you waiting for me?"

"Don't get too excited," he replied.

Too late for that. It seemed like every damn thing about him excited me. *You need help.* "Wasn't going to," I replied nonchalantly.

"Wanna go for a drive and talk? I'll bring you back to your car later," he said.

The muscles around my mouth ached as I tried not to smile like a fool. "Sure."

CHAPTER FIFTEEN

I fiddled with my fingers as we sat silently in Blake's bedroom.

"Who do you think killed them?" Blake asked, staring up at the ceiling. Neither of us had said a word since we'd arrived twenty minutes ago. It hadn't taken me long to calm down. Although Blake couldn't find the words to comfort me, he'd had no trouble letting his actions do the talking.

I shrugged. That was a question I asked myself about a thousand times an hour, and the answer never changed. *I don't know.* "I don't want it to be any of them."

"You'd prefer it to be me," he whispered, his hand freezing on my knee where he'd been making small circles since we'd sat down.

"No," I replied. I should've seen that coming. I hated that he felt like an outsider with everyone. As far as I was concerned, he was stuck with us. He was part of our group now. "I should probably want that, but I don't."

He pushed himself up on his elbows and raised an eyebrow. "Of course you do."

"I don't. Honestly. I don't want the killer to be anyone I know. There has to be another explanation."

"But there isn't, is there? We both know Lawrence was pretty pissed off, but it's not him."

Deep down I knew that, but I couldn't admit it aloud and make it real. "Eventually you're going to have to accept that one of your friends is a killer."

"Who do you think it is?" I asked. He had said Kyle a couple of times before, but Blake's reasons were ridiculous. I think his suspicions had more to do with the fact that they'd got along the least that night.

"I don't know." He flopped back on the mattress. "No one's saying much. I still think Kyle, but I'm not ruling the other two out just yet."

They have said much, just not to you. I had learned things about my friends recently that had shocked me. Everyone had a reason for wanting to hurt Josh and Courtney. Should I tell Blake and see if he could figure it out from what I knew? He wasn't as close as I was to the others, so perhaps there was something blindingly obvious that I was missing.

"Blake," I said slowly, still mentally debating whether I should say anything or not. *Bad idea, Mackenzie.*

"Yeah?"

I couldn't stop myself. "There are some things about Megan and Kyle you don't know." I was officially the biggest bitch on the planet.

His expression didn't change. "What things?"

"They had motives," I whispered.

The air turned so thick I thought I was going to choke. I kept forgetting that Blake wasn't just around to help me out; he was a "person of interest" too *and* Josh's brother. "Go on…"

Why had I ever thought it was a good idea to tell him? Of course he was going to think their secrets made them guilty. He wanted someone to pay for Josh's death and already thought one of them had blood on their hands.

Not only was I a horrible friend, but I was an idiot too.

But I'd gone and told him they had motives, so I couldn't backtrack without him getting suspicious and thinking the worst—of me. He'd probably think *I* was trying to cover *my* tracks.

"Josh blackmailed me. You resented him," I said, making it clear we each had motives and he couldn't just jump into blaming the others. "Megan spiked Gigi's drink, which forced Courtney to drive the night of the crash that killed Gigi and Tilly, and Kyle was having an affair with Courtney." The words left a bitter taste on my tongue.

"Courtney was cheating on Josh?"

"Yeah. Kyle said it ended a few months ago, but it went on for a long time."

Blake snorted. "Well, my brother was a cocky, arrogant bastard and probably deserved it."

My spine straightened in shock. That wasn't the reaction I'd expected. At all. "Blake, what…?"

"Come on, like you didn't think the same. Something like that would have deflated Josh's ego a bit. I'm just disappointed he never knew. What about Aaron?"

"What?" I shook my head, trying to keep up. Now Blake was on to Aaron? Talk about doing a one-eighty. "What about him?"

"What's his deep, dark secret?"

"Um. He doesn't have one."

He smirked and looked at me as if to say *ah, bless.* "Of course he doesn't. He's squeaky clean."

"You think he does?"

"What I think is that nothing would surprise me anymore. Everyone has at least one skeleton in their closet, and you need to ask yourself why Aaron is still hiding his."

"It's possible he has no secrets, or no secrets to do with Josh and Courtney, anyway."

Blake was up and in my face so fast it made me dizzy. His close proximity made my head do that swimming thing. If he wanted to have a serious conversation with me, he was going to have to keep a distance. "Mackenzie, you are far too naive and far too trusting."

I pushed myself back, putting a little space between us. I was flat against the wall, so I hoped he didn't move any closer because I was finding it hard to breathe as it was. "So I've been told."

"People will take advantage of you."

I wrapped my arms around my stomach. "Sorry for not wanting to believe my friends are murderers."

"I'm not saying it's a bad thing, but you need to be careful. Your need to see the best in everyone is going to bite you in the arse. You're blinded by the faith you place in other people, even strangers."

"Are you talking about you?"

"Yeah, me too. You believe I didn't kill Josh and Courtney, but you know so little about me other than that I resented my mum and brother, and put a man in hospital."

My lungs burned with the need for oxygen but I couldn't get them to work. *What's he saying?* "Are you telling me you did it?"

He sighed. "No, Mackenzie, I'm telling you that you wouldn't be able to tell if I were guilty. Which one of your friends is most likely to have murdered Josh and Courtney?"

"I don't know. None of them."

He smiled and cocked his head to the side. "There you go. You know it's one of us, but you refuse to face it. You know them more than anyone else. You know which one of them is the most likely, even if you won't acknowledge or accept it."

I bit my lip hard enough to taste blood.

"Gut instinct, Mackenzie, who is it?"

"I don't know, Blake!" I hopped off the bed and paced his room. What was he doing to me? He watched me like a hawk. "I don't know. I have no bloody idea!"

"You do."

"No, I don't!" I shouted. "Stop it, you…you arse!" He broke out into a full smile that was filled to the brim with amusement. "I want to punch you so bad right now."

"Look, I'm not trying to piss you off—"

"Then stop pissing me off."

"You want my help or not?"

I shook my head and walked out of his room. "No, I just want you to leave me alone. I'll walk to get my car."

He didn't follow me as I left his house, but I didn't expect him to. He wasn't the type to run after a girl. It was getting late, and the dim streetlights just about lit my way. I was supposed to be at

Megan's, but I couldn't face it. The air was warm, it being August and the middle of a "heat wave," but I still wrapped my arms around my chest.

I was halfway home when my phone beeped with a text message. I still had to pick up my car from the station at some point.

80% of victims know their murderer. Think about who you know, Mackenzie.

My feet planted to the ground. Sucking in a shaky breath, I reread the message. What was this? A threat?

It was from the same number as the other sinister text messages. My heart raced and pulse throbbed in my ears. I looked over my shoulder, clenching the phone in my fist. No one was around—that I could see, anyway. I held my breath and strained to listen for footsteps or some other sound that someone was following me. The wind blew softly, rustling leaves on nearby trees, but I couldn't hear anything else.

Because maybe they're standing still watching you.

A shudder ripped up my spine and I started walking faster.

I was breathing too hard to hear anything else. Taking another glance over my shoulder, I scanned the surrounding area. Somewhere behind me, I heard a door slam. The thud sounded wooden, as if it came from a shed. I didn't care what it was. I broke into a sprint.

I didn't see or speak to any of my friends that night because I was too freaked out. *One of my friends is probably the killer.*

I found myself obsessively reading the mysterious text messages and googling the cell number. There were no details listed. Of course.

I sat on my bed with my legs crossed, staring at my phone. Was I being told I knew who'd killed Josh and Courtney, or was someone trying to tell me I could be next?

What did it all mean?

Blake thought I already knew the killer. Could these messages be from him?

Could it be Megan, Kyle, or Aaron?

Monday, August 24

That night, I barely slept. In the morning, I rubbed my stinging eyes and reached for a bottle of water on my bedside table. My head hammered with a splitting headache.

"Morning, sweetheart," Mum said, poking her head around my door. "Are you OK?"

"Morning. I'm fine. Are you and Dad going to work now?"

"Just about to leave. Are you sure you don't want to come to the office with me?"

"I'm sure, Mum."

She leaned against the doorframe and folded her arms over her chest. "OK. Promise you'll call if you need anything?"

"I promise, but really, I'm OK."

"Are you seeing anyone today?"

"And by anyone you mean?"

"Will you be seeing any of your friends?"

"No, I'm not feeling very sociable today. I'm just going to lounge in bed and watch rubbish daytime TV."

"All right." She smiled and grabbed the door handle, ready to close it again. "We'll see you later. Call if you need anything."

"I will. See you later."

I looked at my phone. There were so many missed calls and text messages. I'd blown everyone off last night and stayed home instead of getting pizza at Megan's, and although I felt bad for letting them down, I wanted to be alone too much to care. The secrets Kyle and Megan had hid from me kept picking away at my sanity. I was exhausted, fed up, and emotionally drained. I just wanted the truth.

And someone had sent me that scary text, which I didn't know what to make of.

I wanted to go and see Aaron, but I didn't. I wanted to see Blake, but I couldn't handle another one of his theories or lectures. I wanted to be alone, but I didn't want to be by myself. And then there was Pete. He had been hurt, possibly because he found out who killed Courtney and Josh. Or possibly because he was in the wrong place at the wrong time.

Groaning, I gripped my hair and flopped down onto the mattress. Why couldn't it be clear? If one of my friends was the murderer, they were not only hiding the truth, but they were also allowing the rest of us to be suspects. How far would they let it go? If I were somehow charged, would the real killer let me go to prison?

That wasn't friendship. I would never put myself before someone I love. Wow, Blake was right. I was too trusting.

Somewhere between overthinking and throwing clothes from the heap on my floor in frustration, I had a moment of clarity. One of my friends was lying to me, and I had to look at the details the way Blake did.

This was beyond proving our innocence now. Those texts were threatening. My stomach turned over in fear. The killer could want more blood.

CHAPTER SIXTEEN

Thankfully, Aaron's car was the only one in his drive when I got to his house after walking to get my car. There wasn't a single person in this world that didn't lie; it was just that some lies were harmless and others were dangerous. Sometimes, it was hard to figure out the difference. I was going to find out what secrets Aaron was keeping, what lies he had told.

It took me longer than it should have to get out of the car. I had one friend left who, as of right then, I still trusted. That could change soon.

The front door opened, and I knew I had been sitting in the car too long. Aaron had obviously seen me. He stepped onto the lawn, looking at me like I'd grown another head. "Kenz, what're you doing?" he asked over the sound of my car engine humming.

I turned the key and opened the door. "Sorry, I was in another world." *One where I could still pretend at least one of my friends wasn't lying to me.*

"You OK?" Aaron looked so innocent. He was all angelic blue eyes and blond hair, kind of like a grown up version of the Milkybar kid but without the glasses. I couldn't imagine him doing anything bad. Ever.

"Yeah, I'm fine. Are you?"

"Sure. You skipped Megan's last night. We missed you."

I shrugged, stopping in front of him. "Didn't really feel up to it."

He reached out and stroked his thumb under my eye. "You're not sleeping well either."

"Do I look that bad?"

"No!" He rolled his baby blues. "Just a little tired and maybe stressed. Come in."

"Your mum out?"

"Yep, you've got me all to yourself. Go on up and I'll bring chocolate and tea."

He still seemed like my protective Aaron, and it warmed my heart. "You know me so well."

I went upstairs to wait for Aaron and curled up on his bed. My phone beeped with a text. It was Blake.

Check his drawers. Text BACKUP if you need me and I'll fire up the Batmobile!

I shook my head, grinning to myself. He was an idiot. I'd told him that I was going to Aaron's, this morning. We'd completely made up after our fight and were pretending it never happened. That was fine with me. I didn't want to talk about it.

I punched back a reply. Catwoman doesn't need help.

Do you have a Catwoman costume??????

I flipped my phone over and laughed quietly at his latest message.

"What're you laughing at?" Aaron asked as he walked into his room with chocolate bars stuffed in his pockets and a cup of tea in each hand.

"Nothing," I replied, sitting up to take my mug. Aaron didn't have a very high opinion of Blake, so I didn't want to start our conversation by talking about him. "Thanks." I sipped my boiling-hot tea, not caring how it burned my tongue, then set it down on the bedside table.

Aaron's phone beeped. He froze, his face falling before pulling it from his pocket.

Oh God, was he getting messages from the stalker too?

"Everything OK?" I asked.

Grunting as he read the message, he tightened his grip on the phone, his forehead creasing. I wanted to tell him about my text but I was scared to. I…I didn't really trust anyone right now. But what if Aaron had received one too?

"Aaron?"

He lowered the phone and a smile spread across his face. It didn't reach his eyes. "Sorry, Kenz. I didn't mean to be distracted by my phone. That's rude of me." Clearing his throat, he took a sip of his drink.

"What's been going on, then?" I asked. He wasn't going to tell me who the text was from and I couldn't really blame him. I was doing the same.

Aaron sat down and scooted closer to me. "What's on your mind?"

I blinked. Did I look nervous? Afraid? Confused? "Why do you think there's something on my mind?"

"You're doing that lost-in-thought thing where you look miles away."

Now how was I going to ask him what his secret was without it being obvious? "Nothing much. What's been going on with you? We haven't talked in forever."

"I know. It's been intense with what happened to Courtney and Josh. And Tilly's birthday is soon."

"I know," I whispered. "I miss her."

"Me too. I just wish we could have sorted things out, so we could've been together more than we were argued. I'm not dealing well with never knowing if we could have made it work or not."

I knew it wasn't always easy for Aaron to open up about his feelings, so I appreciated his honesty. I felt I had to respect that by being honest too. "Aaron, I don't want to seem harsh, but you and Tilly were a nightmare. I think if you'd had a relationship when you were both a lot older and had had the time to be with other people, it would have worked. But neither of you were ready for anything serious so young. You can't beat yourself up about that."

"No, you're right. I still love her though. I wished we had that chance to turn us into something more serious."

"I wish you'd had that chance too. Do you want to do something for her birthday?" I asked. For Gigi's birthday, I had made a cake and we'd all gotten her cards. It was silly really, but even though they were gone, it seemed important to mark the occasion. They still deserved a celebration, and we needed time to honor their memories.

His eyes turned serious and filled with pain. "I'm going to get high and reminisce about the good old times."

"Get high?" Get high as in… No. Aaron didn't do drugs. Or so I'd thought.

"Come on, Mackenzie. You've never done it?"

"No," I replied. He had. Obviously.

"Such a good girl," he muttered under his breath but loud enough for me to hear. "Well, you're missing out. It's very good when you don't want to give a shit about anything."

I couldn't have been more shocked if he'd pulled his jeans down and peed on the floor. We never really spoke about drugs, but I didn't do them, so I assumed none of my friends had either. Aaron was open about drinking and, unfortunately for the rest of us, sex, so it didn't come as a shock that he'd admitted it—just that he did it.

"Did Tilly do drugs too?"

"Sometimes. I have some weed if you wanna give it a go."

"What's wrong with you?" I snapped, snatching my arm away as he reached for me. Standing up, I spun around. "I don't know what your problem is, but don't bring me into it. I'm not going to sit here and get high with you, especially with everything else going on!"

"All right, all right," he said, raising his hands above his head. "I just thought we could cheer ourselves up."

This wasn't the Aaron I knew. He didn't use drugs. What he was doing now was completely out of character. *Maybe you don't really know his character.* Was he high now? His eyes looked fine, but I had no idea what was going on inside his head.

"If you want to cheer me up, be the Aaron who makes me

laugh and feeds me chocolate." I shook my head. "Look, I'm going. Call me when you want to do something other than get high."

Aaron didn't follow me as I left his house. I didn't even care that I hadn't found out his deep, dark secret that could make him want to kill Josh and Courtney. There was something wrong with him if he thought I was going to do drugs with him.

I got in my car and slammed the door, taking all my frustrations out as I pounded on my steering wheel. It took only a few seconds for my stomach to free fall. Aaron did drugs and we were all drugged at the cabin. Weed wasn't like Rohypnol, but if he was doing one of them, he could surely get ahold of the other.

Without thinking about where I was going, I drove straight to Blake's house. I really needed his snarky comments. I used to absentmindedly go to Kyle's if there was something on my mind, but now it was Blake's.

I rang the doorbell and waited. As soon he opened the door, I pushed past him. "Come in," he muttered behind me. Ignoring him, I walked upstairs to his room. His mum wasn't in again, or if she was, I didn't see her. Maybe she was still at the hospital with her brother. Blake's footsteps following me were all I heard. Not even more sarcastic comments. He must've been tired.

"He's on drugs!" I said, dropping down on his bed and throwing my hands in the air.

"What? Aaron?"

"Yep. Weed."

"I hardly think that's a confession of the year."

"He does *drugs*, Blake."

"I wouldn't paint weed smokers and Rohypnol users with the same brush."

I'd thought the same thing, but…still. It was suspicious. "Do you smoke weed?" I asked.

"No, but I know it's not exactly on the same level as what we were drugged with."

"Yes, thank you. But doesn't that mean Aaron would be able to get ahold of Rohypnol?"

"Anyone can get ahold of anything."

"I couldn't. I wouldn't even know where to start! What do you do, hang out on a dodgy street and ask whoever looks like a criminal to sell you drugs?"

Blake's dark eyebrows rose and his mouth dropped. "OK, promise me you won't do that. Ever."

"Why? Is that how you do it?"

He laughed from deep in his belly and shook his head. *At least one of us finds it funny.*

"No, that's how you get yourself raped or murdered, little miss innocent. Seriously, your naivety is worrying."

"Well, I'm sorry. I don't know how to score drugs."

He laughed again and flopped down on the bed beside me. "We need to move on," he said, shaking his head and grinning so wide he looked like a bloody cartoon. "So now you think it was Aaron?"

"That's not what I said," I replied defensively.

"It pretty much is. You think he can score Rohypnol. You're considering the possibility he killed Courtney and Josh, aren't you?"

"I don't like you anymore, Blake." He didn't bite back, knowing that was untrue. "I don't know what to think," I replied, sitting cross-legged on his bed.

He looked up and his blue eyes were icy and intense. "Mackenzie, stop fighting so hard and open up your mind. Distance yourself from your feelings."

"I tried that already and it doesn't work. You're distant. Why can't you just tell me what happened?"

"I'm distant, not an oracle," he replied dryly. "Anyway, I've told you what I think, and you continually dismiss my theory."

"Because you think it's Kyle!"

"Well, now I think it's Aaron."

His response gave me an instant headache. "But…" I whispered, trailing off, trying to search for the words to defend Aaron.

"But you think so too, don't you?"

"I think if he was into that whole weed scene, then maybe. He still loves Tilly, or what he thinks is love, anyway. Whatever's going on, he's seriously messed up right now," I said.

"Why did you say it like that, Mackenzie? You think there's something mentally wrong with him? Like a breakdown?"

"No. But Aaron and Tilly weren't good together. Not for longer than a few weeks. Everything ended in an argument and them breaking up. I know they both liked each other, or they wouldn't have kept going back for more, but I don't think they were in love."

"Is that motive enough, then?"

"Is anything motive enough? People kill randomly because they enjoy it or because someone looked at them a funny way. That's not the important part. If Aaron killed Courtney and Josh, it was driven by revenge or jealousy about their relationship, which have always been strong motives."

His smirk was back. "Maybe you should be a judge or—"

I clicked my fingers in front of his face and said, "Stay with me." We didn't have time for him to go off on a tangent. "You think Aaron, so I think we should look into him more."

"I'm a little hurt that you're using me."

"Using you how?"

"You think it could be Aaron too, so you're using me as an excuse to drive down that road, to collect evidence. You've dismissed everything else I've said or told me I'm an idiot, but now you agree—"

"I haven't dismissed everything," I said, playing with my fingers. He was right though: we both thought it could be Aaron, and though I couldn't quite bring myself to admit it out loud, I was using Blake's suspicions to stand in place of my own.

"New rule," he said, lifting his hand. "If you're going to use me in the future, it will only be when we're both naked."

I stared blankly. "I knew you were no gentleman, but that is pushing it."

"Baby, you won't hurt my feelings."

"No, but I'll hurt yours when I'm left frustrated and complaining about your lousy performance in the sack," I deadpanned.

He lunged for me, making me yelp in surprise. "Blake!" OK, that wasn't supposed to happen. I saw his room tilt as he pinned me to his bed and held my wrists up over my head.

He was on top of me and all coherent thought flew out of the window.

"You're being mean. And you've cruelly insulted me and mocked my performance, which you know is off the charts since I remember *vividly* the way you reacted to my every touch last time."

Last time and first time. That night meant so much to me and not only because Blake had made sure it was all about me. It was the first time that I'd been with someone since the abortion. He was the first person I'd trusted since Danny.

I laughed breathlessly from beneath him. He was both too close and too far. "Thanks for the offer but I'm busy." I tried to say the words evenly, but they probably came out in a frazzled rush.

"What part of that did you take as being an offer? Clothes off, Mackenzie."

I pouted as the fire in my lower abdomen burned out of control. "See, that is why I know you'd be rubbish right now. How unsexy is it when someone tells you to take your clothes off like that?"

"I kinda like it."

Yeah, I kind of did too, but he didn't need to know that.

"That's only because you're a man." *Lie, lie, lie.* I squirmed. "You kiss a woman and remove her clothes as you go. You can have that tip for free. Let me know if it works," I replied, pulling my arms to try to get him to release me. "Come on. You're heavy and we have things to do." I frowned and looked up at him. What was taking him so long to make his move? "Hello?" I called to his perfect imitation of a statue face.

"You might have something there," he whispered in reply and lowered his head.

My heart thudded against my chest.

Oh sweet Jesus.

He was going to kiss me. No amount of obsessing over my friends was going to stop me from returning that kiss. This was for me, for us, and I think both Blake and I needed it.

"Blake!" Eloise shouted from downstairs. Her footsteps thundered up the stairs. "Blake!"

Blake spluttered a string of swearwords and pushed off me.

His mum calling him right when things were heating up felt like I'd just done the Ice Bucket Challenge.

Eloise burst through the door just as I'd gotten a grip on myself and sat up. "He's dead," she sobbed. Her knees gave out, and she collapsed to the floor, gripping the door handle. "Pete's dead. He's *dead.*"

CHAPTER SEVENTEEN

Oh God. I dropped to the floor beside Blake's shaking, broken mother. She had just lost her son and now her brother, and she looked as if she was about to die too. Blake looked at me like a lost puppy. "Mum…" he said, his voice cracking.

I reached out and wrapped one arm around his mom's back, scooting closer to her. "I'm so sorry, Eloise," I whispered soothingly, pulling her closer to me. She fell limp into my lap and cried. I shook from the heavy vibrations that rocked Eloise's sobbing body. "Shh, it's OK. Are you alone? Is there someone we can call?" She had a friend who'd come by most days since Josh had died.

"Yes, I'm alone," she croaked. "I'm alone."

She said it in a way that broke my heart for Blake. She may have lost one son and her brother, but she wasn't alone. She still had Blake.

"OK," I said. "I'm going to take you to bed so you can lie down and then Blake and I will sort out who to call and what to do next."

She didn't reply, but she didn't try to stop me when I hooked my arm under hers and lifted her up. Blake stepped in and helped, doing most of the lifting, and we carried her to her room.

Practical things Blake could do, but with the emotional stuff, he was about as useful as a teapot.

"Blake, don't you...don't you do anything stupid. Don't you get yourself killed," she whispered and started to sob so hard her weight seemed to double.

"I'm not going anywhere...Mum," he replied, sounding about a thousand miles out of his comfort zone.

Eloise cried harder when he called her Mum. She didn't stop when we laid her down or when we promised we'd help her through losing Pete. She hugged her pillow, pressing her face into the cotton as she broke down. Her fingers gripped it with such force her knuckles turned white.

"Do you need anything? Water?" I asked, stroking her hair.

"N-no. Look a-after him," she replied, curling into the fetal position.

"I will," I promised her. "Would you like us to stay?" She shook her head and curled up tighter. "OK, we'll check on you soon." Standing up, I nodded to the door, telling Blake we were leaving.

"How do you know what to do?" he asked as we left the room. He looked like hell, like he hadn't slept in weeks. But even though he wasn't at his best, he still made my heart beat faster.

"I'm so sorry for your loss, Blake." I wrapped my arms around his waist and his body tensed. I knew he wasn't exactly a cuddly person, but with me hugging and him not hugging back, things quickly got awkward. *This was a mistake.* I was about to pull away, but he very slowly lifted his arms and snaked them around my back.

I answered his question, "I don't really know what to do. I just did what I would want someone to do for me. All you have to do is look after her, think about what you would want if the tables were turned."

"I've never had to do that," he whispered, tucking my head under his chin.

"You do now. I know you've not had a lot of experience or the best relationship with your mum, but she needs you now. You need her too."

"Hmm. So when you fall apart, I need to remember to put you to bed."

I pulled back, but he didn't loosen his grip, so I couldn't quite see his face. "I'm falling apart?"

"Not yet. You're not done protecting everyone yet."

I wasn't sure who I was trying to protect. I didn't know who was guilty and who was innocent. "Does that mean you're sticking around, then? Even after you're allowed to leave town and go back to your dad's?" I asked. If he said no or told me only until this was all over, I'd be broken. We'd not known each other long, but it was long enough for me to willingly hand over my heart. It was his.

"I'm not sure what I'll do yet. Back home I don't have much going, but at least it's home. Whatever I decide, I'll come back. I promise to be the one to tuck you into bed."

It was better than a straight-up no, but I selfishly wanted more. "You really do care, don't you? As hard as you try to push every-one away and be Mr. Independent, you do care, Blake."

"No, you just have this way of bulldozing into someone's life and bloody staying there."

I smiled and closed my eyes. With his chest against mine, I felt like I was home, and although he wasn't the romantic type, he made me feel cherished. Through the worst time in my life, he was there for me, being the rock I needed.

"That was sweet on some level," I teased him.

"I don't do sweet, Mackenzie."

"Too late! You were sweet. Inside, you're made of little pink marshmallows."

"Why pink?"

I opened my eyes and grinned. "They're cuter."

"You think I'm cute?"

I let my arms drop and this time he took a step back. "No, actually I think you're an idiot." He smirked, looking proud of himself. "Whatever, Blake. Stop distracting me." People were being murdered around us and we were messing around. Only he could turn me into my old self when my friend was dead and we were possibly on someone's hit list.

"Sorry," he replied, not one bit sorry at all. "I think we should follow Aaron, Kyle, and Megan."

"You want to stalk my friends?"

"No, but I think Pete found out who killed Josh and Courtney, so they killed him. Whichever one of your friends did it, they're getting desperate. If they think people are starting to catch on, they might do something or go somewhere that'll lead us to the truth."

"So we're going on a stakeout?"

"Yep. We just need a different car."

"A rental car?" I replied, feeling a flash of adrenaline and maybe excitement. *What's wrong with me?* "Can we even do that?"

"Why can't we?"

"Don't you have to be twenty-three or whatever age it is?" Although Blake was twenty and had been driving for three years, I didn't think he'd be allowed to rent a car.

He snorted. "Please, I have fake IDs that put me well into my thirties. I'll get the car and pick you up tomorrow morning. This needs to be sorted out before…"

"Before?" I prompted.

"Before someone else gets hurt."

"Watch out. You're caring again."

His dark eyebrow lifted. "I meant *me* getting hurt."

"Sure you did." I bumped his arm with my own.

"Go home, Mackenzie," he joked.

"OK, fine. When your mum wakes up, remember to—"

He gripped my wrist, eyes rounding in fear that I'd actually leave him alone with his mum.

"All right, all right, I'll stay for now," I reassured him.

"That's what I thought. Come on." He pulled me back to his room.

"Are you OK?" I asked. "You've not said much since Pete…"

"Since I learned he died, you mean," he said, sitting on the bed and holding his hand out for me. I took it with a smile and sat down, kicking my legs over his.

"He was a stranger. I barely saw any of them after I moved with my dad."

"Did you want to know your mum?"

"Are you going to psychoanalyze me again?"

I smiled. "Maybe a little."

"I wanted to—of course I did. That's not always how it goes though. My parents split and so did our family. There were times growing up when I wanted Mum to be in my life, properly be in it, not just the odd phone call every couple of months, but she was busy raising Josh and had her own life to deal with."

"That doesn't mean she was allowed to be less of a mum to you," I replied, anger burning in my chest for him. No matter how far apart they were, she should have been the best mum she could have to her son. A phone call every few months wasn't being a parent.

"Mackenzie, it's fine. I'm a big boy, for shit's sake."

It wasn't cool, but I dropped it because Blake wasn't known for spilling his heart and I didn't want to fight. "OK, I'm sorry. What does this mean for us?"

"Wright is going to try pinning Pete's death on us too. Whoever the killer is, they've just entered serial territory."

I felt like I'd just been punched. "What?"

"Serial killer, Mackenzie."

"Yes, but how do you know that?"

He sighed sharply as if he was frustrated. "Three murders and you're serial. Although I think that might only count if there's time between each one, so Josh and Courtney might just count as one."

I swallowed bile. "Stop." God, how could he talk about death like it was nothing?

"Sorry," he muttered, wincing.

"Blake, what if we're next?"

He cocked his head to the side and brushed his fingertips along my jaw. "You know that's the first time you've put yourself before your friends. Don't look so confused. A few days ago, you would have said something like, 'What if we're all next?' Now it's just *us*."

"Because I don't know which one of..." I stopped midsentence. *Which one of them is the killer.* I moved off Blake like he was on fire.

Blake watched me with sympathetic eyes, and if he said anything to try to make me feel better, there was a good chance I'd gouge them out. "Do you want me to speak to Wright about Lawrence? Maybe—"

"No," I said, cutting him off, thankful he wasn't trying to make me feel better. "It's not Lawrence, is it?"

Taking a deep breath, he replied, "No. I don't think so."

"God," I whispered. "I'm so stupid. One of the people I trusted the most is a killer." I knew that now, without a shadow of a doubt. I couldn't pretend anymore. I had to look at facts. Someone already inside that cabin murdered Court and Josh.

"You're not stupid. You're loyal."

I snorted. "Same thing."

"Stop doing that. You're putting yourself down for being a good friend. Don't ever feel bad for not wanting to believe one of your friends could be a murderer."

"OK, fine. I won't feel bad. But I would like to be able to better see through people to who they really are."

He tilted his chin in a nod. "Yeah, you're fairly atrocious at that. If it helps, I promise to tell you when someone is lying to your face."

"So you do care, Blake?"

Rolling his eyes, he replied, "Yes. Happy?"

"Happy about?"

"Women," he muttered. "Fine. I care about you. There, satisfied?"

My eyes widened. Satisfied was the biggest understatement of the century. I'd expected him to say he cared about his family, not just me. Though I'd take it. Mr. Heart of Steel had just told me he cared about me—specifically me. As if I needed reason to fall for him more.

My little thing for Blake had become an Everest-sized thing for Blake.

"Hmm, it's not often you're speechless, Keaton. Why does it surprise you so much?"

"You're trying to make it sound like nothing." If he was going to play this down, I was going to kick him in the shin. This was huge for me. I didn't trust men after Danny, so I couldn't pretend our hookup was casual for me.

"You know it's not nothing," he replied.

"Yes, I know that," I said, gritting my teeth. "But you're trying… Oh, you know what, never mind."

"Just a heads-up, I'm going to kiss you now."

My insides squirmed. "Blake, Pete has just died. Your mother is distraught in the next room, and we're possibly next on the hit list." His eyes were on my lips and it made it hard to think about the right thing to do.

"All the more reason to take advantage of the moment, then. This is what people do in helpless situations like this. Don't you watch movies?" he murmured.

I didn't have time to reply before his lips grazed mine so lightly it tickled. Every other thought fell out of my head. I stopped breathing as he pulled back and stared into my eyes. He was giving me a second to put a halt to this.

To hell with it. If it was good enough for the movies... I pressed my lips to his and kissed him. I knew it was probably a bad idea, but what I felt when he kissed me—the burning fire and the feeling of being home—spurred me on. No one had ever kissed me as passionately as Blake did. No one had ever made me feel so safe before.

His hands rested on my hips, and then he picked me up as if I weighed nothing and set me down on his lap. It sent my body into overdrive.

My hands quickly found his hair, and I grabbed fistfuls and pulled, which he seemed to like a lot. Usually, I could show a little restraint and self-control, but with him it was lost. He moaned into my mouth and threw us back on the bed.

Once again, he was hovering over me while he kissed me until I was breathless, on the verge of passing out or spontaneously combusting.

"We shouldn't be doing this," I murmured against his mouth.

"Yes, we should. Stop overthinking. Actually, just stop thinking."

I did.

CHAPTER EIGHTEEN

Tuesday, August 25

The next morning, I sat in the living room with Mum, drinking tea before she went to work. Blake and I were following my friends today, which was officially the most ridiculous thing I'd ever done.

"Are you OK, love?" Mum asked.

Since I had gotten back from Blake's last night, she'd been suspicious and hovering over me like I was hiding something. It wasn't like I wanted to hide my...whatever I had with Blake, but a sort-of boyfriend along with everything else was a lot for my parents to deal with.

"I'm OK. Eloise was completely broken over her brother's death. You should've seen her, Mum. It was awful to witness. And Blake doesn't know what to do with himself."

"Where's his dad?"

"He's dealing with Josh's death by immersing himself in his work. Apparently that's how he deals with everything. Blake's kind of like the parent to his parents without ever being shown how to support someone else."

"You like the boy," my mum said, giving me a gooey smile. At least she wasn't telling me it was bad timing and I was a horrible person for liking someone at a time like this. Also, I was so far past just liking Blake it wasn't even funny.

"I do."

"Does he feel the same?"

As I did for him? Doubtful. But he certainly had feelings for me. "I think so."

"Of course he does," she replied, giving the typical parent response.

"We'll see what happens, I guess."

"As long as he treats you well, you have my blessing."

Wow. I had expected more of a fight, especially given the short length of time I'd known Blake, but the deaths of my four friends in under a year put things into perspective. My parents only had to deal with me having a boyfriend. Tilly's, Gigi's, Courtney's, and Josh's parents had to deal with never seeing them again.

"Thanks, Mum. That means a lot to me."

"Will you promise me one thing?"

"Of course," I replied, taking a sip of tea.

"Tell me when you two are together. I don't want secrets."

My gut bunched with guilt. Of course she was talking about when and if we became an official couple.

"I will," I replied, the words burning on the way out.

Mum left shortly after and I'd never been so glad that she had to work before. I hated lying to her, but I couldn't exactly say that I'd slept with Blake. There were things she just didn't need to know.

Throughout the day, Blake and I texted about spying on my

friends. He promised he would pick me up in a rental car. I waited in the front hall for him. I loved that through all of this craziness, I could still get excited over a boy. It felt so normal.

A car outside beeped its horn and I knew it'd be him. I grabbed my keys and went outside. All excitement I felt turned to sheer disbelief as I saw what Blake had rented.

"Are you serious?"

Leaning his arm out of the car, he replied, "What?"

I gestured to the bright-red convertible. "We're supposed to be *inconspicuous.*"

"Ah, but I figured they would never expect to see us in a flashy car. We'll be more inconspicuous in this than some sad, old Focus." He tapped his head as if he'd thought of something deeply clever.

Really now.

I closed my eyes and rubbed my forehead. *This can't be happening.* "I genuinely don't know what to say to you, Blake."

"Thank you, maybe?"

"I'm not thanking you for being idiotic," I replied and got in the car. "Bloody hell, can you at least put the roof up?"

"Later. Wanna pretend we're Bonnie and Clyde?"

"Sod off," I replied, sighing in discouragement and throwing my bag on the backseat. "What do you think we're going to find?"

"Probably about as much as we've found already, which is bugger all, but what choice do we have? Everything is ten times more serious now. We can't just sit back and wait for the police to figure out what happened. Pete's dead, and we don't know how far the murderer is going to go," he said.

I wasn't sure if I believed one of my friends would or could kill me. They all had their issues with Josh and Courtney, but as far as I knew, I'd never pissed any of them off—not enough for one of them to want to end my life. Would that matter though? Someone was obviously messing with me by sending text messages, and I wasn't sure why or what I'd done.

"Do you really think they would want to kill us?"

"I'm not willing to take that chance, Mackenzie."

I shook my head. "We're discussing this as if we're talking about deciding on a day's outing."

"Would you prefer me to panic?"

I rolled my eyes. "No."

"Kenz, this is all we have left. We find who's done it or end up six feet under…or, third choice, be wrongfully imprisoned. I don't know about you, but I don't fancy option B or C. Like you said, there will be time to grieve later. Right now, we fight. OK?"

"OK," I replied. That was what I'd been doing all along, only now I was trying to prove Blake and myself were innocent, rather than Megan, Aaron, and Kyle. Out of all of them, Blake was the only one I was one hundred percent sure was innocent. And I hated that.

"Let's drive to Megan's—you need to direct me, by the way— and check out what's going on there first. Please remember we're here to catch a killer, so keep your hands and lips to yourself for the next few hours."

I rolled my eyes again. At least he could still keep it light. "Take a left at the end of the road and get your head out of your arse."

Blake's smirk lit up his whole face. I loved carefree Blake. I settled in to spy on my friends and hopefully keep Blake in check for a while too.

"This isn't as fun as I thought it'd be," Blake moaned, reclining his seat and throwing his arm over his forehead. We'd been parked outside of Megan's for no more than fifteen minutes. I felt like a copper trailing a suspect.

"And you expected what?"

He shrugged with one shoulder. "Megan carrying a suspicious-shaped black bag or a rolled-up rug. A truckload of Rohypnol being delivered."

"You'd make a rubbish detective."

He looked at me out of the corner of his eye. "Oh, sorry, do you know who the murderer is, then?"

"That's not the point. I'm looking beyond the obvious."

"The obvious being Aaron?"

Sighing, I looked out of my window and back at Megan's house. Blake was exasperating. "Who had the time to drug our drinks?" I turned my body back and pulled his arm away from his eyes. "Why're we assuming it was the drinks that were drugged?"

"You think it could have been the food?"

"Maybe. We all helped to cook."

"We also all got drinks at some point in the evening too."

"Yes, I know, but the food is still a possibility. There were only two people who finished up cooking the dinner." My mind reeled with the new possibility.

"Who was that? Aaron and…?"

I gulped. "And Josh."

Blake stilled, and I waited for his reaction. After a minute, he frowned. "A murder/suicide? How could Josh stab himself like that? And it doesn't explain Pete."

"Perhaps that was random. You know Pete, always shouting his opinions down at the pub. Maybe he pushed someone too far and they snapped. Maybe someone used Josh's and Courtney's murders to cover up Pete's. Come on, it's a possibility."

Pete was punched once for telling someone they were a "tosser" for supporting the wrong political party. He spoke his mind and didn't care who he offended.

"You're asking me to believe my brother murdered his girlfriend and then himself?"

The cogs in my head turned and possibilities slotted into place. "What if Josh found out about Kyle and Courtney?"

"Then wouldn't it make more sense to kill Kyle than kill himself?"

I shrugged. "I don't know. His mind was obviously messed up. Blake, it could have happened. Call Wright!"

Closing his eyes, he groaned. "No, Mackenzie. Remember Lawrence? We were wrong about him." *We think we're wrong about him.* "I don't want to do anything that'll make it seem like we're desperate to divert the police."

"But we *are* desperate."

"We don't want Wright to know that. We need to think it through first."

"OK," I replied, feeling myself deflate. "Then we'll go to Wright, yeah?"

"Let's just see how tonight goes and talk it through some more. We'll go tomorrow if we need to." He smiled at me and looked out of the window. "Hey, hey, hey," he said in a rush and nodded to Megan's house. She ran to her car, ripping the door open. "Now, where's she off to in a hurry?"

"Start the car!" I hissed as Megan sped off.

He peeled off the side of the road and we followed Megan to the churchyard. Who would be in a flustered rush to come here?

Deep in the graveyard, I saw exactly why she'd raced over. Kyle was waving his hands around, shouting something that I couldn't hear. He stumbled and arched his back, drunk and clearly angry. My heart plummeted.

"Oh God, what's he doing?" I shoved the car door open and leaped out. Blake's footsteps were right behind me as we ran toward Megan and an angry Kyle. Blake spat out a swear word as he gained on me. It was a stupid thing for me to have done since we were "undercover," but I couldn't not go to my friends when they clearly needed help.

"Kyle!" I shouted.

Megan was already with him, and she was the only one to look up. Kyle clawed at the ground like he hadn't heard me.

"I don't know what he's doing," Megan said. "He called me

ranting about what a slut Courtney was and that he wanted to dig her up!" I froze in shock. That wasn't Kyle. He didn't say things like that. Hell, he didn't even *think* things like that. "I don't know what to do, Kenz."

"I hate her," Kyle spat, taking a few steps toward me. It was the first time in my life that I was actually scared of him. I had no idea what he would do.

Blake stepped between Kyle and me and Megan. "Calm down. So Courtney picked Josh. Man up and stop acting like a little bitch about it," he growled.

I wanted to kick Blake. He couldn't have given tact a shot?

"You don't have a clue!" Kyle roared. "You pathetic loner, you don't have a clue what it's like to love someone. The only person you care about is yourself."

That's not true, I wanted to insist but remained silent.

"What?" Megan said. "What the hell is he going on about? You were with Courtney, Kyle?"

"Kyle, that's enough!" I yelled, ignoring Megan's confusion. The cat was out of the bag and she'd catch up. "What's wrong with you? You've lost it. How much have you had to drink?" His eyes were bloodshot and he was noticeably stumbling, which was unusual for him—unless he was drunk off his face. We absolutely needed to implement a no-drinking rule because this was getting out of hand.

"She chose him, Kenz. How could she choose him?" His eyes narrowed and his lip curled in fury. "It's all her fault. It was *all* her fault."

"Kyle, don't," Megan said. Her voice was weak and she sounded as if she had just been kicked in the stomach. "Courtney's dead. Her death wasn't her fault, and you shouldn't talk about her like that."

I was with Megan on that one.

"I don't care!" His eyes were fierce and distant from being so worked up. "She deserved it after what she did to me. Everyone's going around saying how they didn't deserve to die, but they *both* deserved it!"

"They deserved death?" Megan repeated in shock, both appalled and heartbroken as she looked at Kyle. I was too. My stomach turned at his words. That was just disgusting.

Kyle squeezed his eyes closed. "I want her back. I want her with me." His shoulders hunched over, defeated. "I love her."

I stepped forward, wanting to comfort him but was stopped by Blake's arm. Kyle narrowed his eyes at him. "Oh, piss off. Kenzie's my best friend! I'm not going to hurt her." I could see by the way Blake's eyebrow twitched that he was thinking Courtney was someone he loved and he was saying horrible things about her. Blake didn't trust Kyle one bit, and right then, I wouldn't have been willing to leave my life in Kyle's hands either.

"It's OK," I muttered, gently pushing Blake's arm down. Kyle wouldn't hurt me—at least not in public. Blake made no attempt to stop me again, so I walked to Kyle and wrapped my arms around his waist. I was hyperaware that I could be hugging a murderer, but at that moment, he was just my lost, heartbroken, messed-up friend. "You're going to be OK," I whispered. We all were. We had to be.

Kyle gripped me so tightly his fingers bit into my skin. I felt how badly he was hurting and it was heartbreaking. "I don't know what I'm doing," he sobbed. "I can't think straight. She's *gone*." His legs gave way and we dropped to the ground with a soft thud. "What am I going to do?"

"I don't know," I whispered, shuffling so he wasn't on top of me so much. I hadn't figured the "after" part out yet. Eventually, we would all have to face up to what had happened and deal with it, like we did when Gigi and Tilly died. I would have to let the good memories back in and accept they were gone. I didn't know if I was strong enough to do that all over again.

"It hurts," he hissed and gripped me tighter. "I can't... God, I can't..."

"Shh," I whispered, rubbing his back and choking as my throat clogged up. "We'll get through this just like we did when Tills and Gigi died."

Megan knelt beside me. "But this isn't the same, Kenz. Tilly and Gigi were an accident. This," she said, shaking her head, "this was deliberate."

"We can't just give up," I replied, sobbing. "We have to stick together. I know this is harder, but we can get through it. I need you both. Aaron too." *And Blake*, I added silently. Especially Blake. But now was not the time to include him—not when my friends were still banking on Blake being the killer.

"You're right. Why don't you come back to Kyle's with me and we can talk about all this stuff? Maybe we can figure it out together," Megan said.

Behind us, Blake scoffed. "You mean so you can try to find a way to pin it on me."

I turned around, giving him my full attention. "That's not what she meant."

Kyle pushed off the ground and scowled. "The hell it isn't! We all know you had a problem with your brother."

Folding his arms over his chest, Blake grinned sarcastically. "We all know *you* had a problem with my brother, and since he was getting in the pants of the girl you love, I think your motive shoots you to the top."

"Stop!" I yelled, standing up and holding my arms out between them. "You guys have to stop this."

"Why are you always defending him?" Kyle spat.

"Because he's in the exact same position as us. Just because we didn't know him before doesn't—"

"Mackenzie," Kyle said, cutting me off. "We don't know him now."

I sighed sharply. "Then trust *me*, Kyle."

"You're shagging him," Kyle sneered, stumbling back a step.

"No," I lied. I had slept with him. "You need to go home. I'm not talking to you when you're like this."

"Whatever," he mumbled, walking toward the parking lot in a wonky, alcohol-fueled line.

Kyle refused to get in the car with Blake, so I helped Megan get him into her car and she took him home. I got back in the stupid flashy sports car and closed my eyes. "Is it Kyle?" I asked Blake as he turned the engine on.

"I don't know. He's mad, but he seems more self-destructive rather than murderous. Wanna check Aaron before I take you back to my place?" he replied.

"I'm going back to yours?"

"Yeah, my mum's still a mess, and I don't know how to handle women upset, you know that."

I shook my head. "Fine. I'll text my mum to tell her where we are. Aaron's next. Wright tomorrow."

"You think we'll find anything at Aaron's?"

"What're you expecting? Aaron to be carrying a suspicious black bag or a rolled-up rug?" I replied.

"Ha-ha," he said flatly. "Buckle up."

I did just in time for him to step on the accelerator, pinning me to the back of the seat. We arrived at Aaron's far too quickly, because Blake was mental behind the wheel, and parked a little way down the road.

"Can I talk to you about something?" I asked.

"I think it was Aaron in the kitchen with a knife."

I rolled my eyes. It was so hit-and-miss whether Blake would take what I had to say seriously or not. "You know one day you'll have to deal with what happened to your brother too, right?" Blake's defense was to joke around and make light of every situation. It was probably something he had done his whole life. I could picture him joking about what a crap mum he had even though it must have left its mark.

"Sure. Not looking forward to your breakdown, I have to say."

"Because you don't do hysterical women."

"No, because I don't want to see you upset," he said quietly.

"Oh."

He smirked. "Not what you expected me to say, huh?"

"Nope, not really."

"I'm not a complete arsehole, you know."

"Oh, I know. No, not a *complete* one."

"But seriously, what did you want to talk about, Mackenzie?"

I licked my lips, debating if this was a good idea or not. But I didn't have anything to lose. "I've received a couple messages."

His eyes locked onto mine. "No number, cryptic shit?"

My spine straightened. "You had them too?"

"Yeah."

"Why didn't you tell me?"

"Why didn't you tell *me*?"

Sighing, I leaned closer and handed him my phone. "Show me yours."

"Mackenzie, I'm all up for—"

"Don't finish that sentence, Blake. Show me the messages you received." I held out my hand and wiggled my fingers. He dropped his phone in my palm, already looking at my messages. I read the ones he had received.

Did you tell the police just how much you hated Josh?

You're not fooling anyone.

I looked up at Blake, but he was still engrossed in my messages. Who did the sender think Blake was not fooling?

Poor Uncle Pete. He should've kept his nose out.

I placed my hand on my neck, feeling warm. What kind of

person would send a message like that? Blake may not have been close to Pete, but he was still family.

Go to the police and Mackenzie will be next.

I shuddered and put Blake's phone down, feeling sick to my stomach. I didn't want to see more. Now I was being threatened? "Do you think Megan, Kyle, and Aaron have been getting these too?" I asked. My heart thudded and my hands trembled. Someone would hurt me. They'd *threatened* to hurt me!

He shrugged. "I think at least two of them have."

"Come on, do you really think whoever it is wouldn't text their own phone too?"

"Worth you asking. Their reaction might give away a clue."

"Yeah, maybe." I bit my lip and handed his phone back.

"Mackenzie, what you just read on there…"

"We don't need to discuss it."

"No one is going to hurt you."

I hope not. Giving Blake a smile, I pulled myself together. This was not the time to freak out.

Blake tapped my knee. "Aaron's door!"

Someone in a hooded black jacket and dark jeans was talking to Aaron on his doorstep. They exchanged a few words and then Aaron retreated back inside.

"Bloody druggie," Blake muttered. "Well, I think it's safe to say Aaron would know where to get Rohypnol."

I wanted to run to Aaron, flush whatever he'd just bought, and slap him until he saw sense. There wasn't a thing I could do if he wanted to spiral though. All I could hope was that he'd snap out of it. Josh's and Courtney's deaths had clearly brought back all he'd felt when he'd lost Tilly. But he wasn't going to be able to smoke away his guilt over their relationship. Not forever.

Even though I couldn't deny what I'd just seen, I still felt a stab of honor. I wanted to defend Aaron. "I thought you said weed and Rohypnol were two completely different things and we shouldn't—"

"Yes, Mackenzie, but how many people do you know that do a bit of weed dealing like that? And own nice, flashy Range Rovers like that? Which, by the way, total cliché. It's the drug dealer's car of choice."

"I don't know any drug dealers. Drugs don't appear in my world."

He smiled sarcastically and nodded toward Aaron.

I added, "That I knew of."

"This is pointless. Driving this around was fun, but we're not undercover cops. Let's take the car back and head to my house," he said.

"Today was a complete waste of time."

Blake stroked the steering wheel. "I enjoyed driving this."

"Oh, I stand corrected," I replied sarcastically.

"I liked spending time with you," he said quietly.

Well, that did things to my heart that had me falling even harder for him. "Yeah, I enjoyed it too."

He flashed a boyish grin. "Let's go chill on my bed and I'll let you take advantage of me."

I shoved his arm, then gave him my best smile.

CHAPTER NINETEEN

Wednesday, August 26

Since Blake and I admitted we'd both received threatening texts, we wanted to check out Josh's room, in case he had also been getting threats before he'd died. We didn't have access to Courtney's place, but if we found anything suspicious at Josh's, I was going to find a way to get into her house.

"I just don't get it," I said into the phone to Blake while starting up at my ceiling. Mum and Dad were downstairs, and I couldn't handle them constantly questioning if I was OK. I wasn't and pretending was draining.

"To be fair, you don't get any of it. Don't yell, because neither of us do."

I ignored him, half because I couldn't be bothered to bicker and half because I knew he didn't mean to make it sound like I was stupid.

"If Josh and Courtney were being stalked before they died, why wouldn't she tell me? It's a long shot, isn't it?"

"Probably, but it's a scenario we should consider. Maybe they figured out who it was and that's why they were killed."

OK, that made sense. If Megan, Kyle, or Aaron had been

sending threats and Court and Josh figured it out, they'd want to shut them up. Maybe something the stalker had sent to Josh was still in his room. I had kept the texts sent to me.

"So we need to find something that links Megan, Kyle, or Aaron to evidence we may or may not find in Josh's room?" I said, putting the phone on speaker so I could lay it down.

"Piece of cake, right?" he said sarcastically.

"I'm scared, Blake. Whoever is sending those messages has made sure we're too scared to show the police. That message said they'd *kill* me." Betrayal burned like acid. Whoever sent that message didn't care who they hurt, and that made them dangerous.

"Do you want me to pick you up?" Blake asked.

"No, it's OK. I'll be over in a few."

"All right, see you soon."

I rolled onto my side and ended the call. When I got to Blake's, I would feel better. Something about him made me feel safer. He was big and strong, and I knew he wouldn't let anything happen to me. I might not have known him long, but I trusted him above any of my friends—he was the only one helping. Whether Courtney and Josh were already dead when Blake and I went upstairs, I didn't know—and I believed that Blake didn't know either.

Since the murders, going outside left me full of nerves, and today was no different. I got ready and slammed the front door as I left. The local knitting club was walking by on their way to the village hall for their weekly meeting. Five old biddies judged me, stopping to get a good look.

Before the murders, they would have stopped to chat and tell me I needed to put some "meat on my bones." This time, they whispered to each other, stealing glances at me out of the corner of their eyes.

Mildred, the eldest and brightest-purple rinse of the bunch, was the first one who would usually call me over. Last winter, she knitted me a pink-and-brown-striped scarf because I didn't wrap up warm enough, apparently. It hurt that she turned so easily.

People weren't supposed to be guilty until proven innocent. Ignoring them, I got in my car and got the hell away from all the judgmental looks.

Blake was sitting on his front doorstep when I arrived. "You're waiting for me," I said as I got out of the car.

"Did Josh have something going on with Tilly and or Gigi?"

"Tilly and or Gigi? Where did that come from?"

He shrugged. "I get them mixed up."

"No, he didn't have a thing with either of them. Gigi was a lesbian, remember?"

"Megan was straight, remember?"

Fair point.

"Why'd you ask, Blake?"

"Because," he replied, holding out a handful of photos of Tilly, "I found these in his sock drawer."

Cocking my head to the side, I took them from his hand and flicked through them. They were all close-up pictures of Tilly. None were too odd, most candid ones, as if she hadn't known they were being taken.

"Tilly," I whispered, unease seeping into my bones. "Why would he have all these?" There had to be at least twenty pictures. When I reached one of the bottom photos in the stack, it was just of her cleavage. I shoved them back at Blake. "Why does he have those?"

"I dunno."

"Oh God, was he cheating too? No," I said, shaking my head at how ridiculous the thought was. Tilly wouldn't go near Josh. Like, even if he were the last man on earth. She may have thought less of him than I did. "They don't look right, do they? If you were posing for your piece on the side, you'd actually pose a little. Half of them look candid and the other half look like general pictures."

"General pictures?"

"Yes!" I exclaimed, having gone way past my tolerance for his smart remarks already. "You know, a smile for a picture anyone would take."

"All right. Josh has general and candid pictures of Tilly. No sexy posing." He shook his head and said, "I still don't know where you're going with this…"

"Really?" I replied flatly, pushing past him to go inside. "Blake, they mean Josh had a thing for Tilly, but it was just *his* thing."

"She didn't have a thing," he muttered and closed the front door behind us.

"I'm going to hit you very soon."

He grinned and stepped far too close to me. "OK, I'm done."

I stood my ground, not letting him know he affected me, even if every single nerve in my body fizzled. He would just love it if he knew how my legs turned to jelly when he stood just inches from me and how his voice gave me goose bumps.

"Lead the way," I said, waving my hand to the stairs.

"Ladies first," he replied. His voice was low, husky, and incredibly sexy. "Ah, but you're not a gentleman." I already felt boneless, so knowing his eyes were on me as we walked upstairs would probably make me collapse.

His lip curved with amusement. "You're right."

Blake walked ahead. As soon as there was some distance between us, my clouded mind cleared. I shouldn't have even been thinking of a guy with everything that was going on, and I couldn't even talk about it with anyone because things with Megan were weird and my only other girlfriends I could talk to about boy stuff were dead.

I stopped at Josh's open door. Blake had already gone inside, not caring that we were about to breach the privacy of his dead brother. "You waiting out there all day?" he asked.

"It feels wrong."

"Do you want to get us off Wright's little list, or do you want to respect Josh's privacy?"

I walked straight in.

"That's what I thought. There's nothing else in any of the drawers. I've not looked anywhere else yet. You look under the bed, and I'll look in the wardrobe."

"Great," I muttered. Now what kind of grossness was going to be lurking under an eighteen-year-old guy's bed? That was something I was more than happy never to know the answer to, and I needed an answer for everything.

Turning my nose up in anticipation of all things disgusting, I knelt down and lowered my head to the floor. If there was a used condom, I was out. "Nothing," I said, shocked. Everyone had at least a sock that had been kicked under their bed. Josh's was so clear I could see right through to the other side.

"Huh, what a pansy. You should see what's under my bed," Blake said. I couldn't see his amused, cheeky little grin, but I knew it was there.

"No thank you," I replied and stood up. "So where does he keep the things he doesn't want anyone to find then?"

Blake shrugged, holding up a black plastic box. "My guess is in here."

My first thought was *Please let there be some useful clue in there*, and my second was *I really don't want to know if there is*. What if there was evidence that he'd been in a secret relationship with Tilly, and Aaron had found out about it? Stranger things had happened. Not a lot stranger, but still.

"You ready to see what deep, dark secrets my brother had?"

I shook my head. "Not really."

"Good," he replied as if I'd said yes. "Let's open it then." He dropped the box on the bed, steadying it with one hand as it bounced. I held my breath as Blake took off the lid.

"Car magazines. Why hide those?" I asked. My heart dipped, thinking it was just a box full of old rubbish Josh hadn't got around to chucking. We were never going to find what we needed.

Blake cocked his head to the side and smiled as if to say *aw, bless*. "Underneath," he said and lifted the two magazines that hid the real contents of the box.

My eyes widened in shock. "What the…"

"Ohhh, Joshua!" Blake exclaimed, laughing. "What were you into?" He lifted out a black gag and swung it around his index finger. *I think I'm going to vomit.* While Blake was playing and picking out metal handcuffs and something that looked like it belonged in a medieval torture chamber, I was motionless and speechless.

"OK," I snapped. "Put it all back."

"Oh, we got pictures!" he said, waving a pouch of disposable camera prints.

I raised a hand. "I don't want to. We can't."

"These might be a clue. What if some are of Tilly?"

"Then they would be with the others you found." *And I'd want to see them even less.* I knew it was likely to be photos of Courtney, handcuffed, bound, and whatever else they did together. "And why didn't the police find all this when they searched his room?"

"Because I might have found it in the loft last night and brought it down before you arrived."

I threw my hands up in the air, exasperated. Blake was worse than a naughty toddler. "Well, why did you put it in his wardrobe, and why did you tell me to look under the bed?"

"I could hardly leave it on his desk, could I? My mum could have walked in and found it. And making you look under the bed was purely for my amusement." He laughed and shook his head. "The look on your face when you thought you were going to find something disgusting under there…"

I took a deep breath. *Count backward from ten…*

"Mackenzie, we have to look at the pictures. The whole point of snooping is to find evidence."

"Something that lead to him killing Courtney and himself, not the kink he got off to!"

"How do you know it's not all linked? Who knows what he was into or how deeply?"

"What if it was some satanic…something?"

"Not sure you have to worship the devil to enjoy a bit of rough sex."

I rolled my eyes. "I'm not saying that, but what if *he* did?"

"Why don't I look?"

"Oh, you'd love that, wouldn't you?"

"Ain't denying it, sweets." What the hell was wrong with him? "Oh, don't look at me like that. It's not my thing, but whatever tickles your pickle."

I laughed—properly laughed. "Tickles your pickle?"

"You must have heard that phrase before?"

I shook my head.

"You poor, sheltered girl." He pulled the photos from the sleeve and his eyes widened. "Whoa."

"What? What does that mean?"

He looked up over one of the photos, white as a ghost. "You really don't want to see."

The very tips of my fingers tingled. "What is it? Don't show me, just tell me. Is it Courtney?"

He nodded. "And some of Josh." His eyes rounded even more. "OK. That's going to take a lot of therapy." Throwing everything back in the box, he shuddered and put the lid back on.

"Blake, what were the pictures of? How bad is it?"

He shuddered again. "Bad. Let's talk in my room, yeah."

It must be bad if he can't even be in Josh's room anymore.

"Well?" I said, closing his door and shaking my hands.

"They did things to each other."

"Yeah, I got that. What…what things?"

"Whipping. I saw a whip and…marks on Josh. Blood."

My pulse thumped in my ears like a drum. "Blood? What were they doing? And whose blood?"

"Josh's. There was a cut on his chest. He had the camera at arm's length, taking a picture of Courtney…"

Oh, no, no.

"Courtney. Courtney doing what?"

"Licking it."

"Bugger off," I said. *If he thinks I'm falling for that…*

"Mackenzie," he whispered. His face was dead serious. He was *not* joking. My stomach lurched, and I slapped my hand to my mouth. "You might be right with your satanic thing. I know some guys get off on pain while they're balls deep, but that…"

I turned my nose up. "Oh my God, can you never refer to sex as 'balls deep' again?"

He half smiled but mostly still looked sick.

"Damn it," I muttered and sat on his bed. Courtney never mentioned being into that kind of stuff. Not even being tied up or blindfolded. We confided in each other about our intimate lives. Was she ashamed?

"You didn't know about any of it?" he asked.

I shook my head slowly, still trying to process the blood thing. "She never said a word."

"I'm not surprised."

"Me neither. Not about the really…odd stuff. I thought she would talk about lighter things though, but she hadn't—not even when Tilly admitted she loved being tied up and Gigi confessed her chocolate mousse fetish."

"Please tell me you recorded your sleepovers."

I arched my eyebrow, and he held his hands up, surrendering.

"Courtney never said anything," I continued. "Not anything out of the ordinary anyway. Do you think she really wanted to do that stuff?"

"Lick her boyfriend's blood during sex? Does anyone want to do that?"

"Do you think he forced her?"

Blake shrugged. "I have no idea. I am thinking that maybe this murder/suicide thing is a definite possibility. But I'm thinking Courtney did it."

"No. No way. She couldn't."

"Think about what she was doing to Josh, Mackenzie. If you saw a way to make that stop, if she really didn't want to do those things, wouldn't she take it?"

"She could have just broken up with him."

"Maybe there was more to it than that. Think about how she would have felt if he had been forcing her to do that stuff."

Disgusted and belittled.

But murderous and suicidal?

I rubbed my aching head. "I have no idea what to think anymore."

"We take this to Wright and let him investigate."

"Yeah," I replied, sagging into the mattress.

"You OK?"

I shrugged. Tears stabbed at my eyes. "What if Courtney didn't want to do that stuff?" Oh God, how scared and alone would she have felt?

He dropped to his knees and leaned his forearms on my thighs. "I don't know what to say, Mackenzie. Saying the right things in situations like this isn't one of my strong points."

"You don't have to say anything. Sometimes there are just no words."

"What do you want me to do?"

What could he do? What were you even supposed to do when you found out your dead friend may or may not have been taken advantage of and abused? How did she feel? Why couldn't she have told me? I could have helped her.

"It might have been Courtney," I whispered.

"It can't just have been Courtney. Who's sending the messages?"

I shook my head, squeezing my eyes closed. "I don't know. None of it makes sense, but we have to go to Wright with this. It could help uncover what really happened." Was I actually considering that Courtney had help to kill Josh and then kill herself? Or had someone else just figured out who the murderer was first and was now messing with me and Blake?

"I don't think it's a good idea. He's just going to think we're trying to get the heat off of us," Blake said.

"Come on, we can't keep this to ourselves."

"Why not? We're keeping the text messages to ourselves."

OK, he'd gotten me there. "No, we've only kept those secret because I was threatened. You said yourself we'll tell after they arrested someone and it's safe. That way, they'll have extra evidence against the killer. But this could help the police solve the crime."

He groaned and covered his eyes with his hand, clearly not OK with taking these pictures to Wright. No one had to know we'd handed it in, so I wasn't any more scared for my own safety than I already was since I'd read the text threatening me.

"Please." I moved closer and put my hand on his arm. "I understand why you wouldn't want to share those pictures of your brother, but we don't have a choice. Come on, please? Let's go to the police now, Blake."

Dropping his hand, he looked straight through me. "Fine. But this will be a waste of time and only make us look worse."

I wasn't sure we could look worse in anyone's eyes. Most of the town had already condemned us, and Wright was suspicious as hell.

We didn't have much to lose, but we had our innocence to gain.

CHAPTER TWENTY

"This is a good idea, isn't it?" I asked Blake for the tenth time, needing reassurance as we looked on at the police station doors from his car.

He cut me a look. "No."

"Why are you so against this?"

"I told you! This is a bad idea but, hey, it's your show."

"Show?" I spat through my teeth. "This isn't a game, Blake! And if it is, I'd really like someone to explain the bloody rules."

"Chill," he said, lowering his voice. "I didn't mean it like that, OK? I'll follow you in there, but don't be surprised if this comes back to bite us on the arse. I'm just worried that this is going to make us look more suspicious."

"Blake," I breathed, leaning closer and putting my hand over his. "We're in this together. I know you're innocent and soon everyone else will too."

His fingers stretched and weaved between mine. "I wish I could share your optimism."

"I'll be optimistic for us both."

He took a breath and grabbed the box of Josh's kinky, and frankly horrifying, sex stuff with a death grip. It was as if he felt guilty that he was about to expose his brother's dark secret.

There was a possibility that the killer could have been Josh or Courtney. Maybe. I didn't particularly want anyone else knowing what they got up to in the bedroom, because it was clearly something Court wanted to keep quiet, but we were running out of options.

"Are you ready?" I asked.

Blake smiled, but it was forced. He got out of his truck and I followed behind. My heart buzzed with nerves and the palms of my hands started to sweat. *Oh God, this is one of the worst ideas I've ever had.* I just hoped Wright wouldn't think we were only sharing our theory to cover up our own guilt, specifically Blake's. He probably would, but we couldn't ignore what we'd found, unfortunately.

Wright stood beside the front desk talking to a colleague and he turned as if he'd sensed us walking in. My stomach knotted. How did he just know? The man wasn't human.

"And to what do I owe this pleasure?" Wright asked, threading his fingers together over his swollen belly.

Blake's eyes narrowed. "We'd like to talk to you. If it's not too much trouble."

"Have you come to confess, Mr. Harper?"

"We want to talk to you about another possibility," I said, cutting in before Blake could bite back with a stupid remark. "If you can spare us the time?"

"For you, Miss Keaton, anything."

Cocky, sarcastic bastard. I smiled, or what I hoped looked like a smile, and followed him into the all-too-familiar interview room. "How has no one ever killed him?" Blake whispered in my ear.

I shrugged. Wright must have rubbed enough people the wrong way. I wondered if he conducted every investigation the way he was this one. Surely not. My knowledge of policing and detective work was limited to TV shows, but he didn't seem professional. He was too eccentric in a pushing-unprofessional manner.

"Take a seat," he said, gesturing to the metal chairs. Being in an interview room made me feel like a criminal. It was like when a police car followed you on the road. You'd done nothing wrong, but you're positive you were going to get in trouble anyway.

Blake was sitting so close his arm brushed mine. It wasn't accidental. He knew I needed the support and I leaned on him like a lifeline.

"So," Wright said, waving his hand, "you have the floor."

"Um, we found something and we have something to show you," I muttered, stumbling over my words nervously.

Wright nodded, smirking a little in a patronizing way that made me grind my teeth. "Another suspect? I see you have a box of tricks with you."

I frowned. "Yes." He wasn't even taking this seriously, and it made my blood boil. The contents of the box would probably wipe that smug smile right off his face.

"We think that Josh could have done it," Blake said. "Or Courtney."

"What an interesting theory, Mr. Harper. That would certainly pan out very well for you, wouldn't it? That would solve *all* of your problems."

Yes, it would.

"Josh had jealousy issues. He saw Courtney as his. Their sex life was far from the comfortable, old missionary. I don't know. Maybe he was mad at her or something. Or maybe she'd had enough. Can you just look into it, please?" I asked, sliding the box over to him.

He cocked his head to the side, ignoring what I had said completely. "You've thought about this a lot, haven't you?"

"Clearing my and my friends' names? You probably won't be surprised by this, but yes, I have." *Calm down. Don't let him get to you.*

"Let me share some information with you, just to make your own little investigation easier," he said. "Josh and Courtney were both murdered. From the angle of the knife wounds, it would have been very, very difficult for either one of them to have done that to themselves, and given the brutality and quantity of stab wounds, at this point, I'm ruling them both out as suspects, because the stab wounds were made by the same person. I'm quite offended you assumed I hadn't already investigated that possibility."

Blake shrugged. "Well, you don't tell us much so you can see how we got there."

I kicked him under the table, which only made Blake smirk. "Look, we just want to know who did this. They were my friends."

"Except for Joshua. If I remember correctly, you didn't like him," Wright replied.

I clenched my jaw. Why wasn't he listening to us? "That doesn't mean I wanted him dead."

"Perhaps not."

"Definitely not," I snapped. "Do you have any idea who it was at all?"

Wright leaned forward on the table and smiled. "Mackenzie, I have *five* ideas."

Blake stood up so fast his chair made a horrible scratching noise on the floor. "That's a no then. Come on, Mackenzie. He obviously doesn't have a clue. Want us to leave you with that box so you can flick through the photos and work out if Courtney would have been capable of stabbing her boyfriend so brutally after what Josh put her through, or are you still ruling that out?"

"Thank you, Blake, I'll have someone look through this and we'll return it when and if we can."

Blake snorted, shaking his head. "You really don't know anything, do you?"

I got up and we walked to the door. I was as done as Blake was. What was the point in going to the police if they wouldn't even hear you out?

"I do know one thing," Wright said just as we were about to walk out of the room.

"What's that?" I asked over my shoulder.

"Your friend Aaron has been talking pretty loudly about Mr. Harper's motives. We all know he had the opportunity."

My face fell. I spun around. Aaron had been talking to Wright about Blake? "What?" I whispered.

"I'm not surprised Aaron's bad-mouthing me. He's not a huge fan," Blake replied and shrugged, showing Wright that he wasn't getting to him.

It was getting to me though. Big-time. How could Aaron do that? I would never share their secrets with the detective just to help myself out. Aaron had no proof that it was Blake, so he shouldn't be spreading rumors. I wasn't, and I knew he was dabbling with drugs.

Wright's smile faded so slightly I almost missed it. "Is there anything else you'd like to discuss, or are you all out of—"

"We're done," I snapped and stormed out of the room. I wanted to request a proper detective, but I had a feeling he wasn't technically doing anything wrong. He kept details from us until he wanted us to know—but that wasn't a crime. That tactic was readily used in police investigations.

Since my parents were out, we went back to my house and headed to my room. "We're screwed, aren't we? They're going to pin it on one of us if they can't find out who really did it." I said.

"If there's no evidence, then no."

"But innocent people go to prison. What if the jury does that beyond-a-reasonable-doubt thing?"

His smirk widened. "Good thing you chose detective as your career path and not lawyer."

I flopped back against my pillows. "You're not funny. I hope you know that."

He rolled over, hovering above me. "Please, you think I'm hilarious."

"Yes," I said, "but probably not in the way you're thinking."

His eyes turned serious and I wanted him to kiss me more than I wanted to breathe.

"Really?" he whispered, inching closer. I was pretty sure if I continued teasing him, he would get payback by pulling away, so I bit my lip. There was plenty of time to tease, but this was a time for kissing.

"Blake," I breathed.

"Yes?"

"You're being horrible."

"I'm not doing anything," he replied innocently.

Narrowing my eyes, I gripped the sides of his T-shirt and pulled him closer. "If you're going to kiss me just do it or—" His lips sealed over mine, kissing me deeply, fiercely. His mouth moved against mine with a desperation that made my toes curl. We attacked each other like animals.

We didn't have long though. My mum was due home any minute, and I really didn't want her to walk in on us.

"Blake," I managed to murmur against his mouth. He groaned and shook his head, gripping my hips and cementing my body to his. I pushed at his chest when I could barely breathe, and he pulled away, smirking. "You're like some horny fifteen-year-old."

His eyebrows knitted together. "Actually, I kind of feel like it again."

"Blake Harper, are you admitting you like a girl?" I teased.

"Whatever," he muttered and sat up. I hated having any space between us. He was under my skin now whether I liked it or not. And I liked it. "We should go back to my house and check on my mum."

"We?"

"Not sure if I've mentioned this but—"

"You don't do hysterical women," I said, finishing his sentence. "You may have mentioned it once or twice. I'll come."

The whole way to his house, Blake was silent. I watched him drive for a minute and then decided, since he wasn't filling the silence with anything idiotic, I would talk to him about something that had been on my mind.

"Blake, will you tell me more about your relationship with Josh?"

His lips thinned into a grim line that reminded me how much he didn't like sharing his feelings—and how he didn't like his brother. "What do you want to know?"

"You didn't have a good relationship?"

"It wasn't the best, but then we had barely spent any time together. I think I saw him about ten times through our teenage years. We weren't really brothers, not properly anyway."

"Did you want to be?"

"I guess. I've not really thought about it much. We weren't a family. That was fine though. Dad and I managed." He smiled at a memory. "Though we ate crap all the time. We should be at least double the size we are."

"Your dad isn't a big cook?"

"Not really. We can both make a few things, but we ate a lot of takeout, mostly from laziness."

"Why do you feel like your mum preferred Josh?"

"Because she does. If you have a son that you spent every day with and another you barely spent a week a year with, who would be your favorite? It's fine. I favor my dad, and I'm sure Josh favored Mum. It's natural to love who you're with most, isn't it?"

I bit my tongue. *Not if you're the parent.* "Yeah, maybe," I replied. "Why did you decide to come with us to the cabin? Don't get me wrong, I'm glad you did. I just don't understand why."

He turned onto his street. "My dad started working away even more. When you come home to an empty house every day, your mind eventually wanders to the other half of your family. Josh and I had spent some time together a couple months before, and it went OK. I thought that maybe we could be brothers now that we could control where we went. Before, it had always been our parents pulling the strings, and that was usually in opposite directions."

So he really did want to reconnect—or connect—with his brother. "I'm sorry you lost him before you had a chance to do that."

Blake gulped and nodded. His jaw tightened. I knew I should change the subject before our conversation got too emotional. I didn't want him to withdraw from me again. "I'm going to cook for you and your mum tonight. What's your favorite dinner?"

He blinked heavily. "Doing a conversation one-eighty. Nice. I like spaghetti Bolognese. I think my mum does too."

"Sounds good." I smiled at him, and he smiled back, as if he was trying to figure me out. He pulled into his drive, and that was when I noticed the police car beside Blake's mum's. "What're they doing here?" Blake muttered, frowning.

We jumped out of the car. I prayed Eloise hadn't done anything stupid. If she was dead too, then what was Blake going to do? As much as he didn't think he needed her, he did.

Blake unlocked the door, and I raced past him into the living room. Two officers sat on one sofa, and Eloise was on another. I sighed in relief when I saw she was OK, physically anyway.

"What's going on?" Blake asked.

The officers, who I didn't recognize, moved quickly, grabbing Blake's arms and twisting them round his back. "Blake Harper, I'm arresting you for the murders of Joshua Harper and Courtney Young." The officer launched into telling him his rights. Then the officer said, "Do you understand?"

"What?" I said numbly, my body going into shock. "Why?"

Blake's jaw was tight, tense. "I get it," he bit out.

"I found them under his bed," Eloise cried, rocking on her chair.

"What? Found what?" I questioned.

"Courtney's earrings and Josh's chain. He did it. He killed them. He killed my Josh."

My mouth dropped open as my heart fell through the floor. I shook my head. "No…"

The two officers shoved Blake forward and out the front door. It took me a few seconds to force my legs to walk, but when I did move, I sprinted back out the door. "Wait!" I shouted. They had made a mistake.

The officers had just opened the back door for Blake when I reached the car. Blake looked at me, and his expression— defeat—made my heart ache. "I didn't do it, Mackenzie," he said just before he disappeared into the backseat. He watched me as the car drove off, his eyes pleading with me to believe him.

I believed him. Of course I did, and watching him being taken hurt so much I was breathless. I'd fallen in love with him.

CHAPTER TWENTY-ONE

The car turned out of my sight, and my heart cracked. This wasn't right. To be accused of murder by your own mother!

But there's evidence.

There were things belonging to Courtney and Josh in Blake's room, which anyone could have put there. Josh was never on edge or nervous when I was in his room, not once, and he didn't even think of his place in his mom's house as his real bedroom. Why would he hide the jewelry there if it was his?

Someone's setting him up.

I sprinted back in the house. "Eloise!" I shouted, gripping the doorframe for support and to stop myself before I fell over.

Eloise had her arms around her knees, huddled in her chair as she sobbed. I gritted my teeth as anger boiled inside my stomach. She was crying over her son being guilty. Why couldn't she have faith in him?

Stay calm. I slowly walked over and perched on the edge of the sofa next to her chair. "What happened?"

"They found that stuff in his room." She shook her head, wiping her tears. Her face was tearstained and blotchy. "I can't believe it. I don't want to believe it."

"Then don't. *I* don't believe it. Blake didn't do this and you know it. The police searched the house before and found nothing. It doesn't make sense for him to put their things there now."

"Yes, it does. He thought the searches were done, that it'd be safe now."

I shook my head. "No. Someone must've planted those things to make him look guilty. Blake is being set up, Eloise. Who else has been in the house?"

She had to have let someone else inside.

"I-I'm not sure. A lot of people have come by to check on me." Her voice cracked and she sobbed again, wiping her tears on the back of her sleeve.

Taking a steadying breath, I asked, "Did Aaron, Megan, or Kyle come over?"

"They were here after Josh's funeral."

"But that was the only time?"

She nodded. "Yes, that was it."

I closed my eyes and tried to think back to that day. The police had searched our houses straightaway, well before the funeral. We were together most of the time, but I had been flitting between them and Blake. Who had gone off alone? None of them had really moved from the spot I'd left them in, and I was never gone too long, but they could have had enough time to get upstairs and back. Which one of them would be so bold as to bring trophies from our dead friends to the wake and plant them in Blake's room? I couldn't picture any of them being brave enough—or stupid enough—to do that.

"Why would Blake want to hurt his own brother and uncle?" Eloise asked, breaking me away from my loop of questions.

"He didn't. This wasn't him. You *have* to believe that. Think about it. Someone tips off the police and they miraculously find Josh's and Courtney's things in Blake's room. It's too convenient. It doesn't make sense for him to have put those there after the first search. He would have dumped them. Please don't give up on him. He needs you."

She buried her head in her knees and gripped her hair. "I have nothing left to give him."

I clenched my jaw and my hands shook. "He's your son! You have to find some compassion inside you, the same as you would have for Josh. I'm serious, Eloise. He needs you. You can't honestly think it was him."

She frowned, shaking her head. "I don't know. I just... I don't know."

"Whatever!" I spat, walking out before I said something that I probably wouldn't regret.

We had driven Blake's car, so I had no way of getting anywhere other than walking. I didn't want to call either of my parents or any of my friends. I still needed to figure out who put that stuff in Blake's room, and I was going to start with Aaron.

He was the one with a temper.

I left Blake's and walked to Aaron's. My mind swirled with possibilities and theories. Blake must be terrified. He'd been arrested for something he hadn't done. I didn't want to believe it could be Aaron, but he could turn in an instant if someone pushed him.

It was the middle of a warm day, but the roads were deserted. I took a deep breath. Someone was cutting grass somewhere. It looked and smelled like summer, but it sure didn't feel like it. Summer before university was supposed to be fun, and I'd never been more miserable.

I rounded the corner and heard what sounded like light footsteps. Stopping so I could hear properly, I turned my body to get a good look in both directions.

The only thing I could hear was my heart jackhammering in my chest.

You're paranoid. There's nothing there.

Spinning back, I picked up my pace until I was at a comfortable jog.

It's fine. Just get to Aaron's.

I pushed myself, my thighs beginning to ache from the exertion. If this didn't motivate me to get back into exercising, then nothing would.

Thud. Thud.

Shit. I lurched forward and took off in a sprint. My lungs burned as I gasped air. Feet slammed down on the concrete, sending pains shooting up my shins. *Keep going, almost there.*

Someone was coming after me.

Did they want to hurt me like they had Pete?

Had Pete stumbled on some evidence?

Go, Mackenzie!

Aaron's house came into view, and I wanted to collapse in relief. I was running too fast to look behind me to see if anyone was there, and I couldn't hear through my loud, shallow breaths, but I kept one foot in front of the other as I flew toward my destination.

Hurry.

I slammed into the wall surrounding Aaron's family's front garden and almost toppled over it. My hip bone screamed as it came into contact with the brick.

I cried out, bending over and gripping my side for dear life.

I gasped and looked around. There was nothing but a cat sitting on a fence in the distance. I took deep breaths and held my chest, my lungs feeling like they were going to explode.

"Calm down," I whispered, clenching my free hand. "You're an idiot."

There was no one following me and probably never was.

What the hell was happening to me?

I straightened my back and walked around the side of the wall to Aaron's front door. My hip stung, but I didn't care.

I raised my arm and knocked.

"Just a minute!" Aaron hollered from somewhere inside.

My phone beeped.

No, please not again.

I took it out of my pocket tentatively, like it was going to burn me.

The number. My eyes pricked with tears, but I was determined not to cry as the text came into view.

Careful, there's a killer out there.

I stumbled back and dropped my phone. *Had* someone been following me?

Who'd sent this?

It couldn't be Blake. He was at the police station, and I doubted they'd let him sit there on his phone. I knew he was innocent. I *knew* it.

But Aaron, Megan, and Kyle? Or someone else?

Aaron's front door opened, and I jammed my phone in my pocket and shoved my hands behind my back so Aaron wouldn't see how much they were trembling.

"Hey," Aaron said, his smile stretching across his face, lighting up his baby-blue eyes as he pulled the front door wide-open.

"Hi." He stepped aside, and I walked in with my heart in my stomach. "Can we talk?"

"Sure. My parents are home, so let's go upstairs."

I climbed the stairs and headed to his room. Accusing Aaron of murder, which was pretty much what I was doing at his house, was one of the hardest things I'd had to do. I was torn between wanting him to admit it and deny it.

"So what's up?" he asked as he sat on his swivel chair by his desk.

I lowered myself onto his bed, facing him. I let my eyes wander around his room, looking for a phone I'd not seen before. It was clear, besides all of his junk. "Um, well, Blake was arrested today."

His eyebrows shot up. If he had planted the evidence at Blake's, he faked shock well. "Jesus. For the murders?"

"The police found something of Court and Josh's in his room."

"Wow…" He shook his head. "Can't say I'm surprised."

"No…you always thought it was him."

"Well, I was right, wasn't I?"

"No. He was framed."

"Mackenzie, come on. How long are you going to defend the

guy? Open your eyes! I know you don't want to think badly of anyone, but this is bordering on ridiculous. We barely know Blake. On the night he randomly decides to play big brother, two people end up dead. How does that look?"

"I understand how it looks, and I know you don't trust him, but please trust *me*. Blake didn't do this."

"So the evidence fairies left the stuff in his room, did they?"

I gulped. "No." Raising my eyes to meet his, I waited and then watched his mouth slowly drop. He looked winded, like I'd just punched him in the gut.

"You think it was me?" he ranted, pushing himself up. "What's wrong with you, Mackenzie? I think the guy is a creep, and yeah, I think he did it, but I would never frame anyone, let alone *murder* our friends!"

"OK, OK," I replied, standing and holding my hands up. "I'm sorry, but Wright said you've been telling everyone how much you think it's Blake, and—"

"So you believe that arsehole and not someone you've known for years? I thought better of you."

It was his turn to wind me. My eyes welled with tears. He was right. I shouldn't let what Wright said get to me. I'd never felt lower. "God, I'm sorry, Aaron. I don't know what to think anymore. I don't know how to handle all of this. Everything was already so messed up and now Blake has been arrested."

Aaron grabbed my arms and bent his head down to my level. "You have to face the fact that it was him. How much more evidence do you need?"

To believe he did it, I need a confession. "It wasn't him, Aaron. Why would he leave Court's earring and Josh's chain there? The police had already searched and found nothing. Did he store them somewhere else and then randomly move them under his bed? That's stupid. He would've dumped that kind of evidence if it were him."

Aaron lifted his eyebrow. "Maybe he thought it was safe. I don't know what goes through his psychotic mind. Do I? If you don't believe it was Blake, then who was it, Kenz? Me? Kyle? Megan? You? We're your only other options, so pick one."

I yanked my arms from his grip. "Don't you dare ask me to choose between you."

Because it'd be him. Blake was the only one I trusted now.

"I don't need to. You came here asking me if I set Blake up. I think it's crystal clear who you think killed them."

"Aaron, I'm looking for answers. All I want is to know what happened."

"So do I! They were my friends too. You're not the only person who's lost someone. You're not the only one who wants justice."

"All right. I was wrong, and I'm sorry. I don't want to lose you too."

Aaron groaned as he watched a tear slide down my cheek. I was exhausted; my energy was evaporating at an alarming rate. "Don't cry. You know I hate it when you cry." He wrapped his arms around me. "What you said hurt, but I don't want to lose you either. I don't know what I can do to convince you that I'm innocent, Kenzie, but tell me and I'll do it."

"I'm sorry," I whispered. "You don't have to do anything. I believe you. Forgive me?"

"You're already forgiven," he replied. "Megan and Kyle'll be here soon. Wanna help me get the drinks and snacks together?"

What I wanted was to check on Blake and make sure he was OK, but I knew Wright wouldn't let me see him. Maybe hanging with them would be a good idea? I knew they all had secrets, but maybe I would be able to see through them to the truth. Unlikely, but I could hope.

"Sure," I said, feeling uncomfortable. "Hey, you still have that farm app on your phone? I feel like not thinking for a while."

"Err." He looked around his room. "I do but I guess my phone must be downstairs. Let's get the food and you can bring it back up."

If he didn't know where his phone was, what did that mean? Was he being honest, or was he the one sending the text messages?

I smiled. "Thanks, Aaron."

I helped Aaron get the snacks together, and then I'd had about five minutes on a game I didn't want to play by the time Megan and Kyle arrived. We sat on the floor in a circle. It was just like any other time we'd hung out, but the atmosphere was way off. There was no easy conversation and a whole lot of prolonged silences.

My fingers wouldn't stay still; I tapped them together and

threaded them through and around. I couldn't tell if their expressions were *grieving friend who'd been through so much* or *guilty conscience*. Each one of them looked the same—tired. Blake was right. I couldn't tell if they'd done it and I probably would never be able to.

I was closest to Kyle because he'd always been an open book. And Megan, I thought, had never kept a secret from me our whole lives. Aaron was the blue-eyed boy, the loving friend who would fight to the death to keep the people he loved safe.

Opening a bottle of some premade tropical cocktail—the only bottle that hadn't had the seal broken—I took a large swig. It was stupid to be drinking, but I no longer cared. My mind was in pieces, and I wanted to forget for a while.

My friends didn't seem to worry that one of us in that room was a murderer and had drugged the rest of us. It was clear they believed it was Blake and there was no danger of being drugged again. Were they all in on it?

"To Tilly, Gigi, Josh, and Courtney," Kyle said, holding up his can of beer.

And to Pete.

I raised my bottle, clinking it against the boys' cans and Megan's glass of neat vodka. "Getting drunk, Megan?" I asked.

"It's over now, Mackenzie. Blake's going to prison for what he did. We don't have to worry about Courtney and Josh never getting justice. I kind of think that's cause for a celebration, don't you?" she asked.

No.

"It is," Aaron replied. "To justice and finally being able to move on." He closed his eyes looking beyond tired. I felt the same.

How many toasts were they going to do? The real murderer hadn't been caught yet. I was drinking with strangers.

Ten agonizing minutes later, Megan giggled. She hadn't had much to drink, but she was drinking vodka. I couldn't even blame her. At least if I were drunk, I could stop worrying for a while. I couldn't do that to Blake though. He was sitting in some holding cell, so having fun, getting an escape—even if momentary—seemed so wrong.

"I can't believe it's just us four. This time last year, my room was filled with eight drunk and very happy people. Remember you girls dancing around the room, singing into empty bottles?" Kyle asked, laughing.

I smiled at the memory and wished we could go back in time. Things were simple and easy then. It was such a shock to see how much could change in just one year. My circle of friends had been cut in half, and I had a not-really-a-boyfriend friend who I could possibly lose to jail before we really got to be together. I was so tired of losing people.

"This is all so screwed up, but at least they have the person who did it. We're all OK now," Aaron said, raising his glass to me.

My hand tightened around the bottle, but I said nothing. Perhaps if they all got drunk, one of them might slip up. I didn't have much hope, but it was the only piece I had left.

"Thank God," Megan added. "I knew we would all get through this. We just had to stick together."

Out of the corner of my eye, I saw Aaron raise his eyebrows, and I knew the gesture was for me. I had pretty much accused him of being the murderer when I asked if he planted those things on Blake.

"I'll just be a minute," I said and left the room. There was a phone call I needed to make that absolutely couldn't wait, so I locked myself in the bathroom down the hall.

Wright was on the other end of the line almost the second as he was informed of my call. "Hello, Miss Keaton, what a lovely surprise."

"Is Blake OK?"

"Blake is fine," he replied.

"What's happening? You know he didn't do this, don't you?"

"Unfortunately, I can't speak about—"

"Cut the bull," I snapped. "We all know you do nothing by the book, so don't try to start now."

The line was silent for a second and then I heard a quiet chuckle. "I admire your spunk, Mackenzie." *Spunk. Who still used the word spunk?* "Blake is being questioned."

"I figured that. You're still looking at who really murdered Court and Josh though, aren't you?"

"If you're asking me if you're still a person of interest, yes."

My shoulders loosened in relief. That meant he wasn't jumping on the Blake-did-it train like everyone else. "Good."

"I find it quite remarkable that you would prefer to still be in the limelight."

"I don't want an innocent man going to prison."

"Neither do I," he replied. "The evidence we found in Blake's room has been sent for testing."

"You mean fingerprinting?"

"Nothing gets past you, does it?"

"Hard to say. You're slightly more transparent than my friends right now though." *And that's the biggest lie I've told.*

"I wish I could say the same about you. Good day, Mackenzie," he said and hung up.

I walked back to Aaron's room, and they hadn't moved an inch. Taking my seat between Megan and Kyle, I picked up my drink and then thought better of it.

They had been alone with it, and I didn't trust them anymore.

CHAPTER TWENTY-TWO

I left to go home shortly after they started on the shots. It was only seven in the evening, and I didn't have to be home until eleven, but I couldn't celebrate Blake's arrest. It made me feel sick, and if Aaron made one more toast, I was going to punch him.

Both of my parents' cars were in the drive, which was unusual on a weekday, since they didn't leave work until about this time. My nerves rattled as I opened the door and yelled out, "Hello?"

"We're in the kitchen," Mum replied, and I took a left, under the arched doorway.

The last time we had a kitchen talk was three years ago when they were giving me *the talk* after I got together with Danny. I could still remember the horror I felt at having them explain contraception. Not to mention when Mum slid a condom over a banana, I wanted the ground to swallow me whole. The day I found out I was pregnant, I burned the remaining condoms Danny and I had.

"Sit down, Mackenzie," Dad said. He and Mum were around the kitchen table with a teapot filled with steaming hot tea and three mugs. I sat down and bit my lip. This didn't look good.

"Blake has been arrested," Mum said, pouring tea into the mugs.

"Yes, but he didn't do it. I know he didn't."

"Mackenzie—" Dad started, but I cut him off by holding my hand up.

"Please, Dad. I know what you're going to say, but I trust him. We've spent a lot of time together, and I know that he could never do what he's been accused of doing."

"How well do you *really* know him though?"

I shrugged awkwardly, knowing I was going to sound like every other teenage girl who was infatuated with a good-looking guy. "I know him well enough. You're the one who always says your gut instinct is never wrong."

"And don't I regret that now," he muttered behind his mug as he took a sip. "We just want you safe, sweetheart, that's why we think you should stay at home until this whole thing blows over."

Blows over. He made it sound like it was a thunderstorm that would pass quickly. "Dad, it's fine. *I'm* fine."

He pursed his lips and put down his drink. "Mackenzie, I made it sound like a suggestion, and I shouldn't have. You will stay in until the person responsible for those murders is in police custody. Do you understand?"

"I'm almost eighteen, you can't ground me." He could, of course, but it was ridiculous.

"I don't care how old you are. You're our child and we will do whatever is necessary to make sure you're safe. Hate us if you want."

Oh, playing the hate-us card. Great. "I don't hate you. I understand why you're *grounding* me, but it's a little over the top and you know it."

"Honey, you're our baby. If anything happened to you, we would never forgive ourselves. Now, if you trust Blake, then I do too. You've got a good head on your shoulders, but if you're going to see him when he gets out of jail, it will be here, when one of us is home," my mum said.

Because that won't be embarrassing at all.

Conceding, I said, "OK. Thank you for trusting me about Blake." I couldn't really argue when they were showing me a *lot* of trust. They'd met Blake only a few times and he'd been arrested for murder. My parents had every right to forbid me to even think about him.

"Is it serious between you two?" Mum asked.

"No," I said cautiously. We had slept together and kissed a couple of times. That didn't exactly equal a serious, committed relationship, to him anyway.

"You're not doing that casual thing, are you?" Dad shook his head. "Mackenzie, you deserve better than that."

"Oh my God, Dad!" My face lit on fire. "That's *not* what we're doing. We're not doing anything." *OK, ground, do your thing and swallow me whole.*

Mum frowned. "But you are together?"

"No, Mum."

"I don't get you kids nowadays," she said. "Why you have to complicate everything I will never know. If two people like each other, they should just come out and say so. Such a waste of time going around in circles when you could be happy."

My parents admitted they liked each other within days of meeting, and about a week later they were a couple. It didn't quite work like that these days. Now, if a girl admitted she liked a guy straightaway she was a bunny boiler, and if a guy did that, he was a pussy. There were modern-day politics you had to consider, rules you had to adhere to in order to be happy. The young people that jumped into relationships nowadays were desperate and no one wanted a *latcher*.

"Can we not talk about this? *Please.*"

Mum put her mug down. "All right. You'll let us know when you two sort it out though?"

"Yeah, will do, Mum." I took a sip of my drink, wishing it were hotter so it would scald my throat and I could go to the emergency room and not have this conversation. "Dad, do you think you could call the police station and try to find out what's going on? Wright won't tell me much."

"You're worried about your not-quite boyfriend?" he asked.

"If you're not going to do it—"

"No, no, I'll do it."

"You guys are being really cool about this. I appreciate that. You don't know Blake."

"We know you. And if you trust him over three people you've known your whole life, then he can't be bad," Dad said, standing up. "I'll make that call now."

I *did* trust Blake more. I couldn't explain it. There was just something about him, about *us*, that made sense.

Mum smiled at me when Dad left the room. A full, toothy smile. She had something she was bursting to say. No doubt it would be about Blake. I sighed. "Go on. Just say it, Mum."

"Have you kissed?" she asked.

"Yes," I replied.

"And you really like him?" My mum was a romantic; she and Dad had been together since they were teenagers. They'd had their whole lives to be deliriously happy, so she wanted the same for me.

"I do."

"You're being careful? And I don't just mean contraception."

"OK, we're done now." Why did "enough" mean nothing to my family? I stood up. "I'll see you at dinner."

"You're hiding out until dinner? You shouldn't be embarrassed to talk about boys with me."

"And good-bye, Mother!"

I left the kitchen to hover around Dad by the sofa.

"No, I know… Well, is there anything you can tell me?" he said into the phone. I knew that meant he was getting nothing as well. I hated waiting around, knowing Blake was innocent. How long would it take the police to figure that out?

He hung up and shook his head. "Sorry, kiddo. No news."

I shrugged. "Thanks for trying. I'm gonna go watch a couple films."

My room wasn't like bedrooms in movies, where you could sneak out down the drainpipe. Outside my window was a flat brick wall and a long drop onto stones. It would be noisy if I tried to sneak out. And besides, where would I go? I felt so useless.

Think. What can I do?

The cabin.

It'd been searched, extensively, by the police, and Blake and I had looked too, but maybe I could search again. My head knew it was pointless, but my heart needed to help Blake.

Curling up on my bed, I tried to formulate a plan, and somewhere between considering my escape options and sleuthing methods, I realized I was a joke. I was one of those people in films who did everything wrong.

I was a disaster and I was exhausted. So I decided that, for once, I would do nothing and leave it to the police. Whatever I tried just backfired anyway, so I wasn't going to interfere in case I made it worse. Blake didn't need that right now. It wasn't fair that he was in the police station being questioned when the murderer was drinking and celebrating, but what could I do?

Burying my head in my pillow, I shut my eyes and fell into a restless sleep.

Someone woke me hours later, shaking my arm. I groaned and looked at my phone beside me. 9:55 p.m. Groaning again, I rolled over to grumble at Mum or Dad for waking me up, but Blake's gorgeous blue eyes stared back at me, gleaming with amusement.

I threw myself at him, unashamed. It took a second for him to hug me back, but when he did, he almost crushed my bones. "You're OK," I said, closing my eyes and clinging to him like a limpet. "What happened? Did my parents let you in?"

"They did, and nothing much really happened. Wright made me sit and wait for him for a good hour before we even started, but my phone was taken until they'd finished with me. They'd already searched my room and taken pictures, so they know that earring and chain weren't there before. Hopefully, they're convinced it's a setup. I'm not being charged, but I'm definitely not off the hook. I could be called back in at any time, and I probably will be, but for now they've let me go."

"So Wright knows you're innocent."

"He asked if I planted that stuff myself to make it look like someone was framing me."

"Oh…"

He raised his eyebrows. "Yeah."

"I don't understand why someone would put it there."

"Come on. If items from victims are found after the police searched, they're going to think I hid it and then they're going to ask why."

"I hate this. Whoever the killer is, they're getting desperate," I whispered.

"Yeah." He pulled back and looked at me with a stern gaze. "That means they're even more dangerous. I don't want you hanging out with your friends alone anymore. I know I sound like a dad, but we have no idea what they could do next."

I rolled my eyes. "I've already been banned from leaving this house."

"Good." He sat on my bed, pulling me by the hand until I was tucked into his lap. "My mum came to the station," he said, his voice thick with emotion.

"She did?" Maybe what I'd said got through to her then.

"Yeah. She was a real mum too, doing the hysterical-shouting shit I imagined she'd do if Josh were in my shoes, even though she was the one who called the police to begin with."

"That's good."

"Yeah… It was weird."

"Good weird?"

"Good weird," he confirmed and laid his chin on top of my head.

"Where's your dad?"

"Home with Mum at the minute. He wanted to make sure she's OK until I get back. They seem to be getting on. Well, they've not screamed at each other, so it's going better than it has been for the last twelve years."

"I'm glad. What happens now?"

"With?" he asked.

"The investigation and you."

"It is still ongoing, which seemed to annoy Wright, so it's not all bad. And I have to pack up my room at home and move all my stuff to my mum's."

"Really?" I said, trying not to sound as excited as I felt. Obviously I did a rubbish job because Blake's chest rattled with silent laughter.

"Yeah. My dad's away more and more, so it makes sense for me to be around family. Family…and you."

Don't happy dance.

"You want to be around me?"

He moved his head back and I tilted mine so I could see him. "That shouldn't surprise you. Apparently it's painfully obvious to everyone else that I like you. I want to be with you, Mackenzie." He admitted that so easily I wondered if this guy was really "my" Blake.

All I could do was stare at him like a moron.

"Speechless is unlike you," he teased, grazing my bottom lip with his own. I think I actually died for a second. Chuckling, he shook his head and then gave in, pressing his mouth to mine. I was done. I couldn't form words and I was struggling to keep my pulse under check.

Blake's fingers knotted in my hair as he kissed me, and I thought I was going to faint. Kissing him was a million times better than anything I'd ever experienced before. When he let me up for air, he looked as elated as I was that out of all this huge mess, we'd found something great.

Blake left my house at half past ten. When my parents were going to bed, they'd dropped their not-so-subtle hint about us not being left alone together—until I was at least twenty. Instead of getting annoyed that he was being kicked out, Blake simply smirked, kissed me, and told me he'd be back in the morning.

I got back into bed, feeling whiplashed from worrying myself sick about Blake, then being ecstatic that he'd finally opened up and we were together. Needless to say, I slept like a baby.

CHAPTER TWENTY-THREE

Thursday, August 27

In the morning, I woke up smiling. Blake and I had agreed to get together later in the day, but before that I had something to do. I wanted to visit Tilly's, Gigi's, Courtney's, and Josh's graves at the churchyard.

Mum was in the kitchen when I dragged myself down. "Hey, what're you still doing here?" I asked. It was half past nine, so she should've been at work by then. I don't even know how I was going to cope when uni started and I had to be up at seven.

"I'm going in a little late. I thought we could have breakfast."

My mind immediately skipped to a dark place. "What's happened?" I asked.

"Nothing new, love. I'm concerned about you. Things are so stressful right now, and I want you to know that you don't have to worry yourself to death, like I know you do."

If she could have told me how to achieve that, I'd have done it. "I'm doing OK. I just wish the investigation were over."

"It will be soon, I'm sure. No one really believes you're responsible for what happened."

My mum wasn't a very good liar. The whole village thought

there was more to it than what we were saying. They'd pegged one of us five or all of us. As horrible as it felt to have people think I was capable of killing another person, when all of this was done, I would know exactly who I could count on.

"You're being very brave, Mackenzie, but you don't have to put on a confident front for me and your dad."

"I'm not. There will be plenty of time to process everything, but right now I *have* to get through each day until it's over."

She made two cups of tea and some toast.

"So…I think me and Blake are a thing," I said.

"It was only a matter of time."

"I'm worried about him. Megan, Kyle, and Aaron think he's guilty."

"It doesn't matter what others think, Mackenzie. It only matters what you think. The truth will out in the end."

"Right, but until then, people are crossing the road like he may give them the plague."

"People make snap judgments without gathering one single fact. You'll never change that."

Great, so it was just something we'd have to live with until the police found out who'd done it—*if* they ever found out.

"Yeah, I know you're right."

"It's hard, darling, but hold your head high and cling to what *you* know. Your father and I will try to speak with Wright today and see if we can get any more information. I don't think you'll be a person of interest for much longer."

I hoped so.

"What are your plans for the day?"

"I was thinking about going to see Megan. We keep missing each other and I think she's only been spending time with Aaron because Kyle's busy being angry at Courtney on his own."

Mum shook her head. "You think you know people..." *Tell me about it.* "Well, OK, but I want you to drive there and straight back afterward. No pit stops, Mackenzie Lauren, I mean it."

She'd dropped in my middle name, so she *definitely* meant it. That was only pulled out when there was absolutely no room for discussion at all.

"I promise," I said, and she smiled.

Mum left for work and I headed out at the same time. She wanted to make sure I left the house safely and then I was to text when I arrived, when I was leaving Megan's, and when I was home. I didn't begrudge doing it.

I drove to Megan's house, blasting the Killers from the speakers. We'd lost touch a little, and the guilt of that weighed heavily on my shoulders. Blake shouldn't come between us, but he had.

Turning the corner, I saw something flash in my rearview mirror, but when I glanced again, there was nothing but an empty street. I immediately went into high alert. Pushing my foot to the pedal a little harder, I sped down the road, looking in the mirror every few seconds. I definitely saw something. A person crossing the road was the most likely explanation, as it moved quickly and then disappeared. Whoever it was could've easily hidden behind the row of trees beside the path.

Megan only lived a few minutes away, so I usually walked. But since Court's and Josh's deaths, my parents insisted I drive everywhere, and right then, I was so thankful they had, because I would have felt ten times more nervous if I were walking.

My eyes flicked to the mirror again and I wasn't sure if it was because I was on edge or if there was really someone there, but I could've sworn I saw something move behind a tree. *Just two more turns to Megan's.*

I took both corners a little too fast and when I arrived, there were no cars outside her house. Sometimes her mum borrowed hers if her dad took the one they shared, so Megan could be home. Part of me didn't want to get out of the car.

I did a thorough scan of the surrounding area and gripped the door handle. It was OK. No one was going to jump out at me. I was being stupid. I glanced around and then got out.

But I didn't get far, not even to her driveway.

Something hard slammed down on my head and pain sliced through my skull. I fell forward and landed on my knees. I'd been hit! I held my head and braced for another attack. My heart beat out of my chest. Over the ringing in my ears, I heard someone's deep breathing. Was it my attacker's or mine?

My head hurt, but it wasn't unbearable. Adrenaline swamped my system until I barely felt a thing. I wanted to get up and run, but fear rooted me to the spot.

I wasn't sure what it was that I'd been hit with, but it was thick and hard, like a bat. My mind immediately went to Pete. It had to be the same person.

The person behind me didn't move. I could feel their presence. It made my hair stand on end and my heart sprint. Clenching my trembling hands, I stared ahead, too scared to look around even though I knew if I did, I'd see Courtney and Josh's killer. I was a coward. I wanted to know more than anything, but I couldn't force myself to turn around. Self-preservation was stronger than I'd ever imagined it would be.

My breath shallowed until my lungs burned and screamed for air. Neither of us moved and time stretched on. Someone had to come by soon. Where were Megan and her family? Their house was pretty secluded but not *this* secluded. I just wanted someone to come by and scare away my attacker.

Whoever it was took a step back…or a step closer, I couldn't quite tell. The noise was loud and clunky, like the solid wooden heel of a shoe. Maybe a boot or dress shoes. That didn't help tell me if this person was male or female.

I gulped, and my stomach bottomed out. All I could think about was my parents getting a visit from the police to tell them I'd been killed. The pain I could see them going through had my eyes filling with tears.

Not being able to turn around and look at the person made the whole ordeal ten times more terrifying. I didn't know what they were doing back there, if they had a hand raised and were ready to strike me again.

I heard another footstep and then another. My heart hammered louder than their shoes on the concrete. Slowly, the thuds got quieter until I couldn't hear them anymore. It still took me the longest time to be able to move. There were half-moons dented into the palms of my hands, where I'd been clutching them tightly, and my head throbbed.

More minutes passed on my knees, and I knew whoever had hit me was long gone. Fumbling in my jeans pocket, I managed to slide my phone out and call Blake.

"Miss me?" he said smoothly.

I couldn't speak. My lungs punched out air too quickly for me to be able to form words. Blake recognized something wasn't right straightaway.

"Mackenzie, what's wrong? Where are you?"

"I," I huffed, taking a deep breath to try to calm down.

"Mackenzie!" he shouted. "Did you go to Megan's?"

I sob broke from my throat, and I clutched the phone. *Please hurry.*

"I'm on my way. Stay on the phone." I heard a clattering and banging as he grabbed keys and opened and closed doors. Then his engine roared to life, and I sobbed again. He was on his way. "I need you to breathe slowly, Mackenzie. Can you do that?"

No.

"I'm on my way, I promise. You're OK now. Just listen to my voice and try to slow your breathing. Whatever's happened, you're OK."

I closed my eyes and listened to his voice. He was worried about me and desperate to get here as soon as he could, but he was doing everything he could to make me feel calm.

"I'm OK," I gasped out.

"Shh," he hushed. "Don't talk, baby. Just take deep breaths."

I did what he said, but it didn't help. Nothing would help until he got here. Whoever had attacked me could come back. I was still outside Megan's house on my knees. I didn't dare turn around.

Seconds rolled into minutes and the sound of Blake's car screeching down the road allowed my shoulders to sag. *He's here, thank God.*

He'd barely thrown his car into park when his door opened and he jumped out. "Damn it, Mackenzie, what happened?" he asked, dropping to the ground in front of me. His hands held my face and I finally felt safe.

Collapsing into his lap, I clung to him. I wasn't going to cry. There was no point. It'd get me nowhere.

Blake held me and kissed the top of my head until I'd calmed down enough that my breathing didn't sound like Darth Vader. "I'm OK," I whispered. "Someone attacked me."

Gripping the tops of my arms, he looked at me. "What happened?" Now that I'd calmed down, I realized how much I was shaking. My muscles screamed. "I thought someone was following me. When I got here, I was hit from behind, enough to knock me over, but that was it. They were behind me, Blake."

He was the maddest I'd ever seen him. "Where did they hit you?"

I let go of him to touch the back of my head, and as soon as I did, he was all over it. A doctor wouldn't have checked me over any more thoroughly. He scanned every inch of my head and face until I started to feel like a zoo animal.

"Blake, I'm OK. I wasn't hit that hard. It was more the shock."

"I should've come with you."

"Don't do that. Don't blame yourself."

"Let's get you home. I don't want you out here anymore."

"OK, but I need to find Megan."

"She's not in?"

I shook my head as my phone beeped. "I don't think so." Blake helped me up, and I looked at my phone and shuddered. "I have to drive my car."

"I can come back for it."

"No, I can't leave my car here. If Megan sees it here, she'll ask questions, and this can't get back to my parents."

He stilled. "You want to keep this between us?"

"I don't have a choice," I mumbled, handing him my phone.

"Mackenzie, we have to go to the police." Then he looked down and his knuckles turned white.

The message read, Tell anyone and I'll finish the job. Stop looking, Mackenzie.

"What the hell," he breathed.

We were in so far over our heads. We needed help. But how could we go to the police when I was being threatened? This proved those threats weren't hollow.

"We can't tell anyone."

He looked at me, as he considered our options. We didn't have many and none of them were good. "I don't know how to keep you safe," he said.

"No one is safe, Blake. Not anymore. Not until the killer is locked up. We can't go to the police, and if we keep looking, I'm going to get hurt…or worse."

"OK, so we do nothing."

I shook my head. "No, we just need to be a lot more careful about how we investigate."

"You can't be serious! Not only do you want to keep these threats from the police, but you also want to keep digging? Mackenzie, you've lost it. Do you have a death wish?"

I rolled my eyes and folded my arms. "I don't give up when I care about something or someone."

"You really need to work on that."

"It's not a bad quality, Blake."

"It is if it gets you killed."

"You're impossible."

Smirking, he lifted his eyebrow. "You love that about me."

"Don't know if I do."

"What's the next step, Detective Keaton?" he asked with mock humor.

"I don't know. I wanted to talk to Megan, Kyle, and Aaron, but right now the only person I trust is you."

He grinned, but it wasn't cocky or carefree. "Careful, Kenzie, sounds like you're falling for me."

Fallen, actually. There was no doubt about that one.

"Follow me back to mine, will ya?" I said, brushing off his comment.

Blake didn't leave me alone until my parents were due home. I'd texted my mum, telling her Megan wasn't in, so I went straight home—but I failed to mention what'd happened and that Blake was with me. Megan replied to my text, letting me know that she was out with her parents and grandparents for the day.

I turned in early because I hated lying to my parents. The day's events had left me feeling like I was going to collapse with exhaustion. Thankfully, Mum and Dad decided to have an early one too, so we were all in bed by ten.

Closing my eyes, I pictured myself the night before we'd left for the cabin. We'd all dropped off our food and alcohol to be packed in his designated food-and-drink suitcases. *Control freak.* Josh had demanded that all the beer, bottles of vodka, and fizzy drinks were delivered to his, so we didn't have to worry about getting it all packed into the car the following day. Any other drink we wanted to bring was to be brought in our own bags.

Megan and I had been standing in the corner of the living room, rolling our eyes at him. Aaron and Kyle were helping him stuff the bottles of booze between packets and boxes of food so they wouldn't get broken.

Most of the conversation was lost to me, but I vaguely remembered it being about packing and getting "rat arsed" all weekend. Besides everyone sticking their finger up at Josh behind his back, no one acted any differently.

I pictured the guys carrying the heavy suitcase out to Kyle's car, us girls following them, then squirming with unease as Josh made a joke about there being enough alcohol to kill us.

Taking a deep breath, I reached for my phone to watch the video Kyle had taken that day. He'd recently sent it to me after I asked. I pressed play with trembling fingers. Kyle had captured a few eye rolls toward Josh, stupid faces we'd pulled at him, and a lot of the cabin itself.

Josh told us to help get everything inside, and Kyle turned the phone to catch us walking outside. My ears started to ring as I heard something familiar. Those clunky footsteps. I was immediately thrown back to earlier in the day when I was attacked. My heart pounded. In front of me, my phone started ringing.

"Hello," I said numbly into the phone without looking at the caller ID.

"Hello." I recognized my friend's voice immediately. It was the next four words that made my blood run cold, "Mackenzie, it was me."

I know.

CHAPTER TWENTY-FOUR

My instructions were to come alone if I wanted the truth, and more than anything, I wanted the truth for Courtney and Josh. I put the phone down with trembling hands and sobbed as the realization hit me. My friend *was* a murderer. Creeping out of my room, I made my way downstairs and out of the house. Walking wouldn't take long. I contemplated calling Blake, but I couldn't risk anyone else getting hurt. My legs carried me forward on autopilot, and I was convinced I was living someone else's life. The house came into view, and I sucked in a deep breath.

The front door was unlocked, so I walked straight in. The eyes that stared at me were the same baby-blue ones that I loved so much, but they'd aged. They'd lost their innocence.

"Aaron," I said, not sure how to go on. I must've missed the chapter in the friend handbook on how to deal with a murderer. He didn't move from his spot on the sofa. "Why?" I whispered, taking a few uneasy steps forward.

"They're all on their way," he said in a monotone that didn't sound at all like him.

The closer I got, the stronger I smelled the harsh scent of brandy on his breath. "How much have you had to drink?"

"Not nearly enough."

"You told Kyle and Megan to come over as well?"

Why the bloody hell was I so calm?

"And I asked Blake. I only want to explain this once."

He was going to have to explain it a few more times for Wright. Unless Aaron was saying he didn't intend on handing himself in. All this time, he had allowed us to be interrogated and sat back to cover his own arse. I could never do that to someone I cared about.

"Why did you call Blake too? You don't need to explain this to him." I could tell him. The thought of Blake being around this made me sick. Aaron hated him, and Blake was bound to be angry.

His mouth thinned into a straight line. "I'll explain when they're here."

"Aaron," I whispered.

"Don't look at me like that, Mackenzie."

He'd killed my best friend and he honestly expected me to see him the same way? He was nuts. "How should I look at you then?"

"I don't know. Just not like you hate me."

I almost laughed. That was brilliant in a completely humorless way.

"Mackenzie?" Blake shouted and burst through the door like he was starring in *Mission Impossible*. "You OK?" he asked, scanning my whole body to make sure.

"I'm fine." I was anything but fine, but I felt stronger now that he was here.

Blake's posture turned to stone as he turned his attention to Aaron. He may not have been close to Josh, but he loved him as his brother, and Blake looked like he wanted to rip Aaron's head off.

I positioned myself between them in the small living room and pleaded with Blake to stand down. He didn't move or say a word, but his steely gaze never left Aaron.

Megan and Kyle arrived together minutes later. They both stopped just inside the door, and both looked as pale as a ghost. Kyle shook his head. "What's going on, man? Tell me this is just a sick joke."

Aaron stood up and properly acknowledged our presence for the first time since Blake had made his grand entrance. I took a step back. The expression on his face made my stomach flip over in the worst way.

"It's not a joke, Kyle," Aaron replied.

Megan let out a sob and pressed her hand to her mouth. "Why?" she muttered against her palm.

"Because they didn't care about what happened to Tilly and Gigi."

"What?" I huffed. "They were devastated by what happened." Courtney cried solidly for weeks, she hadn't driven since, and she often told me about the crushing guilt she felt. Josh felt it too at first, and even though he said some stupid, horrible things, I knew that he felt guilty.

"Were they?" he sneered, lifting his pale eyebrow. "They both moved past it so quickly it was like they never even existed to them."

"Aaron, where is this coming from?" Kyle asked, stunned. "You know that's not true, man. What happened to you?"

I tried to remember if there was something I'd missed. An anniversary of one of the times he got together with Tilly. Something, anything, that would explain what had tipped Aaron over the edge.

"Nothing's happened to me, Kyle. You can't see it. None of you can. You couldn't see what they were like. They didn't care about Tilly or Gigi or anyone else. All they cared about was that they weren't the ones in the ground." His voice was low and monotone, kind of like he'd rehearsed this speech over and over until it was perfect in his mind.

I sighed in disbelief. "That's not true." Courtney loved Tilly and Gigi as much as Megan and I did. We were all more like sisters than friends. Whatever Aaron said, I knew Courtney would never have put her own life above theirs.

"Now, here's what we're going to do," he said, pulling a knife from his pocket. "I'm going to stab Blake." I almost stumbled back in shock. *Aaron must be on drugs.*

Aaron looked and sounded so calm, as if he'd just said "I'm going to grab Blake a beer" rather than telling us he wanted to *stab* him. "And us four…"—he pointed to himself and then between me, Kyle, and Megan—"we are going to call Wright and tell him that Blake tried to kill us too, but we managed to get the upper hand. It will be self-defense."

I felt sick. There was no way Kyle and Megan would go for that. They couldn't.

"Aaron, no," I whispered.

"Cut the shit, Mackenzie," he bellowed, spit flying out of his mouth. "I've had enough of this Team Blake rubbish from you. *We* are your friends, and like you've said a thousand times before, we have to stick together."

"Aaron, man," Kyle said, his face still portraying his shock, "we can't do that. I understand how you feel. I do. I lost the girl I love too, and I'm still sad and angry as hell, but this isn't the way to make it better."

Aaron straightened his back, holding the knife higher. "Shut up! You don't know anything, Kyle. We just have to do this one last thing, and then we can put it all behind us. Everything will be OK. I promise."

He's lost it.

He'd become unpredictable and that was the scariest thing. My blond-hair, blue-eyed, loving friend was a coldhearted killer, and whatever he said, there was no way I was letting him hurt Blake or anyone else.

"Aaron," Megan whispered, stepping forward and holding up her hands. "It's all right. Everything is going to be fine, but I need you to put the knife away. We can talk this through and work something out. Between us five, we can find a way to make this better. Right, guys?" she said, looking at us with wide eyes, begging us to agree.

"Of course," I said.

My mind was focused on protecting Blake. I just needed to get the knife away from Aaron, and then I could breathe easy and help the situation.

Blake nodded once, and Kyle replied, "Yeah. Anything."

Aaron laughed, tilting his head back. "Do you think I'm stupid? The second he's out of here, he'll go to Wright," he spat, glaring at Blake.

"No, he won't. Will you, Blake?" I said, willing him to agree and make it convincing. I could tell by Blake's whole demeanor that there was no way he was ever going to help Aaron, but he nodded along with our plan. "See? This is all going to be all right. We'll all cover, and eventually the case will go cold."

"Mackenzie's right, Aaron," Megan urged. "If we all keep quiet, eventually this will blow over. The cops have absolutely nothing on you."

"No!" he shouted, jabbing the knife at the air. "The only way this ends is if we do it now."

"Calm down!" Blake yelled. "You're not stabbing anyone else, you sick bastard. Now put the knife down."

"What're you doing?" I glared at Blake. Was he trying to wind him up further? We needed to tread carefully. "He didn't mean that, Aaron."

Aaron growled. "Oh, will you stop defending him? I'll stab you too if you keep it up." His eyes rounded in shock at his own words. "Mackenzie, I'm sorry. I didn't mean that."

"What is going on?" I shook my head. This didn't make any sense. Aaron was protective. The only time he'd ever been in a fight was to defend someone.

Something was really off here and not just the fact that Aaron standing in front of me wielding a knife, admitting to murder, and throwing around threats. Something in my gut told me there was a big part of the story missing.

"You so much as touch her, and I'll kill you myself," Blake replied far too calmly. His voice chilled my blood. There was a dangerous side to Blake, and it scared me because I worried that he'd get himself hurt.

Aaron stepped forward, and Blake held his ground. "You need to back off now." There was a double meaning to that. Back off away from him and from me. "I'm warning you, Harper."

I threw my hands up. "Stop it! Both of you just stop."

What happened next happened so slowly it almost felt like a dream. Blake spat something out about Aaron's head being wired wrong. Aaron lunged forward the way he had many times before, when he'd gotten himself into a scrap at school. Blake punched Aaron in the face, splitting his lip. I thought that would be it, but a red-faced Aaron threw himself forward again.

I was rooted in place. My heart thudded. They crashed into me and sent me stumbling sideways. I just about managed to correct my footing before I fell.

The knife. Grab the knife, Mackenzie. But before I could move, Megan's high-pitched scream stunned me. Kyle shouted expletives, making me flinch. It took me a second to register that Aaron had used the knife. He held it up and the end was coated in a red film. Aaron dropped the knife and backed away, wide-eyed.

Regret.

Who had he stabbed? Was it me? I couldn't feel anything. Not a thing. Blake looked down, his hand shooting to his side, and

I felt light, as if my lungs had been vacuum-packed. Dark spots danced in front of my face and I was sure I was going to collapse.

It was Blake.

"No, no, no, no," I whispered. Every word scratched my throat. I pressed my shaking hand against his hand on the wound. "It's OK. It's OK," I repeated, trying to convince us both. I could just about handle losing Aaron as a friend, but not Blake.

My hand soon heated as his blood seeped through his fingers onto mine. He stared at me, but he didn't look as terrified as I was. *I can't lose you.* In the background, I could hear Kyle shouting and a scuffle, but I couldn't take my eyes off Blake. Megan was on the phone to the emergency services, and they couldn't get here soon enough.

"Damn," Blake hissed, falling to his knees. "God that hurts."

I grabbed his upper arms and helped him lower to the floor before he fell farther. I'd thought the most useless I'd ever feel was when we'd found Courtney and Josh. Blake had a chance. He was breathing, and yet I didn't know what to do other than put pressure on the wound.

Blake leaned against the wall. His jaw was clenched tight and his eyes twitched as he tried to not show how much pain he was in.

"You're going to be fine," I said, holding back a sob and swallowing hard. "The ambulance will be here soon. How do you feel? Blake!"

He smirked through his pain. "I feel like I was just stabbed."

"Shut up," I scolded, letting out an involuntary sob. The fact that he could still make jokes made me want to laugh and cry all at the same time. God, I really loved him.

Kyle had Aaron pinned to the floor under his body. It didn't look necessary. Aaron didn't move an inch. The only thing that made him look alive was the way he was staring at Megan.

"I told you it was him," Blake whispered and winced.

I could've hit him, and if he hadn't already been in a lot of pain, I would have. Bloody moron.

"Shut up," I repeated, pressing my forehead against his and mouthing *I love you*.

Barely a few minutes later, I heard sirens, but those minutes felt like hours. Blake sat perfectly still, breathing rapidly and deeply. He smiled at me through his pain, and I knew that he would make it because he wouldn't leave me.

"You're going to be OK," I said sternly. "You are."

"I know that. You worry too much."

Paramedics, followed by four police officers, slammed through the door. I thought I would be shoved out of the way, but they saw I was helping stop the bleeding.

"Hello, my name's Jerry. How're you doing?" one of the paramedics said.

Blake gulped audibly. "All right."

Jerry smiled, seeming to understand that Blake was majorly playing down his pain.

"It happened…um," I stuttered. "Not long ago. I don't know how long it's been. It won't stop bleeding. You have to stop the bleeding."

"OK," Jerry said. He was a picture of calm while I felt like I was swimming against the tide. "Now...?"

"His name is Blake," I said, speaking for him. "I'm Mackenzie. Should I move my hand?"

"OK, Mackenzie. No, not just yet. Stay where you are and keep pressure on that. You're doing really well. Where is the knife?"

"Floor," Blake replied. "I work out, but I'm not toned enough to snap a knife."

Jerry and Blake laughed. I couldn't.

"Well, that's good. Now, Mackenzie, I'm going to get you to let go. We've got this now." I did as I was told and slowly lifted my hand. Blake winced. "Good. Blake, we're going to get you on the stretcher and into the ambulance." He looked back at his colleague, who was speaking to someone on her radio in a hushed voice.

I didn't want to let go. I was scared. I stayed by Blake's side, refusing to find my own way to the hospital. There was no way anyone was getting me to leave him.

The last I saw of Aaron was when I caught a brief glimpse of him being bundled into a police car as we made our way out to the ambulance.

Blake hadn't been in the hospital ten hours before he was home and in his own room. I helped fluff Blake's pillows so he was more comfortable. "You shouldn't be here. You need to be back in the hospital." I sounded like his mum, who'd also said the same thing.

It had been a little after nine in the morning when Blake had discharged himself. I had been awake far too long, and I was exhausted. Last night—or this morning, however you wanted to look at it—I had been too scared to sleep in case something happened to Blake.

"There's nothing they can do for me in the hospital. I'd rather be in my own bed than sleeping next to weirdos snoring all night and catching a staph infection."

I smiled. "Wow, you paint quite a picture. Lie down." He did and winced as he moved. "Are you in pain? You can't have any more pills for another half an hour."

"Half an hour is nothing. Pass me them, please?"

"No!" I frowned. "Not yet. The doctor said to make sure you had them at the right time."

"The doctor also said I should stay another day."

Sighing deeply, I shook my head. "You're not getting your own way with this one too. Most men don't even like taking pain medication and you're wanting it early."

"I'm not most men." *That was for sure.* He huffed. "Fine, but will you lie down with me if you're not drugging me up?"

How could I refuse that offer?

I lay down and snuggled up to his good side. It was over. Aaron was in police custody. Kyle, Megan, Blake, and I were no longer suspects. We were free to move on with our lives.

It's over.

A million emotions rushed inside me, growing bigger and bigger, like a balloon being over inflated. I burst out with a loud sob and dug my fingers into Blake's arm, gripping him for dear life. It was too much. *Everything* was too much.

I wasn't supposed to break down in front of him, especially not now. There was no stopping it though. I'd burst, and there was no way back.

My heart felt as heavy as lead.

"Shh," Blake murmured into my hair, unable to find the right words to say. He didn't need to say anything. All I needed was for him to hold me. He pressed his lips to my head and whispered, "Shh, it's OK. I'm here. I'm not going anywhere. I promise."

CHAPTER TWENTY-FIVE

Tuesday, February 7

"I can't believe it's been eighteen months," I said, stroking Courtney's headstone.

Today marked a year and a half since Josh and Courtney had been murdered. Time had moved painfully slow but also too fast. I missed Courtney every day, but I had finally come to terms with the fact that I'd never see her again.

Blake sat beside me, not really knowing what to say. That hadn't changed. Even after the two of us practically being joined at the hip, he was still a bit rubbish with feelings. Still, he managed to make me feel like the only girl in the world with just one look.

"I know, babe," he said, squeezing my knee.

"I've lost far too many people." I turned to him and gripped the hand that was now resting on my leg. "I almost lost you too..." My throat closed with emotion. It was too difficult to think about that day.

"Nah, was never gonna happen. Aaron had bloody awful aim." I swallowed hard and dropped my eyes to the grass. Blake used humor; I was so not there yet. "Sorry, that was insensitive. You'd think after all this time, I'd get better at that stuff. I'm sorry, Mackenzie," he apologized.

I couldn't help but smile. The most inappropriate things spurted from his mouth, but he never failed to make me smile. I could be so distraught and one awkward word from him would put a grin on my face.

"You're better than you give yourself credit for…sometimes," I said.

"You're just saying that because you want to get in my pants."

Rolling my eyes with my lips curved, I turned my attention back to my friend. "You would have been rooting for Blake from the start, Court."

I had no doubt Courtney would have liked Blake once she really got to know him. She would have been the one sitting on my bed, going on and on about how obvious it was that we would eventually happen.

"She had taste," Blake teased.

Well, that wasn't quite true, but I didn't want to bad-mouth Josh.

"Say it," Blake said in a dead tone. "Whatever you're thinking about Josh, just say it."

I squeezed his hand. "No. You already know what I think. I'm not going there again. Not anymore." Not now he wasn't around. Everyone knew my opinion of Josh, so I didn't feel the need to keep reinforcing it. I'd let it go.

"Such a good girl," Blake muttered.

"You know why, Blake," I whispered.

"I do. I just don't know what the difference is. You think it, so why not say it?"

Blake was the type of person who would stick to his convictions no matter what, whereas I believed that after someone was gone, you shouldn't speak ill of them—aloud anyway.

"Because he's dead. I won't be the type of person that pisses over—" Blake's burst of laughter made me roll my eyes. He loved it when I swore because it didn't happen often. "There's something very wrong with you."

"My life would be very dull without you, Kenz."

I think that's the other way around.

"I never know what to say when I visit Josh or Pete," he continued. "People around are chatting away, and I'm just sitting there like an idiot."

"You don't have to say anything. It's enough that you visit."

"Please," he said. "Josh is definitely up there making some snarky comment."

Probably. At first, when I started visiting Tilly and Gigi, I sat in silence for hours. It wasn't until about a month later that I just started chatting about the things we would have talked about if they were still here, and then I started to tell them about things I was doing and my plans for the future.

"It seems like just yesterday we were bickering on the way to the cabin." I ran my hand over the soft grass that had grown over the mound of dirt. "I can't believe a weekend away ended like this," I said, taking a breath.

"Hey," Blake said, squeezing my hand and leaning over to kiss the side of my head. "You want to get out of here now? It always upsets you."

"Sure," I replied and stood up with him. I would have stayed longer if I had been alone, but I knew how much Blake hated it when I cried. And I didn't want to sit in a churchyard all morning sobbing.

We walked toward the road hand in hand. Being with him wasn't easy, but we'd fought our way through a lot together, so neither of us was going to give up just because things weren't always simple. We got a lot of stares still, and our relationship was judged and picked apart on a daily basis, but people who thought we shouldn't be together only made us stronger.

"Where to now, Miss Keaton?" he asked.

"Megan's, Kyle's, and then back to check on your mum."

"And when you've finished checking up on everyone else, are we going to make sure you're OK?"

"I'm OK. I'll cry later, when I'm home alone."

"First, I'm staying with you tonight. And second, you don't need to schedule your emotions around me. Besides, I'm getting used to the over-the-top, complete head-fuck that are females."

I laughed at his interesting choice of words, shaking my head as we walked toward Megan's house. "Thanks for that. I really am doing OK today though. Better than I thought I would be."

Sixteen months of intense therapy later, and I was actually doing all right. I still only trusted three people in the world: Mum, Dad, and Blake. But I was coping and living. Putting my trust in other people was hard now. Not only had I learned that people were capable of doing truly awful things, but also that my ability to read people may as well have been nonexistent.

There was still a long road ahead, but I was healing.

And I wasn't as angry with Aaron as I had been. He wasn't evil. I truly believed he was sick, and Megan had told me that he was receiving the help that he needed. Maybe if we'd realized what he was going through sooner, Courtney and Josh would still be here. But we didn't know.

Since *that* day, I had seen Aaron once in prison. He'd explained himself, and then I'd left. It was difficult to see him looking so lost and afraid, but he'd done something terrible and he needed to be held accountable. Recently, I had been thinking about going back to visit him in prison though. I had started to *slowly* forgive him. If there was anything good that could come out of this, it would be for Aaron to get better.

No one apart from Kyle, Megan, and his parents had bothered with him. I didn't want to be one of those people who'd turned their backs on him if there was a chance he could change. I wanted the old Aaron back so badly. Blake was constantly reminding me to keep my expectations realistic though. The old Aaron I loved so much might never come back.

With time, I had also started to forgive him for trying to set up Blake and stabbing him. I wasn't there yet, but I didn't want to carry a grudge and hate around. It was exhausting.

Blake didn't talk about forgiveness much, but he did tell me that he wouldn't hold it against me if I wanted to be there for Aaron. I knew I wouldn't lose Blake, so I was all for it.

"What would you say if I told you I want to visit Aaron?" I asked, looking up at Blake, so I could see his reaction.

His eyes turned stormy and he held my hand a fraction tighter.

"I'd say you were crazy. But you have this need to help people and I love you for it. I knew you would want to see him, Mackenzie. I've been fine with it for a while and was just waiting for you to get there. I love you more than I hate him, and that will never change."

My heart melted into a puddle. Blake wasn't the romantic type, so he didn't say I love you every hour. When he said he cared for me, the words meant so much.

Sometimes I gave myself ulcers stressing over how we got together. Would it make Blake feel like he couldn't break up with me? Blake told me I was worrying over nothing and needed to discuss it at my next counseling session.

"I love you so much, Blake."

Smirking, his eyes flicked back to their usual state. "Well, of course."

"Do you think you'll ever grow up?"

"Not if I can help it," he replied.

Good. I loved him just the way he was. We had years before we needed to grow up anyway. I was finally learning how to be a carefree teenager again, so I was determined to enjoy it.

Megan was alone in her house; I could tell that just from looking at it. When her parents were home, there was always a window open, a light on, music, energy.

Groaning, I said, "I bet she's upset."

Blake looked like he wanted to head for the hills, but instead of making an excuse to leave, he squeezed my hand. We walked straight inside.

"Megan!" I called. I found her in the kitchen. She sat at the large pine table. She was wearing her coat, scarf, and gloves, so she'd either just got home or was about to go out. There was a gun on the table. Her dad had a few and I'd seen them about, but not when he wasn't at home.

"Hey," I said, worried. "Megs, are you OK?"

She didn't move.

"Who's is this?" Blake asked, picking up the gun from the table to admire it.

"It's her dad's. Put it down," I said. I'd never liked guns. They kind of intimidated me.

Blake put it back on the table.

Megan didn't move, but her mouth did widen in a grin.

"Seriously, Megan, you're scaring me. Are you OK? Did something happen?"

Have you spoken to Aaron? Is he OK?

Eighteen months ago, he was taking his Rohypnol-laced vodka out of the case and checking where the knives were stored in the cabin's kitchen. Would he be thinking about today?

"Megan, answer Mackenzie," Blake said and then waved his hand in front of her face. "Hey, are you OK?"

I could've kicked him. If I hadn't been so worried about Megan and focused on her, I would have. Her eyes were dull and sunken, like she hadn't slept for days. Maybe she hadn't. Blake, Kyle, and I had gone to the movies yesterday, but Megan had canceled at the last minute. Getting back to some version of normal was still really hard for her, and I think the anniversary brought back the loss of Tilly and Gigi too.

Blake sighed. "Kenzie's worried, Megan. What happened?"

"They killed her. They killed them both," Megan whispered. Her eyes were wide and still fixed on the table.

Blake and I looked at each other. He looked utterly lost. I was right there with him.

"Megan, who are you talking about?" I asked.

"You know who I'm talking about," she spat.

Yes, I do.

"It wasn't Courtney and Josh's fault, Megan. Come on, you know that."

I felt like I'd just been catapulted back a year. Everything I'd worked so hard to put behind me started to crumble. I couldn't go through all of this again.

"Megs, please. Don't let Aaron get to you."

She shook her head slowly from side to side and her lip curled at the edge. "But it wasn't Aaron, Mackenzie. It was *me*."

CHAPTER TWENTY-SIX

The blood drained from my face. "What wasn't Aaron?" I asked. My voice, failing me, was barely a whisper. I could guess—it was obvious—but I needed Megan to say it.

For the first time since we had arrived, she looked up and her eyes bore into mine. They held absolutely no emotion. Her eyes were nothing but dark pools.

"*I* did it. I killed Courtney, Josh, and Pete. Aaron is as innocent as you. He confessed to cover for me, but he can't handle it in there anymore. Now he's going to tell the truth."

My mouth fell open as she confirmed what I was trying to convince myself couldn't be true. "But…why? What?" She did it. She *let* Aaron do that for her. My head spun so I had to hold my stomach to stop myself throwing up.

I'm dreaming. I have to be dreaming.

"I can't go to prison, Mackenzie. You know I'm not strong like the rest of you. I would die in there."

I closed my eyes and held up my hand. "Wait. I don't… How did Aaron know? Why and how?" Nothing made sense again.

Beside me, Blake was still, as if he was still processing what she had said and her words hadn't caught up with him yet. He was usually quick to react with a stupid comment or a smirk, but right now he was stone.

I easily had over a million questions, and they all whizzed through my mind at lightning speed, too fast for me to pin down long enough to ask any of them. The whole situation was crazy. Megan and Aaron were crazy. I was angry, confused, and hurt.

Megan's eyes filled with tears. She was still calm, calm, calm. I envied her that. She'd done this horrible, unforgivable thing, and I was the one who was bloody livid. "Do you have any idea what it's like waking up in the hospital and being told the woman you love is dead?" she asked.

I shook my head. We were going back to Gigi. I wanted to yell, but I knew better than to do it. I needed the truth. Aaron needed the truth to come out. Oh God, Aaron! I had thought he was guilty and so did Josh's and Courtney's families.

"Megan, they didn't kill Gigi. Nobody killed either of them. It was an *accident*."

God, this is why Aaron's confession seemed so rehearsed—it was. Those were Megan's words, not his.

"It's hell," she said, ignoring what I'd said completely. "I couldn't even grieve properly because no one knew about us. I missed her every second of every day. I felt like I was drowning, and there was no way out. There was nothing I could do to make myself feel better or to make someone pay for what had happened. Justice was never served, but they both deserved what they got." She picked up the gun.

What is she doing?

"Megan," Blake said calmly, smiling a warm smile like the ones police give someone about to jump off a building. I was freaking out inside, my heart pumping a hundred miles an hour. "It's OK, Megan. It's going to be fine, but I need you to hand me the gun."

"No," she replied, her knuckles turning white as she gripped hold of the handle. My eyes widened and time screeched to a halt. "The things Josh said ate away at me. He was glad it was them rather than him. How could you wish someone died over yourself?"

I didn't get that either, but I wasn't prepared to kill over it.

"I don't know," I replied, just in case it wasn't a rhetorical question. My eyes flitted between Megan and the gun.

"I kept thinking about them both rotting in the ground while Josh walked around doing whatever he wanted and Courtney followed him. I couldn't stand it. Because of them, Tilly and Gigi were dead. They didn't even care. We all took responsibility and we felt some guilt, but not them. They. Didn't. Care."

"Courtney did," I said, defending my friend who wasn't able to defend herself. Whatever her flaws, she loved her friends. Megan was painting Court with the same brush as Josh, and it wasn't right. She was guilty of letting Josh walk all over her, but she cared.

Megan shook her head slowly, her jaw tightening in anger. "I confronted her the night after Josh said he was glad it was them. Courtney admitted she was glad she didn't die. Can you believe that?"

Well, yes. "That doesn't mean she *wanted* it to be Tills and Gigi. It just meant she didn't want to die." I was glad I didn't die, and I knew that was selfish, but I was. If I had a choice though, I would have swapped with them in a heartbeat.

"Maybe she didn't want it to be them, but it was. She chose Josh over her friends, like she had done a thousand times over."

"So that meant Courtney and Josh deserved to die?" Blake asked. His lip curled in disgust and I squeezed his hand to try and diffuse some of his anger. This wasn't going to a repeat of what happened with Aaron. We absolutely had to stay calm. He had to stay calm. Megan had a gun.

"Yes," Megan replied. "There was a link—a link between Tilly, Gigi, Courtney, and Josh." She held her hand up, pointing at nothing with her index finger. She was gone. The girl I knew was somewhere else. "They were responsible for their deaths, and Tilly and Gigi would never get justice. I couldn't stand that. Two beautiful people were dead, and no one was taking the blame. No one was being held accountable."

"So you took it into your own hands? Megan, that's not justice," I said, tears burning in my eyes.

"You don't understand, Mackenzie. Josh and Courtney caused Tilly's and Gigi's deaths. They had to pay."

"What did you do? Talk me through everything. I need to know. You owe me that much."

"When I had made my decision to take things into my own hands, everything became so clear. It was like the fog had lifted. I instantly felt better about their deaths because someone was going to pay. I knew that it wouldn't bring them back, but there had to be justice. At first I was just going to go to Josh's house when I knew they were there and Eloise was away. You know that wouldn't have been hard because Josh would brag about having the place to himself."

That sounded like Josh.

"When he mentioned going away to the cabin, everything changed. It was better, easier. I knew I was incriminating you guys too, but I thought it through carefully and knew none of you would be arrested. Blake coming along last minute threw me, but it didn't really matter. I had enough Rohypnol."

I laughed humorlessly. Well, thank God she had enough for all.

"Where did you get it?" The idea of Megan getting hold of Rohypnol was ridiculous.

"You remember stoner Richard from school?"

"Yeah," I replied. Rich had been suspended from school countless times for smoking weed. He was good-looking and actually pretty smart, but his home life sucked and he used weed to make everything better.

"He moved on to harder stuff, doing quite well for himself actually." She shrugged. "He can get pretty much anything, so he was boasting. Anyway, I planned to drug you all, only enough so you'd be out of it until morning. I didn't want to hurt you. I put Rohypnol in the liquor and took a second bottle, which I hid in my suitcase, so I could swap them over."

"*Why?*"

Blake snorted. "So when the police tested the bottles it'd be clear."

Megan dipped her head in a nod. "Yes. And I had a change of clothes, matching. I bagged the clothes and bottle, weighted it down and ran up the river as far as I could go before I lost sight of the cabin. It's all somewhere down there. After that, I had a shower, changed into my duplicate clothes, and went to bed."

I wanted to stop listening.

"You missed the part where you stabbed our friends to death," I hissed.

She bowed her head. "You know what happened."

"Who did you kill first? How did you do it? Did they fight? Did they die quickly? Why did you stab them so many times?" I asked, fighting myself to remain calm. I wanted to hit her, scream at her, strangle her. How could she?

"Do you really want those answers, Mackenzie?"

"Yes," I snapped.

She looked surprised, as if I'd just let her walk away without telling me what happened in those hours I lost to Rohypnol.

"I gave you, Blake, Aaron, and Kyle more of the liquor." The spiked liquor she meant. "When you all started looking dopey eyed, I took half a shot myself and gave Josh and Courtney a few too. I needed them to be able to walk around after you four were out of it. I wanted them to know what was happening without being able to fight back. It worked. I waited in my room for an hour after I heard you and Blake go upstairs to be sure you were out of it. I knew you'd both crash pretty hard once you were asleep."

She'd heard us go upstairs. Not once did she mention anything about Blake and me being together that night. My face heated, but the enormity of what she'd done made any embarrassment pale in comparison.

"When I went downstairs, Josh and Courtney were in the kitchen, cleaning up. I think they'd been at it a while, and even though Courtney said she was exhausted, Josh wanted them to do the washing up. I told them I got up to get a glass of water and offered to help too."

Her eyes hollowed. "Courtney stumbled into the counter, laughing as she threw the enchilada boxes in the bin. She laughed as if she didn't have a care in the world."

I wanted to shake her. We had all laughed since Tilly and Gigi died. The world still turned and life still went on. That was just the way it was, and Tills and Gigi would never want us to be miserable forever.

"While Josh was putting the bottles that still had something in them in the cupboard, I…I stabbed Courtney. It was so easy. The knife just slid into her like she was made of butter. At first she didn't make a sound. She looked like she was screaming, eyes wide and mouth open, but she didn't make a sound. I managed to stab her once more before Josh turned around. By that time, they were both groggy, moving slowly and not fully aware of what was going on. I stabbed him too."

"Then you stabbed them both some more for good measure?" I spat.

"Don't say it like that, Mackenzie. I had to make sure they were dead. When they were on the floor, I felt the rage of what they had done to Gigi spilling out of me. I got…carried away."

I threw my hands over my face, squeezing my eyes closed as if that would squeeze the image from my mind. Carried away stabbing our friends. It was too much. I saw red spots behind my eyelids and gasped for air as my lungs deflated.

Oh God.

"Pete?" Blake asked, his voice chillingly calm. "What did he do?"

"That wasn't intentional. Pete found out. I saw him in town a few days later and he saw straight through me. He knew it was me; I'm sure he did. There was an argument, and he said he was going to Wright. I followed him home…"

She did it. Not only had she murdered Courtney and Josh, but she'd killed Pete too. And she'd drugged her friends, hiding behind us to cover her own back.

"How could you do that to us? I thought we were friends."

"We are."

"No. You framed us to get yourself out of trouble."

"I planned it well, Mackenzie. No one was ever supposed to be arrested for it."

"Then why plant their things in Blake's room?"

"You wouldn't stop believing in Blake. Blake had motive. He woke up. Your relationship with him almost ruined it for me. It gave him opportunity. It wouldn't matter to us if he went down; it wouldn't matter to anyone if he did."

Blake's hands fisted over the table. That was low, even for Megan.

I didn't dwell on what she'd said because I had to keep a level head. "And what about Aaron?"

She shrugged. "It all got to be too much and I confided in him. I was a mess and he said he'd take the rap for me."

Lie. Her voice was void of all feeling, like she was retelling a story she hated. It was rehearsed. To Aaron, she would've had to be hysterical and…suicidal. Maybe he knew she had a gun and was afraid she'd take her own life.

"How could you let him do that?"

"I can't go to prison, Mackenzie."

Blake raged. He was quickly losing his temper, and the last time that had happened, he had been stabbed. I shot him a look, pleading with him not to make the same mistake again. Blake gritted his teeth as he tried to calm himself down.

"Aaron was willing to take the fall and I let him. No one ever does the full time. I figured he'd be out in a few years."

"He'll be out a lot sooner than that," I said. "You're telling the truth."

"Aaron stabbed Blake, or are you forgetting that?"

"I can never forget that." Every single time I see his scar, it makes my heart ache. I came so close to losing him. "Aaron's *real* crime isn't murder, Megan. He won't serve time for something you've done. Not anymore. But you, well, you're going to prison for a very long time."

She shook her head. "I won't."

"You're insane, Megan," Blake said.

She looked him square in the eye and her smile chilled me to the bone. "You haven't even heard the best bit yet. I still have the hoodie."

"What hoodie?"

"The one I killed them in. Coincidentally, it's about Blake's size…"

I felt the world tilt. "Megan… What've you done?"

"I told you I won't be going to prison and I meant it. Aaron can't be in prison anymore, and I don't want my parents to know what I've done. The police are going to find a black hoodie soaked with Courtney's and Josh's blood in a shed at Blake's dad's house. Wright is also going to get a frantic voice mail telling him all about how Blake has been threatening me and how I can't take it anymore. He'll know that I'm too scared to tell you, Mackenzie, because Blake has threatened to hurt you if I did. I can't see a way out."

Blake and I listened on in horror at her disgusting plan.

"There are various threatening text messages from a burner phone to all of us." She looked at me and smirked. "They'll find that...somewhere with Blake's belongings too. Oh, don't look scared, Mackenzie. You, Aaron, and Kyle are going to be fine."

Blake scoffed. "You're not ever going to get away with this, Megan. You're insane if you think you are. Aaron's going to confess."

She tilted her head to the side. "You have no idea what I'm capable of. He wanted to confess if I didn't sort it, and I've sorted it. See, Aaron only confessed in the first place because you threatened to kill his family, Blake. Now we both have a way out. When the police find all the damning evidence against you, it won't be hard for him to convince them of that too."

"Stop it!" I hissed. "My God, Megan, what happened? You've never been cruel."

"You'll never understand what I've been through, so let's not even go there. Can you imagine how people are going to think of me when they find out I lost the love of my life and was tortured for weeks by a killer? I was so hurt and damaged from losing the one person I truly loved and so desperate to be free of the pain and abuse that I took my own life. People will mourn, plant trees, name buildings after me. I'll be loved, and Blake will be in prison."

"Megan," I breathed.

She stood up and the chair clattered to the floor.

"Don't, Mackenzie! Don't say a word."

The gun shook in her hands as she turned it on me. Blake froze, his face falling. I lifted my hands, my heart flying in my chest.

"OK, I'm sorry. Megs, please put the gun down. We can figure out a plan, I swear. You don't have to do this," I said softly, trying to calm her. Megan was in constant need of comfort. She was timid and some part of that had to still be in her.

"I don't have a choice," she spat. Her eyes were wild and flicked between Blake and me. The gun stayed fixed on my head.

"You do. There is always a choice. Please, Megan. Please put down the gun and let me help you."

The corner of her mouth lifted. "No one can help me, not even you, Miss Fix It. And you won't be able to help your boy either."

She lowered the gun, holding it in a tight grip by her side, and I breathed a sigh of relief. *Stay calm and show her there's a way out of this.* If anyone could get through to her it was me, and the pressure and responsibility of that gave me a headache.

Blake's future was on the line, and I had to try.

"Mackenzie's right, Megan, you can stop this, and we'll find a way to help you," Blake said, taking a subtle step closer to me. His eyes focused on the gun.

"Don't be stupid," Megan snapped. "There is no way I'll avoid prison, and I already have a plan. I like my plan."

Blake's eyes slid up to hers. "Your plan won't stand up."

Her lip curled as she stared through him. "Oh, really? You touched the gun. Your fingerprints are on it. Leave it in my hand or not, but it'll look like you planted it there. I'm sorry, Mackenzie." She took the gun and held it to her mouth. Before my brain processed what was going on she pulled the trigger.

Bang. My ears rang and Megan's lifeless body fell to the floor like a rag doll.

A scream ripped from my throat, but I couldn't hear a thing. Blake grabbed me as my legs were about to give out, and I clung to his arm. I couldn't take my eyes off Megan. Blood. More blood. I'd seen enough blood.

"Oh God, Megan. Megan. Blake, she's dead. Megan's dead!" I rambled. "She shot herself. Oh God, the blood is everywhere." I looked down, but I was clean. The blood had splattered behind her.

"Mackenzie," Blake muttered. His voice was cold and laced with fear. Gripping my upper arms, he forced me to look at him. "Mackenzie, I need you right now. Calm down, babe, please."

No. He was right. He needed me because he would go down for the crimes Megan committed and Megan would be loved. That couldn't happen. How could Megan and Aaron plan something like that?

"I'm sorry," I whispered, gasping for the air I so desperately needed.

"It's OK." He let go of my arms, cupped my cheeks, and bent

his head to kiss me. I couldn't let anything happen to him. He'd stolen my heart, and as long as he was OK, I would be too. I'd do anything to help him.

There was only one way to prevent him from being locked up.

I pulled back and stared into pretty blue eyes I'd fallen in love with so fast and so hard. Blake meant everything to me. "Run," I whispered.

ACKNOWLEDGMENTS

This book was a lot of fun to write—both times. But without some amazing people in my life, *The Cabin* wouldn't be here now. Thank you to my husband for understanding that his wife turns into a caffeine and words junkie as a deadline approaches.

Thank you to the amazing team at Sourcebooks who worked on *The Cabin* to make it what it is today. And the cover is my favorite!

Last but by no means least, thank you so much to my readers. You guys blow me away.

READY FOR ANOTHER
HEART-POUNDING READ?

DON'T MISS
NATASHA PRESTON'S
THE CELLAR

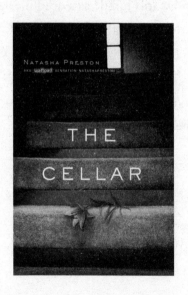

CHAPTER 1

"Summer, are you now leaving?" Mum called from the kitchen.

No, I'm walking out the door for fun!

"Yeah."

"Sweetheart, be careful," Dad said.

"I will. Bye," I replied quickly and walked out the door before they could stop me. They still treated me like I was in elementary school and couldn't go out alone. Our town was probably—actually definitely—the most boring place on earth; nothing even remotely interesting ever happened.

The most excitement we'd ever had was two years ago when old Mrs. Hellmann—yeah, like the mayonnaise—went missing and was found hours later wandering the sheep field looking for her late husband. The whole town was looking for her. I still remember the buzz of something finally happening.

I started walking along the familiar pavement toward the pathway next to the graveyard. That was the only part of walking alone that I didn't like. Graveyards. They were scary—fact—and especially when you were alone. I subtly glanced around while I walked along the footpath. I felt uneasy, even after passing the graveyard. We had moved to this neighborhood when I was five, and I had always felt safe here. My childhood had been spent playing out in the street with my friends, and as I got older, I hung out at the park or club. I knew this town and the people in it like the back of my hand, but the graveyard always creeped me out.

I pulled my jacket tightly around myself and picked up the pace. The club was almost in view, just around the next corner. I glanced over my shoulder again and gasped as a dark figure stepped out from behind a hedge.

"Sorry, dear, did I frighten you?"

I sighed in relief as old Harold Dane came into view. I shook my head. "I'm fine."

He lifted up a heavy-looking black bag and threw it into his garbage can with a deep grunt as if he had been lifting weights. His skinny frame was covered in wrinkled, saggy skin. He looked like he'd snap in half if he bent over. "Are you going to the disco?"

I grinned at choice of word. *Disco.* Ha! That's probably what they called it back when he was a teenager. "Yep. I'm meeting my friends there."

"Well, you have a good night, but watch your drinks. You don't know what the boys today slip in pretty young girls' drinks," he warned, shaking his head as if it were the scandal of the year and every teenage boy was out to date-rape everyone.

Laughing, I raised my hand and waved. "I'll be careful. Night."

"Good night, dear."

The club was visible from Harold's house, and I relaxed as I approached the entrance. My family and Lewis had made me jumpy; it was ridiculous. As I got to the door, my friend

Kerri grabbed my arm from beside me, making me jump. She laughed, her eyes alight with humor. *Hilarious.* "Sorry. Have you seen Rachel?"

My heart slowed to its normal pace as my brain processed my friend's face and not the face of the *Scream* dude or Freddy Kruger. "Not seen anyone. Just got here."

"Damn it. She ran off after another argument with the idiot, and her phone's turned off!" Ah, the idiot. Rachel had a very on/off relationship with her boyfriend, Jack. I never understood that—if you pissed each other off 90 percent of the time, then just call it a day. "We should find her."

Why? I had hoped for a fun evening with friends, not chasing after a girl who should have just dumped her loser boyfriend's arse already. Sighing, I resigned myself to the inevitable. "Okay, which direction did she go?"

Kerri gave me a flat look. "If I knew that, Summer…"

Rolling my eyes, I pulled her hand, and we started walking back toward the road. "Fine. I'll go left, you go right." Kerri saluted and marched off to the right. I laughed at her and then went my way. Rachel had better be close.

I walked across the middle of the playing field near the club, heading toward the gate at the back to see if she had taken the shortcut through to her house. The air turned colder, and I rubbed my arms. Kerri said Rachel's phone was off, but I tried calling it anyway and, of course, it went straight to voice mail. If she didn't want to speak to anyone, then why were we trying to find her?

I left an awkward message on her phone—I hated leaving messages—and walked through the gate toward the skate ramp at the back of the park. The clouds shifted, creating a gray swirling effect across the sky. It looked moody, creepy but pretty at the same times. A light, cool breeze whipped across my face, making my light honey-blond hair—according to hairdresser wannabe Rachel—blow in my face and a shudder ripple through my body.

"Lily?" a deep voice called from behind me. I didn't recognize it. I spun around and backed up as a tall, dark-haired man stepped into view. My stomach dropped. Had he been hiding between the trees? What the heck? He was close enough that I could see the satisfied grin on his face and neat hair not affected by the wind. How much hairspray must he have used? If I weren't freaked out, I would have asked what product he used because my hair never played fair. "Lily," he repeated.

"No. Sorry." Gulping, I took another step back and scanned the area in the vain hope that one of my friends would be nearby. "I'm not Lily," I mumbled, straightening my back and looking up at him in an attempt to appear confident. He towered over me, glaring down at me with creepily dark eyes.

He shook his head. "No. You are Lily."

"I'm Summer. You have the wrong person." *You utter freak!*

I could hear my pulse crashing in my ears. How stupid to give him my real name. He continued to stare at me, smiling. It made me feel sick. Why did he think I was Lily? I hoped that I just looked like his daughter or something and he wasn't some crazy weirdo.

I took another step back and searched around to find a place that I could escape if needed. The park was big, and I was still near the back, just in front of the trees. There was no way anyone would be able to see me from here. That thought alone made my eyes sting. Why did I come here alone? I wanted to scream at myself for being so stupid.

"You are Lily," he repeated.

Before I could blink, he threw his arms forward and grabbed me. I tried to shout, but he clasped his hand over my mouth, muffling my screams. What the heck was he doing? I thrashed my arms, frantically trying to get out of his grip. *Oh God, he's going to kill me.* Tears poured from my eyes. My heart raced. My fingertips tingled and my stomach knotted with fear. *I'm going to die. He's going to kill me.*

The Lily man pulled me toward him with such force the air left my lungs in a rush as I slammed against him. He spun me around so my back pressed tightly against his chest. And with his hand sealed over my mouth and nose, I struggled to breathe. I couldn't move, and I didn't know if it was because he had such a strong iron grip or if I was too stunned. He had me, and he could do whatever he wanted because I couldn't bloody move a muscle.

He pushed me through the gate at the back of the park and then through the field. I tried again to scream for help, but against his palm, I hardly made a sound. He whispered "Lily" over and over while he dragged me toward a white van. I watched trees pass me by and birds fly over us, landing on branches. Everything carried on as normal. Oh God, I needed to get away now. I dug my feet into the ground and screamed so hard that my throat instantly started to hurt. It was useless, though; no one was around to hear me but the birds.

He tugged his arm back, pressing it into my stomach. I cried out in pain. As soon as he let go to open the van's back door, I screamed for help. "Shut up!" he shouted as he pushed me inside the vehicle. My head smashed into the side of the van while I struggled.

"Please let me go. Please. I'm not Lily. Please."

ABOUT THE AUTHOR

UK native Natasha Preston grew up in small villages and towns. She discovered her love of writing when she stumbled across an amateur writing site and uploaded her first story and hasn't looked back since. She enjoys writing NA romance, thrillers, gritty YA, and the occasional serial killer thriller.